Advance Praise for

"*A Dangerous Freedom* is the first .... packed novels. Dylan Reilly is a new protagonist worth following. Enjoy the ride and the read."

—Bob Hamer, Author of *The Last Undercover*

"John Ruane has written a compelling story for our times, seen through the lens of Dylan Reilly and a generation coming of age at a time of profound change wrought by globalism, terrorism, fear, and political insecurity. Fast-paced, action-filled, and a moving commentary on war and the state of the post-9/11 world, *A Dangerous Freedom* is a novel with a statement that will be hard to put down."

—Richard Lindberg, Historian and Author of *Tales of Forgotten Chicago*

"*A Dangerous Freedom* is an action thriller in the vein of Tom Clancy or Vince Flynn. The terror attack on 9/11/01 changed the lives of an entire generation. Some wanted revenge, some wanted to use it to their advantage, and some just wanted to get on with their lives. But as terrorism becomes more commonplace, no one is safe. The only problem is, when it comes time to fight, you find that the lines are blurred and sometimes it's hard to tell friend from foe."

—Tom E. Hicklin, Author of *Road to Antietam*

"Ruane brings the scenes to life and really puts the reader in the middle of the action, which builds to become an exciting thriller!"

—Geoffrey L. Warwick, Author of *A Bruised Reed*

"This action-thriller reminds me of these movies: *Dirty Harry, The Outlaw Josey Wales, Mississippi Burning*, and *American History X*."

—Brooks Kohler, Author of *Sunset in Sylvan Park*

"John Ruane has crafted a page-turning thriller, set against a historic backdrop, weaving many recognizable Chicago places and personalities into the storyline. The reader will enjoy the familiar accents of Chicago as the story unfolds."

—Robert I. Girardi, Historian and Author of *The Civil War Generals*

"John Ruane has deftly taken the world-shattering event of 9/11 and examined its impact on the hearts and minds of those who witnessed it. Some would be inspired to serve. Others would be driven to kill. Still others would strive to seek their own brand of justice against the growing threat of terrorism. With Chicago as a backdrop, this fast-paced thriller introduces Dylan Reilly. As a high-schooler, Dylan witnessed the violence of terrorism. As an adult, he experiences it firsthand and heads off on a mission to defend the innocent, violently if necessary. The lines are blurrier than he remembers them being in 2001 and he finds the players aren't always clearly defined in this new kind of war. *A Dangerous Freedom* will keep you hooked."

—Laura L. Enright, Author of *Chicago's Most Wanted*

A DANGEROUS FREEDOM

a thriller

JOHN RUANE

PERMUTED
PRESS

A PERMUTED PRESS BOOK

ISBN: 978-1-68261-973-5
ISBN (eBook): 978-1-68261-974-2

Cover art by Cody Corcoran

Permuted Press, LLC
New York • Nashville
permutedpress.com

To Mike Reilly, a true hero!

CHAPTER ONE

*D*ylan Reilly vividly remembered that morning, and the exact moment, when he knew for certain that something was wrong, that something really horrible had happened.

It was a bright sunny September morning in a southwest suburb of Chicago. The wonderful traditional fall smell of burning leaves filled the air surrounding St. John's Academy as Dylan Reilly entered through one of the tall, glass front doors of his all-boys Catholic high school for the start of his sophomore year. The tiled foyer floor was shiny and slick from the wax job performed over the summer clean-up months. Dylan walked directly to one of the dozen familiar long, black upholstered benches, placed along the side wall. He sat down next to two of his hockey teammates, Teddy Webb and Willie Mitrovich, who were in a deep conversation about history class.

"Hey fellas," said Dylan softly, not wishing to interrupt their conversation. His two pals glanced over and gave him the quick lift of their respective chins, the greeting reserved for boys their age. Dylan sat back, half-listening to their conversation about Mr. Leesak's class and the importance of not sitting in the front rows. The popular yet somewhat etiquette-challenged history teacher had a bad habit of not covering his mouth when sneezing. This always resulted in an unwelcomed dose of saliva sprayed over the students in the first few rows. Laughing, Willie shared that the educator's sneeze was so loud, it would wake up the wrestling coach, Mr. Mumphrey, who was supposed to be monitoring study hall in the next classroom.

Dylan couldn't help but laugh at Willie's description of Mr. Leesak's most famous disgusting practice in the classroom. Just then, his attention was drawn away by the sight of two teachers down the hall to his right. They looked panicked as they spoke with a great deal of agitation, then quickly walked in opposite directions—one toward the front office and the other toward the chapel. Something unusual was happening and Dylan pointed it out to his two laughing buddies.

"Hey fellas, something's up," Dylan said, watching the two teachers walking too fast. "Look at Mr. Lynch and Mr. Goodkey."

"What's going on?" asked Willie, a thin, brown-haired boy whom Dylan had known since they were seven years old, playing wiffleball in the backyard of their childhood friend, Tommy Mackey.

"I don't know," said Teddy, who was also a member of the student council and a voracious reader of history, dating back to when Dylan first met him on the St. Michael's Catholic Grammar School basketball team in Park Hills.

A buzz soon filled the foyer as other students noticed the same scene of panic that Dylan and his buddies had just witnessed. That's when Georgie Hanlon came running in from the main hallway and yelled, "They've crashed a plane into the Twin Towers!"

No one knew what their wide-eyed, loud-lunged, freckle-faced fellow student was referring to at that moment. Some had never ventured out of the neighborhood and didn't seem to know what he meant by the "Twin Towers."

"An American Airlines jet just crashed into the side of one of the Twin Towers in New York!" shouted Georgie at the large group of students assembled in the foyer, who were waiting for the school day to begin. "There's a big fire! It's pure chaos! People are jumping out of windows near the crash! Jumping! It's terrible! Terrible!"

"What! What happened? What!" echoed across the foyer, students uncertain about what they just heard. Shock, disbelief, and curiosity now filled the St. John's entrance lobby, abuzz with questions, boys moving toward the main hallway looking for teachers, answers.

But Dylan reacted as he always did when there was an emergency or someone needed help. He jumped up immediately to see what he could do to be of assistance. He sprinted through the main hallway to the library where he could check the news reports on television. He believed

Georgie was telling the truth, but he hoped when he turned on the TV that there would be regular programming, and it was all some prank someone decided to play on them for a good laugh.

No such luck. Within a few minutes, Dylan was surrounded by Georgie, Teddy, Willie, then ten, twenty, then hundreds of his fellow students watching the report by Katie Couric and Matt Lauer on NBC's *Today Show*. The picture on the screen showed the North Tower with an extensive fire protruding from the side of the building, gray smoke pouring out from the windows on several floors, halfway up the massive skyscraper in Lower Manhattan.

Couric and Lauer seemed confused. They continued describing the terrible scene as their news team tried to get information about how the plane crashed into the building, providing them with tidbits of information as the minutes passed. They continued referring to it as an accident. A growing group of students and teachers huddled around the television in the St. John's Academy library, some just staring in disbelief, while others began speculating on the event. "Was the pilot drunk?" asked Joe Doyle, another one of Dylan's hockey teammates, who nudged his way through the crowd to join his four pals.

"How do you fly a plane into a skyscraper like that?" asked Willie, equally perplexed.

"Well he's in big trouble, that's for sure," said Teddy, whose dream was to become a prosecuting lawyer someday and put bad guys behind bars.

"No, he's dead, stupid! Can't you see?" scolded Joe, never one to soft-pedal the truth.

Just then, at 8:03 a.m., the boys, the country, and the world, watched a United Airlines jet circle in behind the North Tower. Within seconds, a huge ball of fire shot out from behind the tower, the large fuel-filled jet crashed into the South Tower.

"That's no drunk pilot! It's a terrorist attack!" yelled Dylan, his eyes growing wide in realization that America, the world, had just witnessed a massive act of terror.

A hush crossed the St. John's library as hundreds of teenage boys stared at the blazing Twin Towers. A universal look of shock filled their collective faces. Some looked stunned, some fearful, some even crying. Dylan, however, was not a participant in the shock and fear. No, his jaw dropped and a look of intense anger filled his face. Grinding his teeth and clenching his fists, he was fighting mad. So was his pal Joe.

"Terrorists! We have to kill those damn terrorists!" Joe yelled out. The teachers of the Catholic boys high school looked at the young hockey player, most likely feeling the same frustration and perhaps somewhat envious that the young Irish-American boy could express it. There would be no detention, known as jugs, assigned to Joe Doyle for his outburst. No, this was one time a St. John's student could curse so boldly inside the school without receiving a jug.

Just then, the principal, Mr. James Hushing, entered the library.

Dylan realized that Mr. Hushing had to do what every other school principal in the country needed to do at this time. His immediate objective was to calm the fears and anger of the student body and bring as much normalcy and comfort to the situation as possible.

"May I have everyone's attention, please?" said the tall, middle-aged, salt-and-pepper-haired leader of the school, adjusting his black-rimmed glasses. Dylan remembered him as a man well-known for his vivacious personality and sense of humor, who was recruited to St. John's from St. Michael's Catholic School. "We are all going to go down to the gymnasium. Please walk down in an orderly manner. Talk if you like, but please, let's stay calm."

The voices of the young students filled the long sunlit main hallway. The sun shone brightly through the large windows on the east wall as the army of boys shuffled past the bookstore.

The moment they entered the large black and gold decorated gymnasium with the StJ logo centered at half court of the shiny wooden floor, the noise level grew louder with each passing minute as the terrorist attack was discussed. The boys became more angry, sharing the recollections and opinions about what their country should do next.

"I'm going to enlist in the Marines right after school today," said Joe, which didn't surprise Dylan, knowing the hockey team's best defenseman was always the first one to defend his teammates when a fight broke out on the ice. "I'm going to get those cowards! Killing innocent people, Americans, like that! I'm going to get those bastards!"

"That's great Joe!" Dylan said. "But, of course, you know that at fifteen years old…"

"Sixteen!" Joe shot back.

"Okay, at sixteen years old, you have two more years before you can enlist."

"I'll get a fake ID," he responded, anger filling his face. "Anything to get in. Anything to kill those terrorists!"

The stands along the east wall of the gymnasium were packed with more than eight hundred boys that made up the student body. Mr. Hushing stepped up to the microphone on the wooden podium positioned at center court, a familiar sight to all the students from pep rallies and other events at the school.

"Boys, this is a sad day for America and the world," said the beloved principal, who must have learned by that time that both towers had imploded. "No one could have ever imagined such a terrible act of terror like this could take place in America. What's important right now is for all of us to go back to our homes. You need to be with your families right now. This is one of those moments in time when we have to stop everything we are doing and just support each other, support your loved ones, stick together.

"Those terrorists think they have won today, but I promise you that they haven't won. All they have done is woken up a sleeping giant with the resources and abilities to strike back one thousand times harder than they struck us today. I know I'm saying this to you as a Catholic, the leader of a Catholic high school, but this is one of those times when we can't turn the other cheek. This is a bully tactic that requires a full response, a *Just War* act of defense. And I'm sure that's exactly what President Bush will do.

"Boys, I wasn't born when the attack on Pearl Harbor occurred in 1941, but I can tell you that my parents often talked about the shock and anger they felt and witnessed among their families, friends, and neighbors. Well, that is exactly what you and your classmates are feeling right now and most likely what you will see when you go home today.

"I won't say anything more about this now, except to add that being with your families and talking about what has happened, and what will happen, is good therapy. It worked in 1941 for my folks when they all sat around the Victrola radio, listening to the news. It will work now. Our most immediate goal is to get past this tragic event and move on to the next step, whatever that turns out to be.

"We have the buses lined up outside to take you home. For any of you who cannot go home right now, because your parents are at work, please see Mr. O'Keefe, who has agreed to stay here at the school and show movies until your parents can pick you up."

Once again, the buzz filled the gymnasium, the loud voices bouncing off the walls as the boys filed out in groups to their designated buses. The five friends and teammates—Dylan, Willie, Georgie, Joe, and Teddy—walked to the far end of the parking lot, near the Vikings new astro-turf football field, where their vehicles were parked. Joe, who took his patriotism very seriously, told his four best friends that he had made the life-changing decision to enlist into the U.S. Marines once he became eighteen, following their graduation in May of 2004.

"We're a long way away from graduation, Joe," said Dylan, trying not to let his friend overreact. "You may feel differently by then."

"No, I won't," he informed Dylan, his team's captain and linemate. "This is history. This is one of those moments in time when we all have to make a decision. We have to answer the call to service and kill those damn terrorists!"

"Okay, but do me a favor and please watch the movie, *Born on the Fourth of July*," implored Dylan, who had watched the movie several times. "It's a very different situation than the one we are in right now, but it's a true story and one anyone who joins the Marines should watch. It would be good for you to see, Joe."

Joe agreed, then climbed up into his red 1996 Dodge Ram truck that had an American flag on a long metal pole attached to the tailgate and flag stickers decorating the entire rear bumper. Teddy's 1993 brown Ford Explorer was parked next to him. Teddy, like Joe, had already turned sixteen and had his driver's license, which made him a big shot among his peers, especially on this tragic day when they climbed into the SUV to flee the sadness and anxiety at school.

As Dylan slid into Teddy's vehicle, he looked over at Joe's truck and just smiled at the familiar patriotic decor, which seemed so appropriate that morning. Joe drove off quickly, and Dylan felt proud watching the American flag flapping in the wind created by the truck's speed.

Teddy pulled out of the parking lot and drove quickly toward Central Avenue. Sitting quietly in the backseat, looking out the window, thoughts of revenge filled Dylan's head. The images of what he had just witnessed on the library's television couldn't be avoided or pushed away. Great anger arose inside him, his heart beating faster and faster. From the looks on the collective faces of Teddy, Willie, and Georgie, this was a shared feeling, the frustration of that horrible scene festering in their hearts, minds, and souls.

Dylan thought about Joe's proclamation and to enlist after graduation. Unlike Joe, Dylan had never used a gun and had never even seen a real gun. The idea of joining the military would be a major shift in his mindset and life. He wondered if he had the courage to use a gun. Joe certainly had the courage and experience, since his father had taken him hunting many times.

America was now confronted by an unexpected war and an uncertain future. The terrorists who crashed planes into the World Trade Center killed innocent citizens. Americans! Murdered! Dylan thought, shouldn't it be the responsibility of all young Americans over the age of eighteen to join the fight? As a student of history, Dylan knew all too well how so many generations of young men had made the ultimate sacrifice for their country when it was needed.

Whereas his pal Joe didn't blink about committing to enlisting and couldn't be talked out of it, Dylan struggled with the thought of joining the military, knowing it would change him forever. He would have to embrace guns, embrace killing. That wasn't a choice Dylan was willing to make, but he did consider various scenarios. What if a terrorist showed up at his doorstep one day with an AR-15 assault rifle? Would he just put his hands up in the air and say, "Please don't shoot?" He knew he would be shot and killed. And what if he was married and his wife was standing next to him? Would he say, "Please don't shoot her either!" They would shoot her too. That was the reality.

He wondered if he was just living in denial about not arming himself. Dylan knew the enemy was overseas and would never show up at his doorstep. At least that's what he hoped. But what if someone with a gun did confront him? What would he do? For the time being, he lived as an unarmed American, willing to take that risk, playing the odds against that scenario.

CHAPTER TWO

Dylan and Darlene Reilly were a top-of-the-wedding cake couple. Both twenty-eight years old, they were an attention-drawing, standout pair, perfectly matched spiritually, morally, intellectually, athletically and physically. The six-foot-tall Dylan had long, wavy, brown hair, a symmetrically-balanced face, piercing green eyes, thick eyebrows, strong chin and muscular athletic build from years of weight-training and skating on hockey rinks. Darlene had long beautiful shoulder-length auburn hair, accentuating her heart-shaped face with high cheekbones, green eyes, full lips, small nose and chin, clear and smooth skin, and a slim five-foot-four build from a lifetime of running and tennis.

Yes, when Dylan and Darlene walked arm-in-arm down the streets of Chicago, heads turned and horns honked. Many passersby would mistakenly believe they were seeing two famous movie stars. The couple always dismissed the attention, and on this day, headed toward their B gate at Midway Airport, destined for New York.

After years of discussing and planning their first great adventure together, they finally boarded the 8:10 a.m. Southwest Airlines flight on Saturday, June 7, 2014. When they landed at LaGuardia Airport, they quickly weaved their way through the crowded, dirty gray terminal corridor toward baggage claim.

Even though they were familiar and comfortable living in Chicago, the country's third largest city, seeing New York for the first time was a bit overwhelming. It was bigger, busier. So crowded! Horns blaring, people yelling at each other.

On the cab ride into Manhattan, Dylan thought he may have made a mistake bringing his bride to New York. In only forty-five minutes since landing, he had convinced himself that this adventure did not look like it would be very rewarding. On the other hand, it was a trip he had been thinking about for more than twelve years.

The cab driver pulled into the private driveway of the magnificent-looking Marriott Marquis in Times Square. Up the glass-enclosed elevator, the young Reilly couple traveled to the eighth floor, where they were quickly checked in and sent to a very nice and spacious eleventh-floor room. Finally, they were able to calm down and relax. A few hours later, after unpacking and enjoying a very tasty chicken salad sandwich, courteously delivered by a room service employee named Bob, they ventured out to absorb the excitement of the Big Apple.

They took a short stroll down the traffic-filled, noisy, and bustling Seventh Avenue in the heart of Manhattan. They walked toward the TKTS Booth at 47th Street and 7th Avenue, hoping to purchase half-price tickets to see what promised to be a hilarious comedy starring the great Nathan Lane.

When they reached the Times Square island, they stopped only for a moment to admire the wonderful statue and tribute to one of the great Broadway success stories, George M. Cohan. Besides being a symbol of great creativity and theatrical talent, for Irish-Americans familiar with his story, he symbolized the plight of many who endured the challenges of a making a living in a tough business, maintaining a commitment to his art and family, hard work, and devotion—characteristics so many Americans liked to pride themselves on. As Darlene gazed at the iconic black stone statue of the great Cohan, Dylan just stood back and admired his wife of three years. He cherished the look of happiness filling her oh-so-beautiful face, sparkling green eyes, and bright happy smile of contentment, knowing that she was leading quite a fulfilling and happy life.

Dylan and Darlene originally met in an ethics class at the University of Chicago in the fall of 2007 when they were partnered together on a research project to determine attitudes toward Muslim-Americans six years after 9/11. This turned out to be an eye-opening experiment for both, who hadn't considered themselves racist or bigoted on any level. They soon learned that they, like so many of those they surveyed, made judgments against anyone who looked to be of Middle Eastern heritage after the 9/11 terrorist attack. They knew it wasn't fair, but they also knew that their appearance immediately linked them to the terrorists that had become a constant feature on the nightly news. Those were the looks that identified the enemy to Americans, so how could they not have those thoughts enter their minds; some skepticism?

In 2007, the United States was already four years into the Iraq War. President George W. Bush justified the March 20, 2003 attack known as "Shock and Awe" on the belief that Iraq's President Saddam Hussein had weapons of mass destruction.

Beginning with 9/11 and then the Afghanistan War, followed by the Iraq War, the growing hatred toward Muslims became common nation-wide with news reports of mosques in the United States being damaged or vandalized. After finishing that project, Dylan and Darlene promised each other that they would not make any prejudiced assessments about Muslims or anyone they came in contact with based solely on how someone looked or dressed.

They worked hard to live by the famous statement from Martin Luther King Jr's speech on August 28, 1963 to more than 200,000 Americans on the National Mall in Washington, D.C., when he said, "I have a dream that my four little children will one day live in a nation where they will not be judged by the color of their skin, but by the content of their character." Dylan and Darlene had a wooden plaque created with that quote that hung in the living room of their condominium on the near West side of Chicago, where it served as a constant reminder to them.

After graduating from the University of Chicago in May of 2008, Dylan landed a teaching position at Watson College Prep on the Near West Side, teaching history and coaching hockey.

Darlene took a position with a nonprofit social services agency, Door Opener Chicago, helping the safety net population learn how to navigate the Medicaid and Medicare programs so they could correctly apply to receive health care coverage. She saw firsthand how many families really struggled and go without health care because they became frustrated with the extensive amount of paperwork that had to be filled out and filed, just to be considered for coverage.

Many were Hispanic immigrants or poor African Americans, who were unable to complete the many complicated application forms. Darlene's organization and other non-profits helped them, opening the door for them to Medicaid clinics and hospitals so they could receive quality and efficient health care services. Darlene was more than happy to tell people that her vocation was to help people who needed some assistance to get on the path to a healthier life. When asked about her work, she used to compare it to seeing someone standing in the pouring rain, because they weren't able to get into a locked building. She had the ability to unlock the door to that building. Let them in and dry them off. Give them a helping hand. Darlene felt very good about her efforts, knowing in her heart that she was living her Catholic faith.

Darlene was most certainly a very good person with only good intentions and no overt cynicism to tear down her spirit. From the day they met, Dylan told anyone who would listen to him that he had met the kindest woman alive and would marry her someday. He believed it with all of his heart. He often repeated himself, telling family and friends about this incredible lady.

He knew his caring and loving wife was special, maintaining her personal mission of "agape love," despite living in an increasingly unkind world. He always felt so lucky to have married her on Saturday, August 2, 2011. It was a simple but elegant ceremony presided by Father William Stenzel at Providence Church in the Pilsen neighborhood on the southwest side of Chicago.

The days passed for the young couple, and life changed. The first tradition they started together as a couple, was recording and watching the broadcast of the annual 9/11 ceremony from New York and Washington, D.C. Just a month into their marriage, Dylan and Darlene sat together in front of the large screen plasma television and watched the familiar but always heartbreaking event. Regardless of how many times they had watched it in the past, each year, they felt as Americans that they needed to watch the full ceremony. They needed to see and hear the announcement of each victim's name and the ringing of the fire engine bell to honor the departed and their families.

Dismissing the ceremony seemed a selfish choice, unpatriotic, not one they would ever choose to make. In 2002, they each watched the first annual broadcast of the event from their high school libraries. With each passing year however, the site from which they watched the ceremony would change.

As time passed, the progress was evident. Cranes and trucks continued to haul away mountains of debris from the fallen towers, leaving that mammoth whole in the ground.

During those years, the Lower Manhattan Development Corporation announced a competition for design plans for a new building. And that's when the arguments began. Where should the building be located? What was the best design? Were they planning on building on the land where the twin towers once stood? That was the land those who lost family members or friends during 9/11 wanted to see dedicated as a memorial to honor the remains of their loved ones. The final plans for the new One World Trade Center, also known as Freedom Tower, were unveiled on June 28, 2005.

By the anniversary ceremony of 2006, the once massive empty hole in the ground now had large cranes in it, setting the footings and foundation for the new building. It was a wonderful sight, signaling that America was moving forward. The tragedy of the past would be honored, but the future was on the rise in the form of an impressive new building that would be most often referred to as Freedom Tower.

Just south of the new building, plans were developed for a National September 11 Memorial & Museum. Once again to make it fair, a competition was held to select a design and architect for this project. Michael Arad of Handel Architects was selected, working with Peter Walker and Partners on the design. Together they created a beautiful scene with white oak trees and two large square reflecting pools in the center, marking where the Twin Towers once stood.

A dedication ceremony for the 9/11 Memorial was held on the 10th anniversary of the attacks, September 11, 2011, and then opened to the public. The 9/11 museum was officially opened on May 21, 2014, following the dedication on May 15, 2014. Life was moving forward in a positive direction for citizens of New York and all Americans.

Dylan followed the news about the progress of the building and museum. He strongly believed this was an historic destination every American should visit.

In August 2008, three months after graduation and a year after he and Darlene started dating, they began the tradition of watching the 9/11 ceremony together. Dylan had promised Darlene that once Freedom

Tower and the 9/11 museum were finished, they would make a trip to New York City to see it for themselves.

Since he was a kid growing up in Park Hills in the southwest suburbs of Chicago, the idea of actually visiting New York seemed a distant and unattainable fantasy. Before 9/11, America's largest city was a place he romanticized about living in one day, due to the perceptions created by the many movies and television shows filmed there. After September 11, that image was shattered, but a visit seemed even more appealing for the history-minded young man.

As the young couple stood in the long TKTS Booth line in Times Square, all of those thoughts and memories of that tragic day in September of 2001 flooded into his mind, resurrecting all of those buried angry feelings that had been stored somewhere in his brain. He wondered how he would feel once they arrived at Freedom Tower.

Dylan and Darlene purposely placed that priority item on their schedule toward the end of the trip, knowing it would stir up many emotions. They didn't want that to take away from the fun of seeing the many other popular tourist sites. But the 9/11 Ground Zero Tour was all Dylan could think about once they landed at LaGuardia.

As they drew closer to the window of the TKTS Booth, Darlene looked up to see that tickets were still available for that evening's performance of "A Funny Thing Happened on the Way to the Forum." Nathan Lane was one of their favorites, always so funny in his appearances on *The Late Show with David Letterman*. He always talked about his supposed wife, Marge, and the twins.

The next day, they planned to take the Lady Liberty Boat Tour to the Statue of Liberty and Ellis Island. On the drive to the boat docks in Lower Manhattan, Dylan knew they would be passing by Freedom Tower and get their first glimpse of the historical site.

Dylan, standing next to his loving wife nearly at the front of the line, couldn't avoid thoughts of changing the schedule and just jumping into a cab to travel immediately to the 9/11 memorial. He had to see the place that had caused such an upheaval of anger and frustration on that horrific September day in 2001. He had to see the place where unimaginable terror occurred when ten Al-Qaeda hijackers crashed American Airlines Flight 11 into the North Tower and United Airlines Flight 175 into the South Tower. He had to see the place where 2,753 innocent Americans were killed and thousands more injured. He had to stand in the place that left countless family members and friends affected for the remainder of their lives by those deaths and injuries.

Dylan had to be in the place where the cowardly sneak attack led a wave of patriotic boys across America, eighteen years of age and older, to enlist into the armed forces. That massive enlistment included dozens of senior boys he knew from his high school, St. John's Academy. He had to see the place that motivated Dylan's pal and hockey teammate, Joe Doyle, to enlist into the U.S. Marines immediately after graduating in May of 2004.

Dylan was so proud of his friend, going to war to defend America against evil-minded terrorists. As he stood there in Times Square, he recalled the report he had read in a military publication about his brave friend.

Lieutenant Joe Doyle's 1st Marine Regiment was deployed to Afghanistan where he was serving as platoon commander with the 2nd Platoon, Shilo Company. His platoon received the dangerous assignment of providing security for the parliamentary elections in the Nangarhar province.

Joe was doing his duty, standing guard, looking for potential threats, while a line of fearful voters stood before him. That's when his men, and the voters, came under fire.

"Take cover!" screamed Joe to his men as he stood firing his M-249 Squad Automatic Weapon toward the roof of a sun-dried brick build-ing, where small white explosions exposed the location of the gunfire.

As voters ran and Lieutenant Doyle's men dove behind a stone wall to take cover, Joe bent down to one knee, firing his weapon, picking off three of the Taliban. He saw them in his sight, their angry scowls.

He kept firing with no regard for his own life. And that's when it happened. One shot from a sniper positioned inside a tan rectangu-lar building more than one hundred yards away ended the life of the young and courageous Joe Doyle.

Just like that, Dylan's good friend Joe was gone forever. He would always be his hero.

Joe's death weighed on Dylan. Why were brave young Americans like Joe allowed to enlist and sent to Afghanistan and Iraq to fight for the freedom of all Americans, while most young people, including himself, could just go on with their daily lives in the relative safety of the United States? He wondered if it shouldn't be one-for-all and all-for-one.

If the United States is going to commit to fighting in a war, everyone should be involved, not just the patriots and the poor; those who love their country so much they are willing to die for freedom. That was a big "if" in the War on Terror.

Dylan looked up to see that Darlene was now just a few feet from purchasing their theater tickets. He could feel a constant tug to just step out of line. He was so anxious to stand on the hallowed ground where so many innocent Americans and brave first responders had lost their lives.

Dylan was certain that when Osama bin Laden and his terrorist organization carried out their act of evil, they never expected such an overwhelming response of courage and commitment by so many young Americans.

Dylan had watched the documentary by the Naudet brothers, Jules and Thomas, the French-born filmmakers who had been shooting a documentary on the New York Firefighters of Engine 7, Ladder 1, just a few blocks away from the twin towers when the 9/11 attacks took place. Their film, "9/11", started with Jules joining several of the firefighters who went to check on a gas leak and he saw American Airlines Flight 11 passing overhead.

Jules somehow had the presence of mind to lift his camera and film the jet as it crashed into the North Tower. Like everyone, they were shocked and confused. But the firefighters first instinct was to go to the scene of the crash to help. Jules continued with the group to the lobby of the North Tower where he filmed the fire chiefs setting up a command post. Frantic and fearful people were evacuating the building as quickly as possible.

Worst of all, loud thuds were heard just outside the building from those who were being burnt alive in the blaze several stories above. They jumped out of the building to end the pain of the overwhelming heat.

As Jules captured events in the North Tower, his brother Gedeon filmed the other airplane, United Flight 175, as it crashed into the South Tower. Then when the North Tower collapsed, Jules, still filming, gave the world a view while running for his life. Those were some of the images that lived in Dylan's mind. That was the reality of that day, which for him occurred during the first month of his sophomore year at St. John's Academy, standing in the library watching the television with his fellow students.

Osama bin Laden's cowardly attack on the United States certainly created fear in many Americans, who would begin judging anyone who looked to be of Middle Eastern heritage, anyone who identified themselves as Muslims. The national anger was directed at an enemy who had a certain look and believed in a specific religion, Islam. Whether it was fair or not, those were the only identifiable features Americans could link to the men who brought such devastation to their country.

News stories of American-born Muslims being beaten and harassed filled the pages of newspapers across the country during the first few months after 9/11. They were experiencing what German-Americans endured during World War I and Japanese-Americans faced during World War II. When United States citizens were getting killed and injured by an enemy, all consideration for politeness and rational thought went right out the window. Those who had a link to the enemy, were the enemy, in the minds of many Americans. That was true in 1917 and 1941. And it was just as true in 2001.

The day the United States finally found Bin Laden and sent Seal Team 6 to his compound in Afghanistan to capture or kill him in the middle of the night on May 2, 2011 was a joyous day throughout America. It didn't mean the end of a war on terrorism, but it did mean an end to the terrorist leader who planned and started all of the misery that so severely damaged all of those 9/11 families, friends, and first responders.

So Dylan wondered what he would feel like, once he was standing at the 9/11 memorial. Would he feel differently? Would stepping onto that sacred ground make him see the world differently? He didn't know, but he was eager to find out.

Darlene reached the window of the ticket booth, and Dylan watched his wonderful wife pass her credit card through the small opening under the window.

"Two tickets for 'Funny Thing Happened on the Way to the Forum,'" she said, smiling, excited to see a show that would make them both laugh and have such a wonderful time together. Dylan realized that seeing the show, and continuing their schedule as planned, would be the best idea. He would wait two more days to see the memorial.

CHAPTER THREE

*T*wenty-year-old Haydon Reuben Huff sat in the ragged and worn brown cloth recliner, the favorite armchair of his famous father, and studied the old photos of his father's glory days hanging on the living room walls. Gazing at them helped subside some of the pain he was feeling, following the funeral of his departed parent, Andy Huff.

Despite his father's poor relationship with his mother, Haydon had admired him. He certainly wished they had married and lived together as a family, but that wasn't the priority. Andy Huff's focus as one of the leaders of the 1960s counterculture Yippie (Youth International Party) movement was to make a major impact on America, a country he so desperately wanted to change to a communist nation.

Living in Chicago, Haydon stayed abreast of his father's continuing efforts to change America. However, he had no interest in getting involved physically, intellectually, or emotionally. That was his father's life. He loved his mother, Annie Lennard, and spent most of the days of his youth by her side in their North Side apartment. It was during the infrequent visits to his dad's apartment, a total of twelve over the twenty years of his life, that he learned of the intricate details of his celebrated exploits.

Haydon was most certainly his mother's son. He was short and thin with long, straight strawberry blond hair, pale skin, a narrow face with small cheeks and nose, weak chin, full lips, brown eyes, thin eyebrows, and not a muscle to be found on his body. He had a mild temperament, quiet, and no identifiable talent. He was all Lennard with no evident

Huff traits, other than a birth certificate from Cook County Hospital stating Andy Huff was his father.

When he did visit his father on those "special weekends," as Annie Lennard referred to them, he watched the way so many passersby on the street reacted to the legendary and still recognizable Andy Huff. His father literally could not walk down a street in America without someone yelling profane suggestions to round up his commune of cowardly, dope-smoking, freak followers and leave the country forever.

"Get the hell out of here! You're not wanted here, you Commie!" was the comment most often heard by Haydon during those early 1980s visits. On occasion, but more rarely as time went on, they would be approached by a former Woodstock attendee or counterculture activist who couldn't help but express their great admiration, appreciation, and gratitude for all the Yippie leader did to change America in the 1960s.

However, those complimentary remarks were usually followed by a request for money, loose change, whatever he had on him. One wild-eyed fan, who became frustrated when Huff had nothing to give, pulled a knife and threatened to kill young Haydon. But Huff had been in physical confrontations so often that he was always prepared with a can of mace to spray away any attackers, and that is how he dealt with the disheveled looking old homeless Yippie, who obviously had no one to follow any longer. It was a sad scene, resulting from a sad decade.

Haydon grew to view those old Yippies as pathetic people who really had no direction in their lives. For him, he viewed the 1960s as a time when millions of those lost souls had found a direction with the counterculture, war protests, and the Yippie movement. When that ended though, so did the roadmap for the ragtag, longhaired, pot-smoking, bell-bottom jeans, psychedelic-shirt-wearing youth.

Although most found a path back into society, working and living life like most Americans, there was still a small group who maintained a dedication to the Yippie vision. They would travel from commune to commune, following the Grateful Dead band on their concert tours, and always have a copy of Timothy Leary's book, *Turn On, Tune In, and Drop Out!* in their backpacks. The time, the movement, and energy behind it was long gone. Those Yippies who clung to the Flower Power days of the past found nothing but sadness and desperation.

A few months before his passing, Huff was contacted by organizers of another Woodstock rock festival that he committed to attending, but plans sputtered for the event when the residents of the rural upstate New York town vehemently protested against it and won. Later, he proactively attempted to join the recreation of the historic civil rights march of 1963 but was told by organizers to stay away. They didn't want the face of the Yippie movement branded onto the civil rights messages of Martin Luther King Jr.

Throughout the 1980s, President Ronald Regan had reinvigorated conservatism throughout the country. Greed and selfishness were in, as was voiced by actor Michael Douglas' character, Gordon Gekko, in the popular 1987 movie, *Wall Street*. In just over a decade, the majority of Americans had done a 180-degree turn away from the Yippie movement. The '80s would forever be known as the Yuppie decade.

Undeterred by the setbacks and social trends, Andy Huff developed plans for a protest outside the White House. He would help place a brighter spotlight on all of the lies being told about the Iran-Contra arms-for-hostages scandal. That fell flat as well, since most Americans were well aware of the scandal following Oliver North's nationally televised testimony before a joint congressional committee. His work as an author also failed, mostly because the title of his book, *Don't Pay for this Book*, encouraged readers to steal it. That didn't exactly inspire bookstore owners to carry his radical writings.

Once the face of the 1960s counterculture fully realized his voice of protest had lost support, even in Berkeley, California where he considered running for mayor, he took his messages to a new medium. To the amazement of many, he actually began doing standup comedy, making fun of politicians and anyone else he disagreed with at the time. Haydon had attended one of his performances and felt embarrassed for his father. He had been an important historical figure in America and was reduced to a joke teller. It must have bothered his father as well, because it was only a short time later that he was found lifeless in his second-floor Boston apartment, the cause of death reportedly an apparent overdose of anxiety medication. Many former followers questioned that report, believing the FBI had finally gotten to Huff.

As young Haydon sat in the recliner looking at all of those old photos, thinking about his father, really missing him for the first time in his life, he felt a strange urge to somehow pick up his father's torch. He thought perhaps he could resurrect the movement for those still lingering lost souls. All of those thoughts ran through young Huff's head as he stared at the one tattered photo of his mother and father standing together in Grant Park on August 25, 1968. They looked so happy together.

All of a sudden, he felt very much alone, given that his beloved mother had lost her life a few years earlier, on August 24, 1986, when crossing the street at Clark and Addison. She was struck by 1972 Volkswagen minivan, driven by Joseph Maury, a drunk, out-of-work actor, a longtime bleacher bum, speeding away after a Cubs loss to the Cincinnati Reds.

Haydon cried that day. He cried every day for the next two weeks. His mother was his whole life, his identity, to be sure. He had no friends and his father lived in Boston. It was his mother who raised him, loved him, and named him after the two other leaders who became most famous for protesting the Vietnam War. He missed her so much and was so overcome with depression that he even considered suicide. To get through it, he went on a weed and whiskey-binge for months, putting the pain out of his mind. When he came out of his haze, he hitchhiked to Boston to visit his father, which helped. And now, he was gone forever.

Haydon left Boston, once again feeling lost. He didn't cry a tear after his father died. He didn't need a weed and whiskey-binge to get through it. But he did think about his mother and father every day, feeling so alone.

Several months passed, and Haydon thought he had put it all behind him, when he found himself in a high-backed brown wooden chair, spending hours in the massive Chicago Public Library on Michigan Avenue. He read every article written about his father and mother. He learned about his mother's brother, Nester, and his work with the communists in Oregon. For the first time, his parents' destiny together made some sense. Then, he felt compelled to start calling some of the other leaders who went to trial with him in Chicago. He even made an attempt to connect with his three half-siblings, whom he had tried connecting with during the funeral, but was rejected.

Depressed, he started smoking weed daily, no whiskey this time. Then he tried cocaine. It didn't take long for him to realize he had become an addict. That's when an obsession, he never considered, was suddenly taking over his life. He had to come to terms with his reality. He was the son of Andy Huff, a love-child from a night of passion, during the historic 1968 protests in Chicago.

Before the violence started, the long, frizzy-black-haired, American-flag-shirt-wearing Andy Huff made more news that night than is reported in the history books. His intimate actions under a maple tree in Lincoln Park with Annie Lennard were not found in those historical documents. Annie Lennard was a beautiful pale-skinned twenty-year-old with long blonde hair, accentuated with a daisy flower crown, wearing a tight white midriff top, low-waist bell bottom hip-hugger jeans, and brown leather sandals. She drew the attention of every male protestor that evening, but she chose Huff.

The Yippie leader's appearance, his unimpressive medium-build, hardened dark-toned serious face, steely eyes, long nose, big ears, and thick lips, would have never drawn the attention of someone as pretty as Annie. It was the excitement of his newfound national celebrity that gained her interest.

Later, after testing positive for pregnancy, Annie thought she was destined for national recognition as Mrs. Yippie, the leader's activist wife. Her brother, Nester, would be so proud of her.

Instead, the already-married Huff attempted to pay her off, asking her to keep the pregnancy and birth quiet. After a long quarrel at Hipster's Brew, a coffeehouse located at North Avenue and Wells Street, and an emotional breakdown over his plea for an abortion, she sternly told him that she was having the baby. She took the money, calling him a hypocrite and phony, as the two-dozen hippies around them snapped Polaroid photos of the confrontation. But as she stood there berating him, she demanded that he commit to see his child regularly or she would go to Frankie Flynn at number-one-rated Channel 7 Eyewitness News and tell him the whole story. He agreed.

So on May 20, 1969, Haydon Reuben Huff was delivered at Cook County Hospital, beginning a tragic existence of loneliness and confusion. And twenty years later, on the evening of July 20, 1989, a cocaine-weary Haydon sat in his tiny Northside apartment, watching a retrospective on the new cable channel, CNN, showing Neil Armstrong stepping onto the moon and planting the American flag into the soft gray surface.

It was at that moment, when he decided that he was going to fully follow in his father's footsteps. He was going to reignite the Yippie movement, organize protests, attack institutions, and bring down America. Eyes wide open and pacing back and forth in front of the small Zenith television, he glared at that American flag on the moon, a symbol he had always had mixed feelings about as a kid because of his mother's and father's mutual disrespect for the country. But now, it was all clear: America was his enemy and the American flag the symbol of his enemy.

Over the next decade, he struggled to organize protests that had any impact. He was only able to draw a few hundred followers at most. His largest protest was his first, on August 25, 1989, outside City Hall in Chicago. Huff called for an end to the Dorgan regime.

The mayor, Jimmy Dorgan, was the son of James J. Dorgan, Chicago's mayor during the 1968 Democratic Convention who gave the order to, "Shoot to kill!" to stop the violent protests in Grant Park, which were led by Haydon's father.

With the new millennium on the horizon, Haydon named his new counterculture activist group, Millippies (Millennial International Party), and had them all dress in colorful tie-dye Millippies t-shirts, while he wore an American flag shirt, just like his father had worn twenty-one years earlier. Of the two-hundred-plus Millippies, the only one Haydon knew was Paul Cavon, a journalist for an alternative weekly newspaper, *The Bleeder*.

Cavon hated the Dorgan family more than anything in the world. He met Haydon in Stateville Correctional Center, where he was serving time for harassment of J.J. Mack, an Oak Park resident who was a close friend of the Dorgan family. The police were called as forty-two-year-old Cavon banged on Mack's front door like a little kid trying to get his way, pleading with Mack to turn over dirt on Jimmy Dorgan. It backfired on him.

So the short, brown-haired, out-of-shape, beady-eyed Cavon was the first, and most eager one, to join with Haydon in his efforts to protest against Mayor Dorgan outside City Hall. The profane signs about Dorgan, loud vulgar chants, and finally rocks thrown through the windows of City Hall drew every television crew in town, along with WBEZ Radio and WBBM Radio, to cover the protest.

Seeing the lights of the cameras pouring onto his group, young Huff felt like he was on his path to success. Then, a CBS reporter, Jack "Bulldog" Drummer, pulled him over for an exclusive interview. That was the moment he revealed to the world, well perhaps just Chicago at that moment, that he was the son of Andy Huff, and he was reigniting his father's movement but calling it Millippies. Drummer then asked, "Your father's group, the Yippies, used to have people yelling at them, 'Shut your yappies, ya bunch of Yippies.' Do you think the name Millippies lends itself to easy negative rants like, 'Millippies are a bunch of dippies,' or verbal quips like that?"

Having never considered that response to the name he created, young Huff said, "No, and if they do try calling us such sophomoric names, they'll pay for it."

Once the other television and radio crews found out it was Andy Huff's son, they all came over for an unplanned press conference, Haydon smiling ear-to-ear at the attention.

"We've got to bring the Dorgans down!" he shouted, pumping his right fist in the air. "We've got to bring down the corrupt Dorgan machine!"

The crowd roared, "Down with Dorgan! Down with Dorgan!"

Haydon waited until the crowd had quieted a little, then looked directly into the five television cameras and yelled out, "We've got to bring down America! And we will fight against anyone who stands in our way!"

The crowd of Millippies all roared their approval as the producers and reporters behind the camera lights seemed to give young Huff a unified look of bewilderment, wondering if he had any idea of what he just told the world, and specifically the FBI. None were surprised when the three Chicago Police paddy wagons screeched up to the curb along Clark Street. The bright blue lights flashing atop their vehicles resulted in most of the Millippies running away across Dorgan Plaza, like Ferris Bueller, Dr. Richard Kimble, and Jake & Elwood Blues, the film characters who made the plaza with the strange brown metal Picasso sculpture famous worldwide.

Cavon and Haydon were the only ones left standing as a young Chicago Police officer grabbed Huff's arms, put them behind his back, and slapped the metal handcuffs on. "You're under arrest for intent to incite a riot!"

A huge smile crossed the young activist leader's face as he was led to the back door of the paddy wagon, knowing that was the same charge his father and the other six defendants were indicted on twenty-one years earlier.

"And it is just me, just one Millippie, to incite that right. Isn't that right, pig?" he snapped at the officer, who looked somewhat irritated.

"Yeah, well, it only takes one dippy Millippie. And you are that one. Have fun in jail, dipshit!"

Huff glanced out at the crowd one last time, only to see CBS reporter Bulldog Drummer shrugging his shoulders as if to say, told you so.

Cavon, now also in cuffs, looked at his leader. "Hey, I'm still here, ya know."

"Sorry, Paul," said Haydon. "I didn't see you. I guess it's two dippy Millippies, eh?"

Haydon and Cavon were both convicted and sentenced to a year in Stateville. Whereas Cavon was released after one year, Haydon spent five years, because of his attempts to incite prisoner riots in the courtyard of the massive yellow-stoned prison.

After his release, he tried again to resurrect the Millippies, but other than Cavon, who was writing weekly columns for *The Bleeder* attacking the Dorgan family, he had no takers. Haydon became depressed, frustrated. In September of 2001, he felt so despondent that he travelled back to Boston, planning to end his life in the same room his father had died.

When he arrived at the old wooden three-story apartment on Blue Hill Avenue in Dorchester, Massachusetts, the chipped away white paint on the front of the building was covered with graffiti, indicating people were aware that his father had lived there. There were upside-down peace symbols, several communist sickles, red spray paint reading: "Commie Go Home!" "Shut Your Yappies Yippies!" "Huff = Coward!" "Forrest Gump Won't Save You!"

The building was abandoned, obviously no-one wishing to live in a building that drew such derisive attacks.

Haydon jostled the old wooden front door open and walked up the familiar staircase, which creaked loudly with each step. The door to his father's apartment was open. All of the furniture, old photos, and memorabilia were gone, most likely divided among his other children. But for some reason, his favorite armchair, the recliner, sat right in the middle of the dusty living room with old newspapers strewn across the floor. It looked like homeless squatters may have been there more than a few times over the past decade. The stench was overwhelming, and Haydon couldn't open the windows fast enough to air it out.

He looked out of the large pane front window into the bright lights shining over Boston. This would be his last day on Earth. He wondered if he would see the Heaven so many believed in. Would he see his mother? Or would Hell be his destination? Would his father be there?

He began having second thoughts about his plan. But no, he was done. His life was over. He sat in his father's recliner with an open bottle of Aquafina water on the armrest. He counted to three, opened the prescription of Xanax, and poured the entire bottle into the palm of his right hand. He looked at the pink football-shaped pills; then took a deep breath as he worked up the courage to end his life.

As he lifted his hand toward his opened mouth, his cellphone rang. He stopped, then glanced down at the phone, seeing it was Paul Cavon, his only friend in the world. He thought for a moment, but then decided to answer the call; his last. He grabbed the phone with his left hand, and before he could say hello, Paul blurted out, "Did you see it? Did you see it man? They crashed two planes into the Twin Towers, the heart of Wall Street! They are bringing down America!"

A huge smile grew on Haydon's face, throwing the pink pills into the air and shouting in the phone, "Yes!"

Whoever was flying those planes into the symbol of American wealth obviously hated America just as much as him. He believed he may have found his new ally. He would track them down to work with them to bring down America together.

CHAPTER FOUR

$\mathcal{S}$tanding on the sidewalk in the breezeway outside the Marriott Marquis awaiting their Uber, Dylan was so grateful his beautiful wife was by his side to share the experience of seeing the Twin Towers memorial. This was an important day for both of them, the historical destination they had talked about visiting for nearly seven years, going back to their days as students at the University of Chicago.

Dylan would never forget the moment when he first laid eyes on Darlene Quilty. On that beautiful afternoon in October of 2007, when she turned the corner to enter the classroom, she was most certainly a breathtaking vision of loveliness, pure elegance. Her long, shimmering auburn hair swayed from side to side as she walked, a bright white smile, and such beautiful green eyes; so beautiful!

Dylan was lovestruck. He couldn't take his eyes off of her. She noticed. Smiles were exchanged.

Dylan felt his heart flutter as she looked him directly in the eyes. He knew then that a magical love connection was created that would never be broken.

Partnered together on a research project, he remembered how she would often gaze at him, making him feel so special. Her attention to him never seemed to cease, making him feel like the coolest guy on the planet.

It was a shared head-over-heels, droopy-eyed, endless love. She often voiced her appreciation for his obsession with history and their shared reading habits, including some of the greatest American novels from Thomas Wolfe to Ernest Hemingway to Pat Conroy.

Outside the Marriott, a yellow cab pulled into the breezeway, ending his daydream. Dylan watched the gray uniformed Marriott bellman step up to the cab and open the door to help the passenger out, just as a well-dressed older couple came through the revolving doors of the hotel.

"Do you ever think about our college days?" Dylan asked his beautiful bride, which drew a curious expression and a tilt of the head.

"What brings that up?" she asked, her eyes darting from side to side, trying to read his thoughts.

"I was just thinking of how many times we have talked about this day."

"Oh yes, we did talk about it quite often," she nodded, now understanding the basis for his question. "But when I think about our college days, I mostly remember walking arm-in-arm with you on campus, fending off all of those 'stare girls' who used to annoy me to no end."

"Stare girls?"

"Yeah, you were oblivious to them, but too many girls couldn't help but notice that you were six feet tall, good looking and in perfect shape. They would just stare a hole right through you. Drove me crazy! I thought about putting a sign on you that said 'TAKEN.'"

"Yeah, I never noticed…"

"Yes I know you didn't, because the second you looked at them, they would very quickly turn their head, as if they weren't looking at you."

They both laughed as they watched a black Lincoln Town Car pull up and the smiling energetic bellman opened the back door to help the older couple get into the vehicle, receiving a quick tip for his courtesy.

"You know you had your share of boys staring at you as well. I should have been the one to put a sign on you that said 'TAKEN,'" quipped Dylan, recalling all of the new romance recruits waiting on the sidelines for Darlene, ready to get in the game, if her relationship with Dylan was called on account of rain or poor team support or whatever may cause a split. But there would be no rain or poor team support or misunderstandings, and with each passing year, the couple grew closer and more in love.

"Well those 'stare boys' were hard to miss," Darlene smirked. "Because unlike the girls, they just kept looking and looking and…"

Laughter erupted again. The bellman smiled watching the happy couple.

"But when I think about those days, I really used to love watching you play hockey for the Maroons. You were so fast, so fun to watch. And your team always won!" reminisced the five-foot-four-inch beauty with a healthy athletic figure, developed from years of running and playing competitive tennis.

"Yeah, those were fun days to be sure," Dylan nodded, watching a silver Mercury Grand Marquis drive into the two-lane breezeway.

"This is our car," he said, watching the bellman once again perform the ritual of opening the door, Darlene stepping in first, followed by Dylan, who slipped the very polite and helpful young man a few dollars.

The beautiful married couple sat hand in hand in the back seat of the silver minivan as it drove onto a busy 46th street in the always bustling New York City. As the driver turned right onto 7th Avenue, Dylan couldn't help but feel overly excited, yet somewhat anxious. Yes, the day before, during the drive to the dock to board the Lady Liberty Boat Tour to see the Statue of Liberty and Ellis Island, they actually had a chance to get a glimpse of the great new Freedom Tower. On this day, however, he knew they would see it all. They would experience it all, something he had been thinking about since that fateful day in September of 2001.

After only a few minutes in the Uber assigned SUV, Dylan's thoughts were pulled from their destination to the man driving; a long-bearded fellow who apparently wasn't too keen on taking showers. The vehicle was filled with a stench that was so strong it could knock a buzzard off a dung heap. Several times, Dylan looked over at Darlene who was obviously under siege by an odor that should have been outlawed or quarantined. He gave serious consideration to asking the driver to stop the vehicle, so they could get another Uber or cab or Rigshaw, as long as there was no odor-challenged driver attached. But the fare was already paid and he didn't want to go through the hassle of requesting a refund. Instead, he opened both backseat windows, which seemed to irritate the unfragranced one in the driver's seat, who was forced to turn off the air conditioning. Dylan whispered to Darlene that they would be there in just a few minutes and would have to endure it. They did.

The dented Grand Marquis pulled up to the curb and stopped on Fulton Street at One World Trade Center just after 9 a.m. Dylan and Darlene climbed out of the back seat and stepped gratefully into a warm breeze and fresh air. The sight of the tall, sun-reflective, glass-paned skyscraper, the Freedom Tower, immediately grabbed their attention.

Together, they looked all the way up to the top, Darlene nearly fell over as she tilted her head back and Dylan had to catch her. And there they stood, right in the place where it all happened, gazing up at the incredibly impressive new skyscraper.

It was quite a sight and most certainly a symbol of America's ability to rebound from devastation. Dylan just smiled, holding Darlene's warm hand, and walked toward the Twin Towers Waterfalls, where the two great white-marbled buildings once stood.

This was the place where Osama bin Laden's misguided, brain-washed group of terrorists used jet planes as their suicide weapons to crash into each tower, bringing them down, killing nearly three thousand innocent people.

Dylan couldn't help but remember standing in the library of St. John's Academy as he watched United Airlines Flight 175 circle around the burning South Tower and crash directly into the North Tower, an unbelievably horrifying sight. It wasn't a movie. It wasn't something a writer or director concocted. It had actually happened.

The devastating event had taken place thirteen years earlier, yet the waterfalls were an ever-present reminder of the dangers that will always exist in the world; the damage and harm evil men can deliver when neg-atively influenced and pointed in the wrong direction.

The young couple walked up to the side of the South Tower memo-rial site and looked down at the large square pool of water with an elegant waterfall cascading down each side to the base. They watched it flow further down to the smaller square hole in the middle, the water symbol-izing life, and the dark hole representing the path to the remains of those who perished in the tower.

This was the historic landmark that Dylan had to stand on, look at, feel, pray over. Standing at the corner, Dylan and Darlene read the names etched into the stone:

Vincent Paul Abate, Andrew Anthony Abate, Timothy Michael O'Brien, Glen Wall, Farrell Peter Lynch, Eamon J. McEneaney, Matthew Timothy O'Mahony, Sean Patrick Lynch....

So many names! So many innocent lives lost! So infuriating, mad-dening, thirteen years later!

"I wonder if the victims' families feel any better when they visit here and see the names," Darlene asked her husband, "or if it just pulls them back to that day and the great sadness it brought to their lives?"

"It might be like when we go to the cemetery," Dylan replied. "Yes, it's sad, but somehow you feel like you are visiting your loved ones, praying to God for them, thinking about them. I hope they feel a sense of fulfillment being here, but I'm sure everyone responds a little differently. Either way, let's say a prayer together for them."

Darlene and Dylan made the sign of the cross and said the Lord's Prayer in unison.

"God please bless all of those who lost their lives here on 9/11," prayed Dylan, loud enough for Darlene to hear him. "All of those innocent victims trapped in the burning towers, and the first responders who lost their lives trying to save them. We also pray that you can bring their families and friends comfort as the days of destruction fade further into their collective memories."

"Amen," Darlene said to finish the prayer, then reached out to hug her husband, holding him tight, realizing more than ever as they stood at the historic site, that life was a gift that should never be taken for granted. It could be taken away at any time, immediately, without warning.

As the couple stood embracing, they watched and listened to the clean cascading waters flowing down into the large gaping hole that was once the base for the South Tower. Dylan felt a sense of peacefulness fill his mind and body. Such an awful event happened right there, but now it was peaceful. The sound of the falling water filled his head as he turned to look at his loving wife. Overwhelmed by the emotions of the moment, they kissed, feeling so lucky to be alive.

"I just hope somehow, someway, they will be able to stop something like this from ever happening again in our country," said Dylan, looking high above the waterfalls, fighting off the images of the blazing South Tower, people being burned so badly they jumped out of windows to their deaths. That visual was cemented in his memory which haunted him and so many Americans since that fateful day.

"Shall we go see the museum now?" asked Darlene, a soft smile of happiness accentuating her beautiful face. As they began walking across the plaza to the entrance of the 9/11 Museum, Dylan turned to take one more glance at the magnificent waterfalls only to be distracted by a man in a blue corduroy jacket standing on the other side of the South Tower memorial.

The man caught Dylan's attention because of his blond hair and darkened face. It didn't look right. It looked like he had put something on his face to make it darker, like brown face paint. It was odd to be sure. As he continued staring at the scowling man, he noticed his eyes had a look of anger that set off Dylan's protective instincts. He not only looked very strange, but dangerous.

"C'mon Darlene, let's get inside," said Dylan, picking up his pace into the entrance of the museum.

"What's wrong?" asked Darlene, curious as to why her husband felt it was necessary to hurry.

"I'm not sure," said Dylan, spotting a security guard inside. "I saw a guy out there and he didn't look right. He's very strange looking and had a really angry look on his face! I'm going to let that security guard know about him, just in case."

"Oh, yes, that's a good idea," Darlene said, knowing her husband was not one to overreact as they approached the uniformed museum security guard with "SECURITY" across the back of his bright blue shirt.

"Hello, officer. I just wanted to bring something to your attention," said Dylan to the five-foot-eight-inch, out-of-shape, thick-moustached security guard. "I just saw a strange-looking man outside near the South Tower memorial. He has blond hair, but something on his face, like face paint, to make it look brown, dark. And he had a very unusual expression on his face, just filled with anger. To me, either there's something wrong with him or he's about to do something. I don't know. But I wanted to be sure to bring it to your attention."

A smirk grew on the security guard's face.

"Sure, I get it," said the officer with a strong Brooklyn accent. "You're at the Freedom Tower for the first time, right?"

"Yes," said Dylan, looking around, realizing this guard wasn't taking him seriously.

"You're overwhelmed by the fact that you're standing in the place where the worst attack on American soil took place, and you have to keep an eye out for terrorists, who will no doubt attack again, right?"

"Well, I don't know about that, but I do know that I just saw a fellow out there, who looked like he could be a threat. I have great instincts about those types of things…"

"Okay, look sir, with all due respect," said the security guard with a walkie-talkie attached to the black leather belt threaded through the loops of his navy blue slacks. "I get tourists like you coming up to me nearly every day saying they saw a terrorist. It's okay. The city of New York understands. But why don't you just go ahead and view the museum. It's amazing!"

"But officer…" Dylan said, seeing two armed Port Authority Police, Special Operations officers, outside and thought he had better go tell them.

Too late! Before he could finish his sentence, all of a sudden a burst of gunfire could be heard outside. The security guard's smile dropped and his eyes grew wide.

"Or perhaps you were right," he said and quickly grabbed his walkie-talkie, ran out the door, seeing dozens of screaming people running across the 9/11 Memorial Plaza. The two Port Authority Police Officers had their guns drawn and ran to the side of the South Tower memorial to take cover as they exchanged gunfire with the man whom Dylan had pointed out.

"We have to get out of here, Dylan," said a panicked Darlene, whose husband grabbed her by the arm and hustled her further into the museum, hoping to escape any stray bullets or bombs or whatever dangers might come their way. They found what seemed to be a safe corner to hide. They watched one, then two, then six heavily armed police officers run out of the museum entrance, guns drawn and pointed at the shooter.

"Stay down everyone, stay here!" yelled one of the other museum guards. His instructions elicited screams from several women who looked to be tourists, some apparently of Middle Eastern descent.

"Oh thank God they're not…" blurted Darlene, stopping mid-sentence, and kissing goodbye the ethnic sensitivity training she received in college. Who could blame her? They were under attack! People were being shot.

Loud, long horror-filled screams slammed through the museum hallways. The terrorist was shooting people at random, anyone in his line of fire.

The police kept firing at him. Pop, pop, pop! Pop, pop, pop! Pop, pop, pop! The sound of submachine guns and semi-automatic weapons echoed across the Memorial Plaza. More police arrived on the scene, New York City Police. A dozen guns were firing at the one assailant, who was using the memorial wall for cover. Pop, pop, pop! Pop, pop, pop!

The terrorist desperately shot his AR-15 assault rifle at anyone he could hit—police, citizens, whoever. As long as they were Americans, he wanted them dead. Dylan's eyes were pulled toward the sight of several people lying on the ground with blood splattered across their backs as they laid face down.

All of a sudden, the terrorist jumped up and ran toward Freedom Tower. Police submachine guns blazed at him. The blond-haired, brown-faced killer sprinted full speed toward the tower entrance. The gunfire was loud, rapid. He was fast but not fast enough.

All eyes were on the fleeing terrorist, who was only twenty feet from the tower entrance when his arms and head were abruptly jolted backward. Red filled the white upside-down peace symbol on the back of his blue corduroy jacket as he fell to the ground, his face hitting the sidewalk, bouncing up and then down. Everyone watched the motionless, strange-looking man. No movement. They continued watching. He looked lifeless. It was over.

An army of police officers sprinted to the downed shooter. One furious cop opened up on him with his automatic weapon blazing. The terrorist's body jolted with each round. If he wasn't dead before, he most certainly didn't survive that explosion of frustration and anger. Onlookers watched half-horrified, half-elated. America was far past the point of feeling sorry for terrorists.

Dylan knew that most of the people watching the SWAT officer unload his weapon into that man supported him fully. He also knew it was time to leave but was hoping to spare Darlene from seeing the dead bodies lying in the plaza. Out the door they went, holding each other tightly, Dylan turning her head away from the murderous and bloody scene.

The sound of emergency sirens filled the air with dozens of police and fire personnel arriving on the scene. Television news crews screeched up to the curb in their white news vans with large satellite dishes on top.

Dylan had an Uber waiting for them. Unlike their ride to Freedom Tower, this driver offered a clean car filled with the scent of evergreen. A green Christmas-tree-styled air freshener hung from the rearview mirror.

Once safely back into their eleventh floor room at the Marriott Marquis, they turned on the television news to see the coverage. On CNN, the anchor, Katie Cash, reported that five people had been shot, but they didn't know the extent of their injuries at that time. Veteran correspondent Jim Acuna described the scene. His network showed emergency medical personnel lifting the bodies onto gurneys and then into the back of the red-and-white New York Fire Department ambulances lined up next to each other. Two victims were completely covered by sheets, while the other three were injured but alive.

"Do you think they are allowed to show that footage?" asked Darlene, concerned for the families of those who were shot. "Seems like they shouldn't be showing any of that until after they have contacted the families, right?"

"You're right," Dylan said. "Apparently that's the world we live in now. No consideration, especially for those who have been shot."

They continued watching events unfold, flipping from station to station, wherever they could get a different view, some new information.

On WABC-TV, reporter Rose Abraham was interviewing the New York Chief of Police, Bill Grannon, and asked, "Can you confirm that the shooter is dead?"

"Yes, he is deceased," said Chief Grannon. "In addition, five pedestrians were shot. Two are deceased, and we do not have the extent of the injuries of the other three as of yet."

"Have you identified the killer?" asked Abraham.

"Yes," said Grannon. "His name is Nelson Lennard, son of the deceased communist leader from the 1960s, Nester Lennard. He is a known criminal, having been imprisoned twice in Portland and then transferred to Stateville Correctional Center."

"I see," continued the local ABC reporter. "And we understand that you found something unusual on him?"

"Yes, he was wearing an American flag shirt, reminiscent of the 1960s protestors," Grannon said, throwing his hands up in the air, baffled by the shirt. "Also, he wore brown face paint."

"Any idea why he had face paint on?"

"The only thing we can assume is that he was trying to fool people into thinking he had brown skin, as if he were a radical Muslim terrorist," explained Grannon.

Dylan just looked at Darlene and said, "See, I told you. It was face paint."

"Yeah, not real bright," Darlene said.

"Downright stupid," Dylan said, turning the channel to WCBS-TV and a familiar face appeared. The security guard they'd spoken to earlier was being interviewed. His name was shown at the bottom of the screen: Officer Fred Mizelli.

"We understand that you may have been tipped off to this terrorist just before he started on this shooting rampage?" asked legendary reporter, May Calvin, who became so familiar to New Yorkers from her great 9/11 coverage.

"Yes, I was just inside the entrance of the museum when a man and his wife approached me saying they had seen a fellow near the South Tower Memorial who looked dangerous," said Mizelli. "Well, I responded immediately and ran right out the door to alert the Port Authority Police."

"Oh my goodness!" said Darlene, stunned at what she was hearing. "Responded immediately? No, how about you argued with us saying this happens every day. Liar!"

"It's alright," said Dylan. "What's he going to say? 'If I had listened to that couple, perhaps all of these people wouldn't have been shot?'"

"Well that's the truth of it," said Darlene. "If he had alerted the police on his walkie-talkie instead of dismissing it, maybe he could have stopped some of those people from being shot. It's maddening! That could have been us. That could have been anyone. How do you protect yourself against that kind of attack? How?"

"It's just one bad security guard, just unlucky I picked the wrong guy to tell," said Dylan, watching the gruesome coverage, looking like he had come face to face with a reality he never thought he would have to deal with in his life.

"Darlene, if one of those, or all of those people were carrying a gun, they might have had a chance," said Dylan, words he never thought he would speak.

"Dylan! How can say that? We don't carry guns. We don't use guns!"

"I know, but what if that had been us standing there when that maniac started firing his gun? And he started shooting right toward us, then what would we have done?"

Darlene stood silent, then blurted out, "We would have run!"

"We would have run, just like those people did, five of whom didn't make it to safety. Five of whom just had their families lives impacted forever. Two of whom are gone forever!"

"Dylan, we aren't gun people! We just can't!"

Dylan just stared at the final ambulance pulling away from the scene as the news camera zoomed in on a woman who obviously knew one of the victims. She was crying uncontrollably. The WCBS news anchor, Nancy Drudge, stopped talking and let her viewers listen to the sounds from One World Trade Center where another crisis had just occurred and a lone woman stood with tears pouring down her cheeks.

"I don't know, Darlene," said Dylan, wondering if they would now feel forced to finally purchase a weapon to protect themselves. He knew what that meant and the many dangers associated with bringing a gun into the home. He knew what it could mean for him and his young bride, especially after they started having children.

Dylan was sure he and Darlene would discuss it at great length, but being faced with a potentially life-threatening situation had forced him to accept the hard fact that as long as guns were allowed in American society, the idea of purchasing a gun to protect themselves had to become a real consideration.

CHAPTER FIVE

When the new millennium arrived in Chicago, several new condominium skyscrapers began popping up along the north and south ends of Lakeshore Drive, filling in gaps in the already impressive skyline view. By 2014, that view from the great Lake Michigan could be described as a work of art, ready for printing on the postcards for the millions of tourists visiting the city of Daley, Ditka, Jordan, Payton, Oprah, Royko, and yes, Capone.

In the early morning of the second Sunday in July, on the twenty-third floor of one of the many condo buildings in the River North area, five men in their twenties sat around a large round solid oak table with firearms and explosives organized across the top. Four AK-47 assault rifles, rocket propelled grenades (RPGs) with launchers, boxes of DM-41 hand grenades, .357 Magnum handguns, 50-round plastic ammo boxes, magazine clips, and explosive belts of dynamite sticks. It was a large assortment of weaponry, being prepared for massive destruction and death in the near future.

The four dark-bearded, brown-skinned young men, dressed similarly in black shirts, black jeans and combat-style boots, had a look of universal determination and anger across their collective faces. This was serious business. This day would be the day they would each become a martyr for Allah and receive their reward of seventy-two virgins in paradise, which was the belief of Wahhabism taken from literal belief from writings in the Quran. That was the goal these four angry young men focused on that day.

They would not be thinking about the pain they would endure during the moments of their impending death, when they would walk out onto a busy, traffic-filled, Michigan Avenue and start shooting Americans. Any Americans! All Americans! Anyone who lived in America, walked the streets of Chicago or New York, anywhere in the fifty states. Anyone who did not believe in their extreme Muslim ideology was their enemy. They were infidels. They would have to die. This is what they had been taught, convinced, believed, after viewing many propaganda videos, produced by the terrorist group, Al-Qaeda.

This terror cell's leader, Ziad Haznawi, was a twenty-five-year-old Saudi nationalist and ardent believer in Wahhabism, the faith founded in the nineteenth century following the doctrine of Muhammad ibn Abd al-Wahhab. In line with his faith, Ziad believed that all those who weren't true believers in this form of Islam, infidels, were enemies.

These beliefs had resulted in the violent and murderous actions of Wahhabis across the globe–beheadings, suicide bombings, burning people alive–all of which they claimed was done in the name of Allah, including the 9/11 attack in New York City.

Ziad, wearing his Saudi red and white ghutrah headdress, laid out a map of the Magnificent Mile, along north Michigan Avenue in Chicago. The other three included Ziad's best friend, Fayez Hanjour, a twenty-five-year-old also from Saudi Arabia, who recently dropped out of the University of Illinois-Chicago after struggling for two years to achieve passing grades; Hassan Bahar, a twenty-three-year-old Iraqi who illegally crossed the border into the United States through Mexico; and Malik Morcos, a forty-two-year-old Jordanian ex-convict, released from Stateville Correctional Center after serving ten years for drug trafficking and unlawful possession of firearms.

Originally, Malik had planned to travel to Afghanistan to join up with Al-Qaeda after being released from prison, but while planning his trip with a few friends at a local hookah bar on 87th Street in the southwest suburb of Burbank, he was introduced to Ziad and changed his plans. Why travel to Afghanistan to kill Americans when he was surrounded by the enemy and could carry out his jihad in Chicago?

"Fayez, you will be positioned right here," said Ziad, using a bright blue pen to point to the corner of Michigan Avenue and Delaware. "Malik, you will be directly across the street, right here. Hassan, you will be with me, right here in front of the Walgreens at Michigan and Chicago avenues. Fayez, you enter Water Tower Place through the back entrance, which is always the least crowded area of the building. Take the elevator up to the eighth floor and wait for my group text. Malik, you should be in a good position to shoot both RPGs into the John Hancock Center. That will cause severe damage. Hassan, you will walk into the historic Water Tower building to leave your backpack of explosives. I will go into the Water Tower pumping station and do the same. Hassan when our bombs explode, that's when we take out the AK-47s and shoot every American left standing outside of the Water Tower. It's an open area, so you will have good sightlines for your targets."

They each nodded, looking intently at their leader as their instructions were laid out.

"Now gentlemen," Ziad continued. "I know we are all prepared to die today, but if we do this right, all of us will be able to walk away and live another day to create more chaos, kill more Americans and, most importantly, increase the paranoia among the infidels of this evil Western country."

Hassan then interrupted, "Ziad, I am prepared to die today. I am prepared to go to paradise and receive seventy-two virgins as is promised to us in the Quran."

"As am I," said Ziad, nodding in full agreement.

"And I," said Malik and Fayez simultaneously, all smiling at the solidarity of the moment.

"But Ziad, I must ask you, because I have read it and saw an expert on the Quran talk about this on CNN," Hassan said with some doubt evident in his voice.

"What, Hassan? What are you saying?" asked a curious Ziad.

"A man named Irshad Manji who is an Islam scholar said that there is a mistranslation of the word virgins. He said nowhere in the Quran does it promise seventy-two virgins. He said it only promises something lush and that the Arabic word for virgin has been mistranslated. The real word in the Quran doesn't mean virgins, it means raisins. Raisins, Ziad! Ziad I do not want to die a martyr only to arrive in Heaven and receive seventy-two raisins!"

"You can't believe those lies!" scolded Ziad, standing and walking angrily around the room, looking at his misguided conspirator.

"They had several scholars who had investigated it and had the exact same conclusion that raisin is the correct translation. I don't want to die for raisins," explained Hassan, receiving stares filled with disappointed looks from his three jihadist collaborators.

"That was on an American television network, spewing false propaganda," said Ziad, now growing quite angry. "The Quran says seventy-two virgins! Seventy-two virgins, not raisins."

"With respect Ziad, that's not completely accurate," said Fayez, adjusting his ghutrah, hoping not to upset his leader and best friend. "The Quran never said seventy-two virgins. It says that those who fight for Allah and are killed will be given a great reward, women in Islamic Heaven. It says they will be beautiful virgins with large eyes and big, firm, and round breasts. Companions of equal age. That's what it says."

"Yes, Fayez, but again the term 'virgins' is the issue here," Hassan emphasized. "The Quran experts are saying it means raisins. So big beautiful round raisins, not virgins. Is that what I am to believe?"

"The seventy-two virgins comes from the sunna, you know, the hadiths or practices of Muhammad," said Fayez, imploring his friend to consider these facts. "It's not directly from the Quran. But I've never been told it meant anything other than virgins, women. Are you sure these aren't lies created by the Jews?"

"Well, I don't know," said Hassan, raising his arms up to express his confusion. "But I've never heard it before. And there were several experts, enough to make me think twice about this jihad."

An angry, defiant-looking Malik stepped to the middle of the room, "You're all cowards! All of you! You're making excuses. We all know when you fight and die for Allah, you will receive seventy-two virgins, not raisins! Not raisins, Hassan! Those are lies!"

"Malik, I'm just telling you that what I saw looked credible, not some fabricated story from the Jews!" insisted Hassan, in a conciliatory manner, hoping not to further upset a highly irritated Malik.

"Yes!" said Ziad. "I have always believed it to be seventy-two virgins. I have been taught that since I was a boy. All good Wahhabis know this."

"Taught by who?" asked Fayez, now incredibly concerned about the basis for his closest friend's suicidal plan.

"From devout Muslims like ourselves, Wahhabis, Fayez. Wahhabis!" Ziad insisted.

"Were any of them scholars, or could this just have been a continual misinterpretation of words from hadiths?" asked Fayez, referring to a collection of the prophet Muhammad's statements that provide guidance for Muslims, apart from the Quran.

"Wait, I thought you failed out of college!" said Malik, now furious with Hassan's unwillingness to follow through with the plan.

"I did, but it's not because I'm stupid," explained Fayez. "It's because I didn't care, didn't try. I care about this. Maybe we should just take a step back here and look into this before any of us does something we will all regret. We are talking about our lives here."

"No! I say we kill Americans today!" yelled out Malik, pumping his right fist into the air. "I spent six years in prison. I hate Americans and all of those who put me in jail. I'm ready to kill them all."

Fayez and Hassan just looked at their wild-eyed, revenge-filled conspirator, knowing a challenge to his intentions would be a very bad idea. Ziad could see the fear in their eyes and knew he needed to address this difference of opinion without further infuriating Malik.

"Malik, we are going to kill Americans!" said Ziad, trying to calm him down. "We are going to send those infidels straight to Hell!"

"Yes! Yes we are!" exclaimed Malik, now feeling some support.

"But we have to be all together on this before we move forward, or this plan won't work," said Ziad, appealing to Malik's rational side, hoping there was one. "Obviously, Hassan and Fayez are not ready to move forward. We need to investigate this to help them understand. Then we can execute our plan."

"What are you saying, Ziad?" asked Malik, his blood pressure building as he stared directly at the man he had put his faith and trust in to lead the group. "Are you backing out?"

"I'm not backing out, Malik. I respect that Hassan and Fayez believe there's enough conflicting information here today for us to go back and reexamine the information before we go forward. We all have to be willing to execute this plan or it will fail. Do you understand?" asked Ziad with all eyes now firmly on Malik.

"No, I don't understand," said Malik, who started packing his long black Nike bag with an AK-47, two RPGs, and plenty of ammunition. "And I don't believe what some so-called expert on CNN said about the Quran. I'm going down to Michigan Avenue, and I'm going to kill

Americans. And if they kill me, then I'm going to die a martyr for Allah and be rewarded with seventy-two virgins. Seventy-two beautiful virgins! I will be a hero! My picture will be on the walls throughout the Middle East. I watched the videos. I read the call for a jihad. If you three want to stay here because you don't have the courage to follow through on the call from the Prophet Muhammad, then you stay here. But I'm going. Goodbye!"

Malik slung the strap of his Nike bag over his shoulder and gave his three former conspirators an intense and evil look. Then, he headed out the door of the condo, slamming it hard on his way out. The sound of the loud bang from the door reverberated in the ears and into the souls of the others who stood motionless, mentally-fatigued, looking for an answer from Ziad to quell their mixed emotions of cowardice and confusion.

CHAPTER SIX

When the wheels of the canyon blue Southwest Boeing 737 touched down at Midway Airport that Tuesday evening, the jolt from the impact never felt so good for Dylan and Darlene, who despite the dangerous perception associated with Chicago, knew that they had arrived back to a safe city and their lifelong hometown. It seemed that in only twenty minutes they were stepping off the plane, walking down the escalator, out the airport door, and into a waiting Uber. After 8 p.m., the traffic on the Stevenson Expressway was light. Before Darlene could finish a phone call with her parents to let them know they had arrived safely home, the driver was already pulling his silver Hyundai Elantra up to the curb outside their condo building on Monroe in the now ultra-popular West Loop.

Just forty years earlier, this area was known as Skid Row with alcoholics, mostly World War II and Korean War veterans suffering from post-traumatic stress disorder, lying along the streets and living in the flophouses that lined Madison Avenue. That scene began changing in the 1990s when Mayor Jimmy Dorgan and real estate developers began turning the West Loop into a nice area to live and work. The flophouses and the homeless alcoholic men that once lined the streets disappeared. They scattered to other areas of the city, living in boxes under viaducts or improvised blanket-tents on Lower Wacker Drive. Or, they just moved to warmer climates to endure their misery of loneliness, despair, and addiction.

As much as the young couple loved the neighborhood, which was only a few miles from where Dylan taught at Watson College Prep, they knew that one day in the near future, they would be having children and moving to the suburbs. But for the time being, they enjoyed their life in the West Loop with all of the great restaurants and nightlife. They particularly enjoyed going to City Winery to listen to great music or attending Bulls games at the United Center just a few blocks away.

As they settled back into their daily routine, the tragic experience in New York faded out of their conversations. Within a few weeks after arriving home, it all seemed like a bad dream. Any thoughts Dylan may have had about purchasing a gun faded away due to the comfort of the safe environment they lived in. He and his wife could walk down Madison or Monroe, surrounded by young professionals in their age group. No one looked threatening. No one seemed threatened.

This area wasn't like Park Hills, the southwest suburb where Dylan had grown up, a large village with wonderful schools, parks, and a hockey rink. So many young parents chose to move there in the 1990s and new millennium to raise their children in a safe environment.

Sure, every now and then, even in Park Hills, some bad things happened. A disturbed high school student walked into his parents' bedroom and killed them both while they were sleeping, beating them to death with a baseball bat. Not long afterward, the father of a famous Chicago television reporter decided to murder his wife while she was sleeping, because he was having an affair with a woman he met at church and wanted to cash in on the life insurance policy and start over. Well, he got his fresh start alright, sentenced to sixty years in prison. When those tragic incidences occurred, they were rare. They were shocking—this didn't happen in the suburbs. There was no trend, so no one felt threatened by them, only sorry for the families and the circumstances that led to those killings.

Dylan viewed those tragedies as isolated incidents of family breakdowns that took place in every corner of America, every corner of the world. It was never a threat to him or his family. No, his belief about violence was that the majority of it was predictable. Gang members killed other gang members. Families with major issues took it out on each other. Rejected boyfriends became a revengeful threat to former girlfriends.

People drinking too much in bars could escalate into something dangerous, especially when guns were carried.

The unpredictable dangers, he always believed, were the drug addicts who entered retail stores, banks, or mini-marts to rob them for the money they need to support their addiction. They just might start shooting people because they are so high on drugs and completely irrational. Or the crazed man on the highway who takes great exception to being cut off, or flipped off, and pulls out his gun to settle the score right on the Eisenhower or Dan Ryan expressways. Or armed carjackers who identify their targets in parking lots and then wait until the vehicle owner comes out with key fob in hand to then attack the second the car door is opened, sometimes drawing their weapon to ensure the grand theft.

Reports of those types of shootings seemed to occur more frequently. Home invasions seemed to be another growing trend once the economy went directly south after the Great Recession hit America hard, beginning in 2008.

Desperation! When the average Joe can't afford to feed his family, he will take desperate measures, but usually it doesn't involve killing innocent people.

Dylan knew there wasn't much he could do about being in the wrong bank or retail store at the wrong time if a robbery were to occur. But he did know the odds were long against him being placed in those situations, if he didn't venture outside after 10 p.m. on any evening.

For his home though, like many, he did have an alarm system set up to help protect against an intruder. Home invasion was the number one cited danger most gun advocates in America claimed justification in having a firearm. The elderly were at much higher risk. The saga of the wolves attacking the sheep lived forever in a society of flawed and desperate human beings.

Even though the vast majority of Americans would never be on the wrong end of a break-in and have a much higher chance of having one of their children hurt or killed because they find the gun in their home, about a third of Americans chose to have a gun. They didn't want to take the risk of not being able to defend themselves against a home intruder. They felt safer and had more peace-of-mind, having a gun to protect themselves. Under the Second Amendment, they have that right.

The argument so often voiced against those who were strong gun advocates was if the guns were taken off the streets completely, they'd be taken out of the hands of the mentally unstable, the drug addicts, and the home invaders. It automatically decreased the risk and the number of deaths resulting from gun violence. Gun advocates would never listen to those debate points, arguing that the bad guys will always be able to get their hands on guns. Big guns. *Dangerous* guns.

Dylan knew the debate in America would continue endlessly while more and more innocent people were killed by lunatics or terrorists who had access to guns. He wondered how anyone could have prepared for the crazed man in the Las Vegas Hotel spraying bullets across the area below him which was filled with concert-goers. They were just there to have a good time. Completely innocent people shot for no reason, other than being in the wrong place at the wrong time, targeted by a mentally unstable man.

Dylan was certain that those who hoped that one day there would be no guns in America, except for those worn by the police and military, were kidding themselves. After no new major gun legislation was put in place following the massacre at Sandy Hook Elementary, Dylan accepted the fact that America would always be a country where the dangers posed by guns would be ever-present.

Once he accepted that fact, he then began considering if he too should own a gun to protect himself. He thought that if America was going to be Dodge City, the Wild West, then perhaps he had better think about getting a pistol in case a bad guy in a ten-gallon black hat showed up at his door someday. His experience in New York only served to encourage those thoughts for him.

Terrorists? Who plans for terrorists? Who plans for a killer to walk into a Walmart, shopping mall or school and start shooting people randomly? Well, Dylan knew that all Americans had better be prepared, regardless of the city they lived in. Shootings were occurring everywhere in the country.

Whereas Darlene would never support purchasing a gun, Dylan was giving it great consideration. In the meantime, he told his beautiful wife that both of them needed to pay attention to their surroundings, regardless of where they were at any given time of the day.

"If we keep our eyes open, we may see it coming and be able to avoid being shot," Dylan said to her one evening as they stood on their balcony, gazing at the beautiful Chicago skyline. "Just like I noticed that crazy man with the face paint and scowl on his face at Freedom Tower. If we pay attention to those around us, certain things will stick out that are unordinary. That's what we have to look for and react to for our own safety. Without a gun, it's our only chance."

And life for the Reillys in the West Loop went on with the hope that they would never have to purchase a gun to feel safe.

CHAPTER SEVEN

Amir Farzan and Sofia Abed were both born in Teheran, Iran, just twenty-five days apart during the summer of 1958. They met as young children, having grown up as neighbors, living in the same apartment building on the outskirts of the capital city of Iran. During those early years, Amir and his brother, Ahmad, played with Sofia and her older brother, Kadir. They sang songs and lived a wonderful life.

As a young boy growing up in the 1960s, Amir loved Iran. He loved his country, the friendly people, and the culture. His family was of Persian heritage going back hundreds of years. Devout Muslims, they'd been raised to be patriotic Iranians, which was challenging, given the ever-present political turmoil.

The lasting effects of the abrupt changes to the country's leadership during World War II, when Reza Shah was forced to resign and his son, Mohammad Reza Pahlavi, became the new monarch on September 19, 1941, made life increasingly difficult for many Iranians. Then in the summer of 1952, the shah almost lost power when the government, under a new premier, Mohammad Mosaddegh, attempted to nationalize the oil industry. The American and British oil companies pulled out, creating chaos and economic disaster. Then a year later, in August of 1953, Mosaddegh attempted to depose the shah, who fled the country. However, a military coup followed, led by the United States Central Intelligence Agency and British Foreign Intelligence Service, and quickly restored the shah to power.

From that point on, despite his victory, the shah was viewed as a puppet of the United States and its oil interests. He had absolute power, and like most monarchs in that position, abused it. Stories flowed behind closed doors about the shah brutally killing anyone suspected of being an enemy. All Iranians had to be careful about what they said, what they did, for fear that an agent of the shah may report it and a quick and tortuous execution would follow.

And late one night in March of 1967, the shah's soldiers appeared at Amir's door. They dragged his father, Arman, out the door, never to be seen again. His mother, Sondra, went to the authorities to inquire into the whereabouts of her husband. A gruff, mean, dark-haired policeman stood behind the desk, flashed a cynical smile, and told her that they had no knowledge of what happened to her husband. They never saw Arman again. The family suspected one of his business competitors in the rug trade fabricated a story, which resulted in the abduction.

It was difficult for the Farzan family, but Sofia's parents helped them as much as possible. Her father, Hadi Kardashian, was an orthopedic surgeon and could afford to make a strong commitment of financial support. During this time, Sofia and Amir grew close, with both reaching the age of eighteen in the summer of 1976. Ahmad's mother made the *khaastegaari*, or formal marriage proposal, discussing all of the arrangements with Sofia's mother, including the dowry of 800,000,000 rials.

This was a wonderful time for the young Persian couple, pleased to no end and feeling such a strong love for one and other. The two joyful mothers worked together and guided them through the process, culminating in a beautiful wedding ceremony, the *sofreh aghd*. It was beautiful!

This was a day the two families would never forget and would always cherish, seeing Ahmad and Sofia looking into the mirror together for a bright future. The couple held candles symbolizing energy and clarity in their life together. The combination of seven herbs and spices, the *khoncheh*, was placed on the wedding spread of food to protect against the evil eye. The khoncheh sat next to the flatbread with feta cheese and fresh herbs, symbolizing prosperity in their life together. Eggs and walnuts were also present, representing fertility for the couple—so important! The two mothers took care to weave in so many wonderful traditions into the wedding ceremony.

Smiles filled the hall on this hot and sunny August afternoon. Tears poured, hugs abounded. It was a happy day in an unhappy country. Everyone put their tensions outside the door, out of their minds, for one day.

The Farzan family was not alone in their tragedy and frustration with the government. Decades of brutal rule by the shah resulted in millions of desperate Iranians who reached the point where they felt they had no other choice than to revolt. And revolt they did, beginning in October of 1977. Protests intensified in the fall of 1978 when the Iranian people took their voices to the streets, holding strikes and demonstrations. The anger reached its peak, and patience for the shah's government had come to an end.

The shah and his wife, Farah, fled the country on January 16, 1979. This opened the door for the return of the Ayatollah Khomeini on February 1, 1979, after fifteen years in exile. The long-standing Pahlavi Kingdom, dating back to 1925, officially came to an end on February 11 when a rebel army of citizens overwhelmed the shah's troops in street battles, and Ayatollah Khomeini took power.

Watching the change in the attitudes and actions of so many Iranians after the Ayatollah took leadership, Amir and Sofia Farzan grew fearful about the future of their homeland and their family.

On November 4, 1979, they watched as student demonstrators climbed the walls of the American Embassy and took fifty-two American diplomats and citizens hostage. That was the day the newlyweds came to the conclusion that the country they loved would never see peace in their lifetimes. As passionate as they felt about Iran, they believed the best decision for them—although the hardest decision they would ever have to make—was to move to America where Amir's brother, Ahmad, had moved a few years earlier and was thriving.

Sofia fully realized the importance of going through the small window of opportunity while it is open to pursue a better life, peace, and freedom. In 1941, her grandparents had been killed by the Nazi Schutzstaffel, more commonly known as the SS. They were taken out on the street and lined up with several others, who were gunned down in cold blood. She wished her grandparents would have fled before the German soldiers had arrived. But she also knew that if they did leave the country, she would have never met Amir.

Over the next fourteen months, while the American Hostage Crisis dominated the news worldwide, Amir and Sofia Farzan made their plans to emigrate to the United States. Amir tried to talk his mother into joining them, but she would not leave Iran. She would accept whatever future Allah had planned for her.

On Saturday, January 17, 1981, they left their families, one of the most difficult days in each of their lives. This was truly a sad day, a life-changing decision. Standing with their loved ones in Terminal 4 of the overcrowded Mehrabad International Airport that morning, after long hugs, tears of separation and sadness, they promised to see each other again in the future. The young couple had everything in place and boarded an Iranian Airlines flight to Paris, where they connected onto American Airlines bound for Chicago's O'Hare International Airport.

Upon landing in Chicago and exiting the large, packed airplane, they quickly cleared customs. Amir spotted his smiling brother, Ahmad, standing in a crowd, his eyes dancing back and forth, searching for his beloved brother and his wife.

"Ahmad!" yelled Amir, so excited as he dropped his bags and ran to embrace his brother who he had missed greatly since his move to the States in the summer of 1978. "I missed you, brother!"

"I missed you too, Amir! I'm so glad you are here," said his always-smiling older sibling, known best in the family for his great sense of humor. "And here is the bride!" he said, hugging the beautiful, long, brunette, Persian woman whom he had known as a girl. Her parents were so kind to his family during the worst of times.

Amir and Sofia were so grateful to be in America, a country which would give them a chance to have a good life, get a good education and a good job. They could have a family and practice their Muslim religion in peace and harmony.

There were no riots in the streets, no power-hungry Ayatollahs calling for violence. It was a safe haven for those seeking a peaceful and happy life. Of course, given the great hate in America toward Iran at that time, the Farzans were faced with serious challenges. They knew they would have to maintain a low profile about their country of origin.

Walking through the terminal that Saturday evening, the smell of Garrett's Carmel Popcorn, a Chicago staple, overwhelmed their senses. It smelled so wonderful!

As the automatic glass double doors of the International Terminal slid open, the loud sounds of the vehicles moving through the airport roadway engulfed them. It was at that moment that the realities of January in the Windy City welcomed the Farzans with strong gusts of wind and twenty-below-zero temperatures. Their thin tan coats were no protection for these weather conditions. They shivered their way to Ahmad's Chrysler Town & Country station wagon on the second deck of the parking garage, wondering if they had moved to Siberia.

Riding in the back seat, Amir and Sofia took in the sights of America's second largest city, as they travelled down Interstate 294.

"Is it always this cold here, Ahmad?" asked Amir, still-shivering, tightly holding his wife, who was staring out the window, hoping the heater would soon warm up the car.

"Yes, all twelve months of the year," Ahmad joked, laughing hard to himself at his newly reunited relatives reaction to the severe winter conditions of Chicago. "I'm kidding. In the summertime, it will be great! Ninety-five degrees with a humidity that will leave you drenched in sweat. So it's all good!"

As Ahmad took the ramp onto the Stevenson Expressway, heading toward downtown, the Farzans got their first glimpse at Chicago's beautiful and impressive skyline. They gazed at the Sears Tower dominating the view along with the Standard Oil Building and John Hancock Center, balancing the picture of one of the world's most magnificent cityscapes.

"Have you been to the top of those buildings, Ahmad?" asked Amir, trying to absorb what it would feel like to look down from the top of such a tall structure.

"I have," said Ahmad, smiling as usual. "But it took me quite some time to climb. Couldn't get a good grip, you know."

Laughter filled the station wagon, happiness from door to door. They were so excited to be in a safe country, away from the violence that would plague their homeland. Fortunately, Ahmad and his beautiful thirty-two-year-old wife, Dafne, had a spare bedroom in their apartment where Amir and Sofia could stay until they got settled.

It seemed the year flew by as they all got reacquainted, living in the apartment located on the near Southwest Side, the McKinley Park neighborhood. In February of 1982, Amir was able to secure his own apartment a few miles away on Kedzie Avenue. It was located across from a large and noisy Nabisco plant, which sent the sweet smell of Oreo cookies throughout the neighborhood.

The area they planned on moving into was known as the Marquette Park neighborhood. This was not the best place for an Iranian immigrant, or any other nonwhite person to reside during that time period.

Most of the people living in Amir's new neighborhood were immigrants from Eastern Europe, who made it clear that anyone who was not white was not welcome. The poster boy for the neighborhood's attitude toward people of color was Martin Luther King Jr., who had arrived at Marquette Park on August 5, 1966 to protest for open housing regardless of race.

More than 4,000 residents sent a message to Dr. King and his Chicago Freedom Coalition that they didn't appreciate or accept the movement's "open" point-of-view, throwing rocks and bottles at the civil rights group, and hitting their leader in the head with a rock, just above his right ear.

Amir wished he had known about this racist history of the neighborhood recommended by Ahmad's neighbor. He told him about the Kedzie apartment available for only $300 per month. At that rate, and with the location still fairly close to the liquor store where he was being employed on South Lake Shore Drive, he couldn't pass it up.

There had been no indication of a problem on February 28, the day he signed the one-year lease agreement for his third-floor, two-bedroom apartment with the friendly landlord, Jim Granski. Had he known this was an area on the Southwest Side where anyone who was not white was viewed as a threat to the stability of the neighborhood and its property values, he would have never moved there.

Chicago was the city where Amir's brother lived, which provided an opportunity to move to America. He knew little about Dr. King and less about the civil rights movement he led. He knew nothing about the black population's concerted efforts to progressively move west toward Marquette Park, Ashburn, and Scottsdale. These were white-only neighborhoods filled with city workers, required to live within the city limits in order to maintain employment by the City of Chicago. Anyone working for the city would live in the municipal boundaries, because then they would pay property and sales taxes to their employer, not to the government of some nice suburb on the outskirts of the city.

In these very well-maintained Catholic parish-focused neighbor-hoods, the residents did not welcome anyone of color moving into the area at that time. They feared those minorities would "ruin the neighbor-hood" as was often stated by many of the residents.

This was not purely racism—although for some it was absolutely hate for blacks based only on the color of their skin. No, the argument made was based on the experience witnessed in the Southside neighborhoods east of Ashland Avenue. That area was once very nicely maintained, safe neighborhoods, dominated by Italian, Irish, and Polish families.

When the black population moved into those neighborhoods, prop-erty values dropped. Well-maintained homes were no longer a visual staple of the area, and crime went up. That was the quintessential case study. This was the example anyone west of Ashland would refer to when talking about "black blockbusters" coming into the area and "white flight" by those who were not chained down by a city job and were free to flee to the suburbs.

Despite his lack of knowledge of Chicago's history, it didn't take long for Amir to understand that the Farzans were not welcome there. A pre-cinct captain came knocking on their door in April of 1982 to encourage them to vote for the Democratic candidate supported by the Democratic machine in the 17th Ward election. Of course, when Amir answered the door, the precinct captain with a heavy Southside Chicago accent looked more than a little surprised to see a dark-skinned man standing in the open doorway.

"I'm Bob Smoleski, the precinct captain here in the 17th Ward," said the middle-aged, worn-down, blue windbreaker-wearing, political sup-porter. His demeanor and attitude toward Amir seemed to evaporate into surprise and disgust all at the same time. "Yeah, well, I'm going around asking for those in the neighborhood to vote for our candidate, Jewel Frierson, a great labor leader who is supported by Mayor Jane Byrne, you know what I'm saying?"

Smoleski paused for a moment, then nervously ran his right hand through his combed back Brylcreemed-style, graying quaff. Amir sur-mised that the man was trying to understand how this dark-skinned res-ident standing in the doorway, was allowed to move into the building in *his* neighborhood.

Then the precinct captain blurted out, "Say, are you new in the neighborhood?"

"Yes, we are," said Amir Farzan, smiling politely. "We just moved here in the first week of March."

"Oh, okay, well, just some friendly advice for you mister, uh…" stammered Smoleski.

"Farzan. Amir Farzan."

"Oh, that's just wonderful…Mr. Farzan," said Smoleski with more than a hint of disdain for the obvious Middle Eastern name. "Even though you are an A-rab…."

"Persian," Amir politely corrected him.

"Yeah, Persian, A-rab, whatever! It would be a good idea if you supported our candidate in this runoff election in June to show your good will toward the ticket, you know what I mean? We do not want Allan Streeter to win. He's no longer a party-first guy, so he's got to go. You know what I'm saying?"

"Yes, of course, we would definitely like to support Mr. Free, Mr. Fry…"

"Frierson, Mr. Jewel Frierson. Like the Jewels, ya know? That's our motto, vote for the Jewels. Everyone knows the Jewels."

"What is the Jewels?" asked a puzzled Amir.

"Ya know, the grocery store. The Jewels!"

"Yes, of course, the Jewels. Yes. But I have to tell you, sir, I don't believe we will be allowed to vote yet. We are still new to the country and not eligible to vote yet."

"Oh, is that right?" Smoleski said. "Where are you from, Mr. Farzan? Arabia?"

"Persia. Yes, we came from overseas and are very grateful to be in your country," said Amir, intent on not giving away too much information. "Look, I must go now to attend to dinner. Thank you for stopping by. When we are allowed to vote, we will always support your candidate."

"Persia? Where is that exactly?"

"Have a good day, sir," said Amir then quickly closed the door, leaving Smoleski guessing. Amir looked out the peephole to see the precinct captain turn and knock on the door on the opposite side of the hallway. A young Irish-looking man in his twenties answered the door and Amir listened in on the conversation.

"Hello, I'm Bob Smoleski, your precinct captain," said the political vote salesman, the young Irishman just nodding politely. "Look, you may know there is an important runoff vote happening here in the 17th Ward, and we really need everyone to vote for Jewel Frierson, a very strong labor leader backed by Mayor Byrne. It's easy to remember, just vote for the Jewels!"

"The Jewels, right. I get it," laughed the young man. Amir could readily see Smoleski was far more comfortable sharing his opinions with the young man, assuming he was talking to one of the neighborhood guys, someone who gets it, understands it. No additional explanation needed for "The Jewels."

"Yeah, it's a great catchphrase," laughed Smoleski.

"We actually just moved in here a few months ago, but we are registered voters, so no problem there," said the new resident.

"Oh, that's great!" said the now overly-friendly precinct captain. "Here is my card. You just call if I can ever do anything for you, ya know. Is there anyone else who can vote here?"

"My wife, Mary," said the young man, partially closing the door as the nosey Smoleski tried to glance inside.

"Well, that's good," he said moving to his right, still trying to look inside the apartment. "You're new to the neighborhood, so just so you know, Frierson is running against Allan Streeter, a nigger. And Mayor Byrne tried to be nice to him, support him, but you know how those niggers are."

The young man just stared at Smoleski, looking a bit surprised by his language.

"Also, you should know, you got a sand-nigger living across the hall from you here," informed Smoleski.

"Oh, is that right?" said the Irishman, who looked more than a little puzzled.

"Yeah, I'll tell you, the sand-niggers are the worst," he explained. "I'll take a nigger over a sand-nigger any day."

The young Irishman nodded with a grimace.

"Well, I've got to go here," he said, starting to close the door.

Amir raised his head away from the peep hole. Disappointed, he now realized that perhaps they should have never moved into this area of the city. This was bad. A racist precinct captain was spreading hate toward him, even though he knew nothing about Amir or Sofia. This was not unlike the hate-filled speeches he had listened to in Tehran, only there, it was Iranian's hate targeted toward Americans, any Americans. Apparently, ignorant hatred existed on both sides of the ocean.

"So anyway, if you and your wife can vote for Frierson, the Jewels! We would appreciate it," Smoleski continued, still maneuvering to look inside the apartment. "And anything we can do for you, just give me a call."

"Thank you," said the young man, nodding, then quickly shutting the door.

Despite the support of the Democratic machine, and Mayor Jane Byrne's late night calls to media favorites to leak rumors that Allan Streeter was the target of a federal grand jury probe for allegedly selling jobs and taking bribes while working at the Department of Health, Streeter still won the 1982 election. He defeated Frierson fairly easily with 56 percent of the vote. The winning 17th Ward Alderman went on to predict that Jane Byrne would never again receive the black vote and would lose the 1983 mayoral election. He was right, as Harold Washington won in February of 1983, becoming the first black mayor of Chicago.

Amir and Sofia watched all of this reported by Jason Daly and Frankie Flynn, the top-rated WLS-TV news anchor team, and decided the Southwest Side of Chicago was not the place for them to live. His brother suggested the suburbs, specifically Park Hills, where they didn't have precinct captains and Democratic machines.

So on Saturday morning, February 15, 1983, Ahmad and a few of his friends arrived in a red Chevy pickup truck and large white Ford van at the back door of Amir's yellow-brick three-story apartment building. They loaded all of their furniture and clothing and joyously moved to the beautifully wooded and wide-open spaces of Park Hills, a suburb twenty-five miles southwest of Chicago where he and Sofia hoped to raise their family in peace.

CHAPTER EIGHT

The second Sunday in July of 2014 was a day that Dylan and Darlene would never forget. It was an unusually cool and pleasant summer weekend day with bright beautiful blue skies and blinding rays from a fully exposed sun hovering above the John Hancock Center, lighting up a bustling Michigan Avenue.

The Magnificent Mile was filled with sun-glassed tourists and locals alike, strolling the popular avenue, enjoying the wonderful weather, ducking into stores for some shopping or restaurants for a quick lunch, and, of course, people-watching.

Watching this parade of lazy Sunday folly, the young couple found themselves parked on a bench in the plaza outside the historic yellow-stoned Water Tower building, complete with a wonderful vantage point and shade.

As every Chicago grammar school student is taught, the Water Tower was only one of four buildings left standing after the Great Chicago Fire of 1871. Dylan—always the history enthusiast—liked to sit near that piece of history. As he and Darlene sipped from the long red straws protruding from the large white Styrofoam cups, filled with flavorful chocolate milkshakes from the Ghirardelli Chocolate and Ice Cream Shop, they talked about the items they had just purchased at Water Tower Place. Dylan hoped that the gifts would be to the liking of Darlene's father, who would be celebrating his sixtieth birthday the following Saturday.

"We are always buying him a tie or sweatpants for his birthday," said Darlene, holding up a beautiful green sweater for her husband to see just one more time. "I really think he will like this. He loves sweaters, and I think he will really appreciate this one."

"I agree, Darlene," said Dylan, chuckling at the thought that his wife would make the purchase of this particular gift such an important issue. "After all, you know your dad. So, if you say he will love that green cashmere sweater, then the green cashmere sweater we shall give him."

"Well, I'll drink to that," said Darlene, raising her cup to toast the decision with another sip of the Ghirardelli's chocolate heaven.

Darlene came from a close-knit family in downstate Illinois. She was the eldest of the four Quilty children, two boys and two girls. Her father, Patrick, was a hard-working carpenter, and mother, Ann, a devoted wife and homemaker. Ann took great pride in her loving family, grateful that she was able to stay home and raise the children, a commitment fewer and fewer mothers were making during the 1980s.

The similarities in their families really helped cement the relationship between Darlene and Dylan. He too came from a hard-working blue-collar Irish-Catholic family of five children, two boys and three girls. His father, Paddy, emigrated from Ireland in 1978 and met the love of his life, Mary, in 1981 at an Irish dance at Gaelic Park in a southern suburb of Chicago. They fell in love forever that evening, married in 1984, and moved to a new home in Park Hills, a suburb twenty-five miles southwest of the city.

As the oldest boy behind a very intelligent sister, Dylan believed sports was the right path for him to pursue. Darlene wasn't much different. While she was playing tennis and running track at St. Mary's School, Dylan was playing baseball and hockey for St. John's Academy in the Catholic League of Chicago. They were both good-hearted teenagers, supportive siblings, and hard-working students. And they both excelled in the looks department, which initiated their introduction at the University of Chicago. It was truly a perfect match, and they both seemed to appreciate that from their first hello.

The smiling young couple sat back on the wooden park bench near the Water Tower, enjoying their chocolate treats as they listened to the clip-clop sound of the horses pulling colorful tourist carriages down Pearson Street. Blaring horns from impatient cab drivers completed this symphony of city sounds, a fleet of yellow Chevys maneuvering their way through the ever-present roar of traffic moving north and south down Michigan Avenue.

They people watched, taking turns guessing if the passersby were locals or tourists. The clothes and general look was their best indicator. Of course, it was only a guessing game. Never would they actually ask the people their origin in order to win the game, but they were having such fun enjoying their wonderfully sweet drinks, playing guessing games, and listening to the ambience of Chicago along one of the most magnificent stretches of Magnificent Mile. It was a wonderful day.

As the young couple polished off their milkshakes, Dylan noticed a disturbance was taking place across the street in front of Water Tower Place.

"What's that?" asked Dylan, quickly standing to see if he could get a better look at the commotion just across Michigan Avenue. There was loud yelling. It looked like those in the area, dozens of curious onlookers, started moving up to the corner of Michigan Avenue and Pearson Street to see what was happening. From what Dylan could see of the chaotic scene, it looked like perhaps there had been an accident or a fight. Several people were yelling toward one man, who was screaming in an animated fashion, flailing his arms, venting his anger toward them.

"What is going on?" asked Darlene, now standing next to her husband who quickly took his wife's right hand, thinking this might be a good time to leave.

"I don't know," said Dylan. "It looks like that man in the black sweatshirt is mad about something. Where are the police?"

Dylan combed the crowd for clues and spotted two Chicago police officers about a half block south on Michigan Avenue in front of the Walgreens drug store. They were just talking, unaware of the situation. They obviously couldn't hear or see the disturbance. Looking back toward the scene, he spotted another cop come through the revolving door of Water Tower Place and begin to work his way through the crowd. It seemed the upset man saw the police officer approaching and ran into the middle of a wide open Michigan Avenue, traffic cleared by the red light at Pearson. He had a large black Nike bag slung over his shoulder.

The young couple could now clearly see the upset man, dressed in black jeans and black hoodie. He looked to be an Arab man in his twenties. They watched him place his bag down and take one knee next to it, quickly unzipping it.

Several people in the crowd along the sidewalk continued yelling at him, although Dylan couldn't hear them. The man in black reached into his bag and pulled out some type of large weapon. Screams followed. Long, loud, hysterical screams. Everyone on the sidewalk quickly began to scatter, hoping to avoid being shot by whatever weapon this obvious terrorist had with him.

Dylan would learn later that the man was Malik Morcos, who was following through on a statement he made to his three former conspirators. He was going to kill Americans and die a martyr for Allah to receive his seventy-two virgins. Malik pointed his weapon toward the John Hancock Center. A moment later, a loud burst echoed off the tall buildings along Michigan Avenue as a rocket propelled grenade flew toward the middle of the famed Chicago building. Dylan and Darlene watched the rocket propelled grenade hit the skyscraper and explode, creating a ball of fire and a massive hole in the side of the skyscraper. Debris flew everywhere, the pedestrians below trying to run to avoid being pelted and killed.

When they looked back at the terrorist, he already had loaded another RPG, balanced the launcher on his shoulder, and once again aimed at the tall black skyscraper. All watched in horror as he fired another rocket one hundred feet below the gaping, burning hole created by the first explosion. The ground shook as another ball of fire rained onto an evacuated Chestnut Street below.

The next words heard were words Dylan would never forget. Malik reached into his black bag but this time pulled out an AK-47. He raised it in the air and yelled out, "Death to America! Death to America! Long live Allah!"

Then the wild-eyed, crazed terrorist started shooting directly at those in the scattering crowd who had stopped to watch his RPG attack. Once again screams filled the air. People ran in every direction to avoid the shots. Bodies fell to the cement sidewalk. A river of blood flowed down the sidewalk to the street.

An enraged Malik kept shooting. The police officer who had come out of Water Tower Place now had his gun out and was firing his semi-automatic weapon at the terrorist.

The two cops who had been talking near the Walgreens were now sprinting as fast as they could, running with guns drawn toward Michigan and Pearson. Dylan grabbed Darlene and quickly ran behind the famed yellow-stoned Water Tower building.

They were engulfed in the sounds of rapid gunfire. It had only been a month since their New York trip, and here they were again, running and hiding from someone shooting a gun at people. There was no time to think about the scenarios. All focus was on staying behind the Water Tower building where it seemed hundreds had gathered around them with the same idea. It was lucky for all of them that the other three terrorists hadn't followed through with their part of the plan, or they all would have been shot or blown up by the planted bombs.

Dylan had to see what was happening. He looked around the square corner of the building to see the Water Tower Place cop and Malik shooting point-blank at each other. The cop was shot in the head, and fell limp to the pavement. Horrified screams of shock filled the avenue.

Then, Malik turned toward the two police running at him. He began firing his AK-47. He ran out of bullets. He reached down, grabbed his bag, and started running north, while trying to reload a fresh thirty-round magazine into his deadly weapon.

The first cop to reach Pearson fired a shot and hit Malik in the left shoulder. He fell backward, landing with an audible thud on the hard, black pavement. Everyone watched. Was he dead? Would he move? As he lay there on the hot asphalt about fifty feet from the two Chicago cops running at him, his eyes grew wide as a fearful audience of innocents watched the prone figure come to life. Oh no! Screams, cries.

A bloodied and badly injured Malik was somehow able to push the magazine into his assault rifle. Then he sat up, stood up, and started firing at the two police officers charging at him. One of the cops was hit immediately and fell hard to the ground, bouncing off the pavement and rolling over several times before coming to a complete stop. His stomach was moving up and down rapidly. He was still alive, still breathing.

More screams! More cries! "God help us!" someone prayed loudly enough for all to hear.

His partner kept firing and squeezed off a shot that was a direct hit to Malik's right shoulder. The force jolted him back, up in the air, and flat on his back, the assault weapon spinning away from him.

From behind pillars, buildings, and cars, all hoped the attack was over and the terrorist was dead. All eyes were on Malik. Loud breathing. Panic. Prayers.

The heroic police officer never broke stride and was on top of the assailant in what seemed like mere seconds. He placed his knee on the wounded terrorist's chest to hold him down. Smiles appeared. Tears were wiped. Happy faces evident. Sighs of relief everywhere.

Malik begged the officer to shoot him. He wouldn't. He handcuffed him, and in a matter of minutes, it looked like every ambulance from Northwestern Memorial Hospital had arrived to take the injured to the emergency department. Black SUVs with blaring sirens screamed up to Pearson, tires skidding loudly as they stopped. Bulletproof vested and armed Chicago Police officers jumped out and ran to the scene.

Dylan took Darlene into his arms. The crowd around them cleared out, now safe, heading back to their homes. The warm sun shined upon them. Dylan looked up at the blue skies, so happy they had once again escaped a dangerous situation they never saw coming. As he held his wife, he watched the emergency medical professionals lift and place the injured onto gurneys and into the ambulances. Some were completely covered by white sheets, dead. Dylan wondered how many had been killed.

"C'mon, let's get home," he said to Darlene and used his Uber app to call for a car.

As they drove south on Michigan Avenue in a blue Chevy sedan, Dylan held his wife in his arms. "What are we going to do, Dylan?" she asked. "What are we going to do?"

"I don't know, Darlene," he said, now not feeling quite as safe in the city he loved. "We're going to have to talk about this. I just want you to be safe. That's all I care about."

CHAPTER NINE

Walking into the old Hipsters Brew at North and Wells on Chicago's Near North Side, it felt somewhat surreal for Haydon Huff, knowing that it was the same coffee house his mother and father met to determine his fate back in October 1968. He sat at the last worn-down table in the back, believing it was the same table his mother had described to him so many years earlier.

When his best friend, Paul Cavon, walked through the door, he didn't look happy. Tucked under his right arm was a copy of *The Bleeder*, the alternative weekly newspaper for which he was the lead columnist. He walked to the back of the restaurant and slammed the newspaper on the table in front of Haydon.

"What the hell, man?" he blurted out, which drew the attention of the twenty or so other Hipster customers, most exhibiting long hair, tattoos, purple-colored hair, and vintage-style clothes. "Did you see the news?"

"Yeah, I saw it," he said, grabbing the *Tribune* from the next table and laying it on the table. Cavon just stared daggers at his best friend of more than two decades, working up the courage to tell him something important.

"Look, Haydon, you are my closest friend, the only one I can really trust in the world," the tired and frustrated-looking left-wing columnist began. "But I think we have different priorities. You want to bring down America, and I just want to bring down the Dorgans. I've gone along with this for a long time, too long. But this is the end of the road for me."

"What?" said the stunned looking forty-five-year-old leader of the never-to-be-realized Millippie movement. "What are you talking about?"

"I'm quitting," said Cavon, a stern look across his face. "I should have quit thirteen years ago when you tried to meet up with those Muslims at the hookah bar in Burbank. You're Jewish, Haydon! Jewish! Those Muslims were never going to work with you. They'd rather kill you. Why I went along with that idea…"

"Okay, in retrospect, it was a longshot," Haydon interrupted.

"It was stupid!"

"Okay, it was stupid. But they didn't know I was Jewish. And I'm only half-Jewish. I take after my mother, remember? I look like her, not my father," Haydon admitted to his friend, and to himself, for the first time in his life.

"Well, I'm pretty sure at some point, they would have found out, and then killed you," said the tired and disheveled-looking Cavon.

"Yeah, probably," said Haydon to his middle-aged friend on the other side of the table.

He paused a moment, then held up the *Tribune*, showing Cavon a large article on the front page about the Water Tower shootings, with a big headline that read, "Lone Terrorist's Murderous Mayhem on Michigan Avenue."

"Yeah, I saw it," said Cavon, not understanding its importance.

"That terrorist, Malik," said Haydon. "I met him in prison. He is the one who contacted me to meet with his friends at the hookah bar. He knew I wanted to bring down America and asked if I wanted to join. Had no idea I was Jewish, by the way, even though I had known him for a few years in Statesville."

"So, he just decided to go out there alone?"

"No, there were others, all from the Middle East," said Haydon. "I'm surprised but maybe they all lost their nerve. When I met with them, they were all committed to dying, blowing themselves up if they had to and going to Heaven where they were sure they would each receive seventy-two virgins."

Paul glanced at the article and photo, shaking his head. "You do know that the seventy-two virgin belief is false, right? It's a misrepresentation of the Quran. It's really seventy-two raisins. I wrote a column about it in *The Bleeder*."

"Really! You're kidding, right?" Haydon laughed a bit in disbelief. "You're saying the Muslim terrorists are all dying for raisins?"

"Yeah, I'm surprised a raisin company hasn't signed them up for a commercial," quipped his overtly cynical pal from his years in the newsroom.

"You can't be right about that. They wouldn't blow themselves up for raisins," argued Haydon, thinking his friend was just having fun with him.

"I'm right. Believe me. I've thoroughly researched it and wrote about it. Someone makes a bad interpretation of the writings of the Quran, then spreads that misrepresentation, and before you know it, it becomes a strong belief. Strong enough for people to die for! In this case, seventy-two virgins. In our case, the domino theory!"

"My father would attest to that fact," Haydon confessed. "It's hard for me to criticize someone else's mistakes, given what I did. Nelson getting shot to pieces at Freedom Tower! That's on me. I'm responsible for that. Fifty-two bullets! What the hell!"

Cavon just nodded. "It was a bad idea, but you've got to let it go."

"I can't let it go," Haydon said loudly enough to once again draw the attention of the coffee-sipping hipsters.

"What happened to the others?" asked Cavon with more than a hint of sarcasm in his voice. "You know, the twenty-nine others who were so excited to be working with Andy Huff's son to rise up against America. Did you ever find out?"

"Yeah, I know," said Huff with eternal disappointment in his voice. "They called me after...do you remember Rebel?"

"The tall guy determined to bring communism to America, even if it cost him his life?"

"Yeah, well, that's literally what I was banking on," said Haydon. "When he said that, I completely believed him, thought he would follow through for sure, despite the risks. As it turned out, my cousin was the only one committed."

"Yeah, Nelson should have been committed for believing us, right?" snapped Cavon. "Now, he's dead. At least the news media reported about the American flag shirt."

"I saw that. Only thing that made me happy, salvaged it a bit," Haydon replied, a slight smile crossing his face. "Mentioned my dad, too! Here we are in 2014, and they mentioned my father the minute they saw that shirt. He would have been thrilled!"

"Yeah, would have been thrilled. How thrilled would he have been about the brilliant idea of putting brown face paint on Nelson so people would think he was a Muslim terrorist?"

"Okay, not my best idea, alright! I admit it. It was dumb. I was just banking on him getting out of there alive. People would see the brown skin and think...."

"Think what kind of idiot would dream up such a stupid idea. Nelson has blond hair! Your father would have never pulled a stunt like that."

"Yes, but my mother would have tried it, and I take after my mother," Haydon aggressively barked back, again drawing the attention of the dour-faced hipsters in the coffeehouse. "I'm really more of a Lennard than a Huff. And her brother, Nester, would be so proud of his son, going down in a blaze of glory. Fifty-two bullets! It was a noble attempt to bring communism to this greed-ridden country."

Paul just nodded.

"Well, this is it for me," he said with apparent closure in his voice. "I'm sorry. And I hope you achieve your dream. If you do, I promise I'll write a column about it in *The Bleeder*, if the Dorgans haven't caught up with me by then."

The two friends rose from their old, creaky wooden chairs and hugged. Haydon watched the only ally he had left in the world walk out the door, wondering if the door closing behind Paul signaled the end of his mission to bring down America. He glanced around the coffee shop at a sad and pathetic-looking group of wayward souls, feeling like it was the perfect coffee shop for him to be standing in, among the many lost souls on the north side of Chicago.

He reflected back to the moment when he was sitting in his father's chair about to end his life with a handful of Xanax. He wondered if he would have been better off not picking up his cell phone. At least his cousin Nelson would still be alive, not lying lifeless in a cold morgue in Manhattan, riddled with fifty-two bullet holes.

He grabbed the *Tribune* off the table and walked to the front door, turning to glance one last time at the coffee shop where his chance to live had been determined. He wondered if his parents had made a mistake. Feeling the tears pour down his cheeks, he opened the door and stepped into the bright sunshine on Wells Street. He walked north toward Lincoln Avenue, tears dripping onto the pavement, having no idea what he should do next in life.

CHAPTER TEN

Amir and Sofia Farzan's move to the peaceful suburb of Park Hills turned out to be a good decision. After only a short time following the move, their living environment and surrounding community felt so different, more welcoming, inviting. They knew they would be happy living, working, and raising a family without the violence they would have endured in Iran or the hate they felt in the Marquette Park neighborhood.

Like so many immigrants, the transition wasn't simple or easy, but they made changes to their lives that really cemented their status as Iranian Americans. They were just like the Italian Americans, Irish Americans, Polish Americans, and so many other heritages that had made the boat trip or plane ride across an ocean to the country that offered so many freedoms and opportunities not available in their homeland.

The Farzans had done well. Amir moved his family into a small apartment off LaGrange Road and traveled to the South Shore to continue working at the liquor store, a job his brother Ahmad was so kind to arrange for him. That was a great start.

But once in the suburbs, Amir began looking for new opportunities. After two months, he was hired at a large liquor store in the nearby suburb of Tinley Park, only fifteen minutes from his home. Just a year later, in May of 1984, Sofia delivered their first son, Aaron; then a daughter, Mariam, in 1986. In just a few short years in America, they had the family they had prayed for.

As the young family entered the 1990s, Amir was happy, both at home and at work. He became good friends with the owner of Hennigan Liquors, Bill Hennigan, who was a musician in an Irish band.

There were so many positive changes occurring for the Farzans. Some just seemed to happen, while others were pursued. Knowing they would never be returning to Iran, the family made a concerted effort to Americanize their children as much as possible. They wanted to diminish any reason for attacks against them, while maintaining their identity. They were proud Persians and carried on the tradition with surnames that reflected their native country.

They were aware that it might cause issues for their children at school among some of the other American students, especially bullies, who would find a reason to tease or pick on any child with an obvious difference. Any difference. But Amir and Sofia didn't want their children denying who they were, where they came from, and the pride they should exhibit in their Persian heritage. They believed they could cherish their ethnicity, while at the same time, assimilating into the American culture.

And that's exactly what they did. They registered their son and daughter into sports. Not only would they play soccer, but Aaron would also play baseball, and Mariam competed in United States Tennis Association tournaments. They were typical American parents sitting in the stands yelling at the umpire about his bad calls during the baseball games and stressing out during close tennis matches.

Besides making decisions to help their children fit in, Amir and Sofia were also taking steps to Americanize their own lives. They joined a local book club at the new and large and impressive orange-bricked Park Hills Public Library, where they met several very nice and interesting avid readers. They both found the book club to be a wonderful experience for their growth as Americans, as well as creating new friendships.

The biggest change however, wasn't a strategic decision, but an inspired experience. Neither Sofia nor Amir would have ever imagined stepping away from their Muslim faith in Iran. Now in America, the pressures associated with being Muslim were virtually non-existent, since they didn't always surround themselves with Middle Eastern friends and family. The Farzans could choose the faith of their choice, not the one passed down through the generations of their respective families, with no ability to question the beliefs.

After witnessing his boss, and new friend, Bill Hennigan's exuberance and devotion to his faith, Amir and Sofia discussed their religion at length and thought they would merely investigate Catholicism. They were aware of a trend among some Muslims in the Middle East converting to Christianity, called "Muslim background believers." These men and women had been born and raised Muslim and intentionally converted to Christianity as adults.

There were a variety of reasons for the conversion, but many former Muslims cited the love that Christians exhibited in their relationships with non-Christians and their treatment of women as equals. These were the traits Amir witnessed in Bill Hennigan on a daily basis. Certainly, that had great appeal for the Farzans, who also learned there were nearly a hundred thousand Muslims in America who had converted to Catholicism.

Their curious adventure investigating the faith turned into much more. During the third mass they attended at St. Michael's Church, Sofia felt a strong calling during Father William Sullivan's homily. Amir admitted to her afterward that he too was moved by the words of the passionate and intelligent priest, Father Bill.

After several days of reflection and discussion, they made the decision to enter the Rite of Christian Initiation of Adults program at St. Michael's. They fell in love with the Christian doctrine and were baptized as Catholics. As they continued in the program, they received the sacrament of Reconciliation, then the Holy Eucharist, and Confirmation. They registered their son, Aaron, and daughter, Mariam, into Confraternity of Christian Doctrine classes. This was a major change for the Farzan family and one they did not take lightly.

Amir's brother, Ahmad, was shocked at their decision. He became quite angry. Amir knew he would calm down and come to his senses at some point. His brother hung on to the culture and traditions of Iran, even though he knew he would never return. The two brothers got into loud heated arguments over the issue. It most certainly caused a break in their relationship that depressed Amir to no end, because he greatly loved and admired his older brother.

A few years later, after officially becoming American citizens and saving as much money as possible, the Farzans purchased their own liquor store on LaGrange Road with a small loan from his good friend, Bill Hennigan.

It was quite a day. Amir and Sofia were now Americans, parents, Catholics, and business owners. This was all a dream come true for them as they thought back to where they had come from and how difficult it was for them to escape the new Iranian regime under Ayatollah Khomeini.

Just a year later, they found themselves in the financial position to purchase their own home, not far from St. Michaels and close to several good schools. The red-bricked, three bedroom ranch home had a big backyard and two-car garage. Their lives couldn't have been better, they thought, until Sofia found out in February of 1996 that she was pregnant once again. This was not a planned pregnancy, and Amir and Sofia were in their late thirties, but they prayed together, thanking God for this blessing.

Born on November 12, 1996 at Park Hills Hospital, Arman Farzan, named in honor of Amir's father, grew up in Park Hills a happy boy. The youngest of the three Farzan children was given plenty of guidance from his older brother and sister. Aaron and Mariam were well established in their community and at school. Both were good students with several friends, who had learned the "do's and don'ts" for children of Middle Eastern heritage living in America. As Arman grew older, they passed along their knowledge to him, so he could avoid as many pitfalls as possible.

As the summer of 2001 faded away, Arman and his family viewed themselves as loyal, patriotic Americans. They loved their country and would never leave it. They would lay their lives down for America. Then 9/11 shook the world.

Certainly September 11, 2001 changed attitudes in America toward any citizens who looked Middle Eastern. Like most, the Farzans quickly found themselves rejected by some people in the community. All of a sudden, they were being viewed as possible terrorists because of their physical resemblance to the mass murderers who hijacked the airplanes. They became the target of hateful looks, hateful words. Often, they received glares while shopping at "The Jewels" or filling up their Dodge Grand Caravan at the Shell on 131st and LaGrange.

A few times, it was more than glares. A few times, it was verbal assaults, being called terrorists, murderers. Everyone in the neighborhood knew the Farzans had nothing to do with 9/11. But that didn't matter. They evidently were of Middle Eastern heritage, so hate and frustration was directed at them. Across Park Hills, across the country, vengeful thoughts were being aimed at anyone who looked like those terrorists, those evil men who attacked America and killed so many innocent people.

As a first-grade student, Arman wasn't exposed to those negative attitudes as much as his parents and older siblings. His father's business struggled throughout 2002. When some new customers walked in the door and saw Amir behind the counter, they turned and walked right back out. They didn't have to say anything. He knew.

Over the course of the following decade, the furor from 9/11 calmed down. But then, news of attacks by Al-Qaeda, and later ISIS, made life for the Farzans almost unbearable at times. Their friends, those whom knew them well, never treated them any differently, but many who were unfamiliar with the family would often look away from them quickly, or worse, yell something at them like, "Why don't you go back to Afghanistan with your terrorist friends? We don't want you here!"

This was a bewildering time for the five-year-old Arman. He loved his life, his family, home, friends, and country. He never identified with being an Iranian but viewed himself as a proud Persian-American, who was an American first and foremost. The kids at school never treated him differently. He was Arman, the same Arman they knew before 9/11. A nice boy.

Over the next eight years, Arman became popular at Park Hills Elementary School and then Park Hills Middle School. He was a straight-A student and one of the best soccer players in the Park Hills Youth Travel Soccer Program.

As a talented athlete with a great sense of humor, he had many friends and even more admirers. When he reached eighth grade, nervous, giggling girls seemed to cross his path more often than he could understand. Several of his guy friends tried to clue him in to the fact that the giggling girls liked Arman and hoped he would ask them out on a date, which usually meant to a movie at the Marcus Theater in Park Hills.

Dating had never been part of his family's tradition. Despite the conversion to Catholicism, they still believed in parental matchmaking and arranged marriages. This had already become a point of heated discussion in their household when his older siblings argued with Amir and Sofia, demanding to be able to date anyone they wanted to. Arman certainly was intrigued by the idea of dating girls he liked, especially the really pretty ones who were expressing interest in him. After all, he was a boy, and his ego was continually imploring him to seek out these opportunities to find out where they might lead.

By the time Arman graduated from Park Hills Middle School, he loved America. He loved being an American. He and his entire family were the perfect example of foreigners who had successfully acclimated to the culture. He joined the Boy Scouts of America, and he volunteered to carry the flag at school events where the colors were presented. He thought that perhaps one day, he might even enlist into the U.S. Marines. He had heard all of the stories from his parents about their days in Iran and how difficult it was for them. Arman felt an obligation to perhaps one day join the Marines to give back to the country that had given so much to his family.

Amir and Sofia were proud of their youngest child. They had watched their two eldest children endure difficult times during high school, immediately following the 9/11 attacks. They wanted Arman to have a better experience, wishing to send him to St. John's Academy, which had become more integrated with African-American and Hispanic students, as well as a few boys and girls of Middle Eastern heritage.

Southwest High School, the public school in Park Hills, had a good reputation for academics and sports, but it was somewhat infamous for the stories about fights, bullying, and even a drugged-out student who killed his parents while they were sleeping, beating them with a baseball bat.

Most of Arman's friends were destined for Southwest High. He knew the stories but begged his parents to send him there, thinking his friends would always have his back. He soon found out however, that friendships in middle school often don't carry over to high school.

CHAPTER ELEVEN

The tall, impressive looking, though graying Chicago Police Commissioner, Jerry McAdams, walked up to the brown wooden podium decorated with the red-white-and-blue City of Chicago Emblem on the front. He looked out at a sea of reporters who were quite anxious to ask questions.

"I would like to start with a statement," began the commissioner, with a high-powered group of government officials standing behind him, including Chicago's Mayor Ron Carlisle, FBI Director Jim Toomey, FBI Special Agent in Charge Harold Roberts, and Secretary of Homeland Security John Jackson. "We have identified the shooter in front of Water Tower Place yesterday afternoon as Malik Morcos, a forty-two-year-old citizen of Jordan.

"On Sunday, July 12, at approximately 2:35 p.m., Morcos used an AK-47 assault rifle to shoot thirty-four civilians. Fourteen were killed. Twelve are in critical condition at Northwestern Hospital. The other eight were treated and released. Two police officers were also shot, one killed, officer Raymond Panico. The other was wounded, officer Charlie Piper, who was treated and released.

"Here is what we know at this time. Officer Panico was assigned to patrol Water Tower Place that afternoon and quickly responded to the commotion on Michigan Avenue, where Morcos stood, threatening pedestrians.

"According to eyewitnesses, that's when Morcos took two rocket propelled grenades out of a bag and fired them into the John Hancock

Center. Those explosions resulted in seventeen innocent people killed and tremendous damage inflicted on one of our city's legendary skyscrapers.

"Then, as Panico approached, Morcos took out his assault rifle and fired several shots at the officer, who returned fire. In the gunfire exchange, Panico was mortally wounded.

"A few minutes later, two other Chicago Police officers, Charlie Piper and Joseph McInerney, heard the shooting and immediately ran toward the scene with guns drawn. Both officers were wearing bullet-proof vests. When the assailant saw the two officers running straight at him, he turned and opened fire on them. Officer Piper was hit immediately, while officer McInerney successfully shot Morcos, wounding him, and then apprehended him.

"Our public relations director, Michael Maloney, will distribute the information regarding the victims and wounded. As for the assailant, Morcos is alive and being questioned by the FBI and Homeland Security. Both departments are represented here today.

"For background, Morcos entered the United States in April of 1990 on a work visa. He was arrested in May of 1991 for drug trafficking and unlawful possession of firearms and sentenced to ten years in prison. He was released from Stateville Correctional Center on June 5, 2001. Morcos has already admitted to being a member of an Al-Qaeda terror cell here in Chicago, and we are continuing to work with the FBI and Homeland Security to follow up on the leads and information we now have on known associates of Morcos."

Dylan and Darlene stood in front of their television watching the press conference in amazement. Mayor Carlisle, Chicago's two-term, sixty-year-old mayor, wearing an impressive blue suit, tried to assure Chicagoans that everything was under control. A short, thin man with a narrow face and full head of graying hair, he was a well-educated and a highly-experienced politician. Unlike many of his predecessors, especially the Dorgans, Carlisle could actually speak the English language without "dese, dem, and dose" coloring his sentences.

As each government official stepped forward to answer questions from the host of reporters covering the press conference, both Dylan and Darlene couldn't take their eyes off the proceedings. Dylan couldn't stop thinking about how they could have been shot that afternoon. They may have been killed. Twice in less than two months, they were on the scene of the two major terrorist attacks that took place in the United States. What were the odds of that happening? Zero.

But despite being in the wrong place at the wrong time, twice, they could count their blessings, having walked away from both attacks uninjured.

As WGN-TV's Brad Bentley wrapped up the station's coverage by providing a review of what had been stated at the press conference, Dylan muted the sound and looked at a visibly shaken Darlene.

"A terrorist attack!" he said, just amazed that it happened to them again. "Terrorists! What is going on here? What should we do?"

Darlene looked at her husband, understanding that he never liked to be in a position where he wasn't prepared to meet a challenge. In daily life, that usually meant being prepared to teach his classes or having an umbrella handy because rain was in the forecast. Nothing Earth-shattering. But now they had an entirely new challenge—terrorists showing up in Chicago. This was not New York, the city from which they fled, thinking they had put the dangers of terrorism behind them. No, this was now happening in their hometown, the city they loved.

"Should I get a gun?" asked Dylan, knowing the question would upset Darlene, but it had to be considered. "Just in case. To protect us in case something like this ever happens again."

"No!" Darlene said adamantly. "What would you have done with a gun yesterday? Shot at that man? He had an AK-47 assault rifle."

"I understand, but if we are ever in a situation where we are personally confronted by a terrorist or mugger or whoever...."

"No, Dylan! We are not letting this change us," she said, hugging her beloved husband. "But right now, in this country, it's dangerous!" said Dylan emphatically. "We live in Dodge City! So what happens if the bad guy shows up with a gun? Then what?"

"That won't happen," said Darlene.

"It just did, twice!" Dylan politely argued.

"Yes, but the chances of it—"

"You can't say that," Dylan interrupted. "Not after what we just went through. We have to face the facts. It's the world we are living in right now."

Darlene released him and walked a few feet away, plopping down on the couch. Dylan knew she felt anxious. Conflicted. He also knew he was making complete sense, but Darlene just did not want to allow herself to think that way. For them, up until that point, it had always been taking the risk of no gun over the risk of having a gun. They both knew either way there was a risk. But she had to know he was right.

In only a four-week period, they had been at the scene of two tragic terrorist attacks. Could they afford to keep taking the risk, when it seemed the dangers associated with that gamble continued to show up in their lives?

Dylan sat next to his troubled wife, put his arm around her, and hugged the great love of his life. That's all they wanted—just to share their love together. He looked up at the television screen, where WGN was now showing live footage from the Water Tower Place attack that had been recorded on the iPhone of an eyewitnesses and sent into the station. It was devastating to watch the RPGs explode into the John Hancock Center; horrifying to see the crazed terrorist shooting innocent people as they fled for their lives.

"How could he do that?" Dylan asked, so angry at the thought of such irresponsible violence.

"I don't know, Dylie, I don't know," Darlene said softly as Dylan pulled her close to him and covered her eyes with his arm to protect her from the violent scenes.

"We will figure this out," Dylan said, as he watched the footage of the gun battle between officer Panico and the terrorist, Morcos. All Chicago watched the shot that exploded the officer's head, blood splattering everywhere, Panico dropping lifeless to the ground.

"We'll figure this out."

CHAPTER TWELVE

The day Arman Farzan strode through the entrance of Southwest High School, he was filled with a great deal of optimism and excitement. He was now a high school student, no longer just a little kid.

He had so many friends at Park Hills Middle School who were attending Southwest. Seeing so many friends in the halls, he thought it would be Park Hills Middle School 2.0, the same kids, only now older, more respected, and taken seriously. Sure, he knew there would be plenty of new kids he would meet along the way, but he had his base of friends, and that made him feel very secure about the transition.

High-fives and "Hey, how's it going," were traded between Arman and his old friends every time they passed each other in the halls during the first week on the large campus with over two thousand enrolled students. He told his parents how glad he was that he made the decision to go to Southwest instead of St. John's Academy.

Then, on the Tuesday of the third week of school, Arman became one of the targets of a gang at the school called MG's Boys, named after the two leaders, Rick Mazel and Stosh Gould. This group of five thugs hated anyone who was a minority, but especially the brown-skinned kids whom they mistakenly called "Arabs."

It became very clear, very quickly, that life for Arman at Southwest High would be very different, when his group of Irish, Italian, and Polish friends from middle school, as well as teammates from his travel soccer team, stood and watched him get picked on, harassed, beaten up.

This was incredibly discouraging for Arman. One morning, he was standing with two friends in D-Wing when three of MG's Boys came around the corner. That was the moment Arman's friends should have stood with him and fought back. Instead, it was the moment when Arman realized his friends were not his friends. They quickly departed, distanced themselves from him, knowing they would become a target of attacks by ruthless bullies.

Arman fought back, throwing punches and dodging his attackers, but after a few minutes, with students in the hall standing back to watch the fight, Arman was tackled. It became three-on-one, an unfair fight to be sure.

As Arman lay on the ground, bloodied, bruised, angry, and disappointed with his former friends, he knew he would have to find new friends, loyal friends.

Of the 2,300 students at Southwest High, of which twenty-four percent were defined as minorities, Arman quickly got to know every one of the 123 students with a Middle Eastern heritage that passed through the halls of the fairly new high school. For some reason, the kids in the gang would not accept them as Americans. Or they just didn't like people with brown skin.

Their leader was Rick Mazel, an ugly, pock-marked, melon-headed, pale-faced kid with not an ounce of athletic ability in his body. He was backed up by his enforcer, Stosh Gould, the meanest gang member. Gould took great delight in kicking his enemies as hard as possible in the gut and head, showing no remorse. Nathan Nowicki was Gould's best friend and nearly as mean.

Mike Felder and Benny Kowal were just foot soldiers. Felder was a tall blond-haired boy who played on the basketball team at the school and was pressured into joining the gang or have his legs broken, which would effectively end his sports career. Kowal was told they would burn his house down if he didn't join. Terrorist tactics. He joined.

That was the main group, but Mazel was always working on bringing in new recruits who had to prove themselves to the demented gang leader. If he decided that he wanted them in MG's Boys, it was in their best interests to join.

Arman was no weakling, a fairly tall, slim, but muscular freshman who was one of the best soccer players in the area, a top athlete. MG's

Boys knew it. Any time Arman saw MG's Boys in the halls, he tried running. He tried defending himself, but they attacked him in packs of three or more, making sure they outnumbered him.

Just two days after the first attack, they surrounded him once again in D-Wing, in front of the same lockers where they jumped him the first time. Gould punched Arman hard across his face, bloodying his nose. And when he was hurt so badly that he became dizzy and fell, Gould and Nowicki began kicking him as hard as they could in the stomach, sides, and even his head. These were merciless punks, this band of bullies, each of whose parents had emigrated from Europe to Chicago.

Teachers often saw the beatings and quickly stopped them, but the bullies never seemed to receive enough punishment to deter them from finding another avenue to beat up on Arman, and, as he found out, any other black or brown students at the school they could get their hands on. They waited for him outside of school, or caught up with him in the restroom, shoving his head down the toilet and flushing it. Swirlies!

One morning, the head football coach, Mr. Neal Michaels, spotted Arman coming out of the restroom with his head and shirt soaked. He didn't have to ask, immediately aware of what had happened to the freshman.

The next day, the parents of the five gang members were summoned to the front office, where the principal, Mr. Ben Leonard, informed them about the conduct of their sons and a one-week suspension as punishment. They were also told that if it happened again, they would be expelled.

Principal Leonard was well-liked at the school but was also known as someone not to be challenged. As a former boxer in his youth, he had a competitive determination that was evident in his attitude and actions. The parents got the message and took their troubled boys home, promising Leonard to correct their views and attitudes. The experienced principal just nodded, knowing it was naïve to think the racist mindset wasn't passed down by their parents.

When they returned to school, the other students at Southwest High stayed away from the ill-willed gang, never wanting to be associated with this group of thugs. To most students at the school, they were sure the only thing MG's Boys would ever earn in high school was a prison sentence.

The dean at the school, Mr. Kevin Healy, was also the wrestling coach and didn't put up with any nonsense. He tried to talk the gang of five into joining his wrestling team, where he knew he could straighten them out in a hurry. They would have none of it. And, despite the threat of being expelled, they continued looking for private opportunities to go after minority students.

The principal's ultimatum meant that Arman received a reprieve. MG's Boys knew if they touched him, they would be gone. So throughout the remainder of freshman year, all Arman ever received from any of them were cold, hateful stares as he passed them in the hallways or sat far away from them in class.

But as a result of the attacks, Arman became friends with four other boys who had similar stories to his family. Omar Abadi, Jahan Rahar, Gabe Toma and Dabney Daher were each born in America, all at Park Hills Hospital, just like Arman. Their parents each emigrated to the United States, fleeing the violence in their home countries. Like Arman, both Omar and Jahan's parents came over from Iran in the early 1980s. Gabe and Dabney's parents had fled from Iraq in 1989 when Saddam Hussein was drawing the world's attention to his brutal dictatorship, and life for the average Iraqi citizen became chaotic.

Whereas Arman's freshman year was a time of adjustments and getting accustomed to the high school culture at Southwest High, sophomore year turned into a much more challenging time. The hateful stares from Mazel, Gould, and their thugs, escalated into name calling and threats, which surprised Arman. He wondered if the threat of expulsion was still in place, or if the slate was wiped clean each school year. None of it made any sense to him, and he would scream that fact at the bullies during the verbal attacks.

"I'm more of an American than any of you!" he would shout. "I was born here! None of you can say the same!"

It didn't matter. MG's Boys would stake out hallways where they knew Arman or one of his pals would be walking to class. Then they would surround their prey and start punching them violently, usually a five-to-one ratio. Pure bullies. Pure cowards.

After taking several beatings during the first two months of the new school year, Arman thought about going to Mr. Michaels but decided against it. Regardless, news of the renewed attacks did get back to Principal Leonard. He called a meeting with Coach Michaels, and they agreed that once solid evidence was presented, they would expel all five boys in the gang. Too many bad things had taken place in high schools across America when disputes like this one were dismissed as no big deal, nothing to worry about at all. They did not want that to be the case at their school.

Unaware of what was taking place in the administration offices, Arman and his four friends decided they would have to stick together while in school and coordinated their schedules to work out a plan. After having just researched his heritage in the school library, Arman suggested they call themselves the "Persian Warriors", taken from an elite army in the Achaemenid Empire back in 500 B.C. Omar, Jahan, Dabney, and Gabe loved the idea and from that point on, the name became their bond, their commitment to each other.

Together in strength, they felt if MG's Boys wanted a fight, they would get one. And with that one decision, MG's beatings stopped as the two differing groups of students would pass each other in the halls, the Persian Warriors glaring at MG's Boys, just waiting for them to make the first move. They didn't. Apparently when the numbers were even, they weren't so tough.

CHAPTER THIRTEEN

s Dylan entered Water Street Grill on South Michigan Avenue, he scanned across the long dining area, looking across the high glossy brown oak tables and chairs and similarly fashioned booths on the side. He maneuvered his way past the tall dining tables and bar-counter seating, looking for his pal Georgie Hanlon, excited to see him after nine years.

The restaurant was quite crowded for Wednesday at noon. It was lunchtime for most of the professionals from the many office buildings that lined one of Chicago's most popular avenues, filled with an abundance of restaurant and shopping choices. As he came around the corner to another section of tables, he spotted Georgie outside, seated at a table on the patio with a couple of other fellows, who Dylan immediately recognized.

"Wow!" he said, walking up to the square wooden block table complete with sleek gray chairs on each side. "What is this, a reunion?"

"A surprise reunion," said Georgie laughing with his two St. John's Academy surprise guests. Willie Mitrovich and Teddy Web stood to shake hands with Dylan, followed by the always awkward-looking semi-hug, so popular but so ridiculous. Dylan then took the open seat next to Willie, across from Teddy, who was seated next to Georgie.

Georgie looked much as he did during his high school years, average height with his thick brown hair combed to the side, a pale thin face, thin lips, long chin, friendly brown eyes and looking fit from his one-mile runs each day. Willie was about the same height, also thin, with his distinctive oblong face, tan olive skin, big round eyes, full lips and fairly long but well-groomed thin brown hair. Teddy is the one who looked very different. At six-foot tall with a square face, strong chin, Roman nose, short blond hair, with a muscular build draped in an impressive-looking gray Brooks Brothers suit. He obviously had become a successful professional in a short time period.

"My goodness, you guys don't look that much different," said Dylan. The last time they'd all been together was back in February 2005, for the wake and funeral of their fallen friend and high school hockey teammate, Joe Doyle. "Well, except for you, Teddy. You look grown up and successful!"

"Yeah, it happened overnight," chuckled Teddy. "One day, I was a college kid at Loyola. The next day, I'm a grown up. Who'd of thunk it, eh?"

"You don't look any different either, Dylan," said Willie, smiling wide. "Georgie already filled us in on you teaching at Watson College Prep, coaching hockey, and a married man. Pretty good, Dylan! But I think we all knew you would be doing something to help people. Teaching and coaching sounds right to me."

"Thanks, Georgie," Dylan smiled. "Just trying to do the best I can with what God gave me, just like they taught us at St. John's, right?"

"Hundred percent!" said Georgie, who had received the call from his old high school pal Dylan, just a week earlier, asking to get together. He was surprised but also really happy to hear from him after nearly a full decade had passed. "Well, why don't you tell them the latest news?"

"At lunch?" Dylan said. "Kind of a downer, wouldn't you say?"

"Believe me, they are going to want to know," Georgie adamantly insisted. Dylan paused a moment and looked at his three friends, who were staring at him with great curiosity.

"Okay, well, my wife and I have been present at two terrorist attacks in the past three months," Dylan informed them, then picked up the menu. "So, what looks good here?"

"I didn't know that, Dylan," said Teddy, shifting forward to hear this startling news. "Were either of you hurt? What happened?"

After Dylan politely provided a quick summary of the terrorist experience in New York and then the horrific experience outside Water Tower Place, he paused to let his friends absorb it. Then, he turned to his once-freckle-faced hockey teammate and said, "So Georgie, how about if you fill us in on your exploits since the championship hockey game when you let that Marymount center blow by you in the final seconds of the game to score, costing us the trophy."

A burst of laughter exploded across the table, information that wasn't so funny on the day of the loss, but a decade later, seemed such a distant memory that the four teammates could laugh heartily. Seeing his friends' attitude actually made Georgie feel better about his failure on defense that day. This was literally the first time anyone had brought up the embarrassing moment to him since that day at Orland Arctic Ice Arena.

"Thanks, fellas!" Georgie said, smiling widely. "Yes, I sucked that day!"

More laughter and high-fives for Georgie, letting him know they still loved him.

After St. John's, Georgie went on to graduate from the prestigious Notre Dame University with honors as a finance major, and he thought hard about going into the banking industry. He considered becoming an investment banker where he could earn the big money. But at twenty-two years old, he really wanted to pursue his passion, his dream job in life. He really wanted to become a radio personality at his favorite station, WXRT-FM in Chicago.

WXRT was the most popular station in Chicago for anyone who loved what was termed alternative rock, but more accurately, just great rock music. XRT, as it was most often referred, was a station willing to take risks and play new artists if the on-air talent thought they were good enough to receive the airtime. So many famous bands across the country credited XRT for their courage, including Collective Soul, The Bo Deans, The Smithereens and so many more. There was no bubblegum pop music, no rap, no country, just great rock music with the station playing songs from a variety of eras including the Beatles arrival to America in 1964 all the way through the present day.

Although the news of pursuing a radio career didn't exactly thrill Georgie's parents, he promised he would pay them back for helping to fund his education. His dad was a hard-working, middle-class, blue-collar worker and not really in a position to shell out the big dough required to attend Notre Dame University, but Georgie vowed that if he didn't achieve an on-air position within five years, he would make a change and enter the world of finance.

"So, how did you come up with this reunion brainstorm?" Dylan asked Georgie, as Willie and Teddy sipped their waters while viewing the lunch menu, but still listening with great interest. "I was just calling you to see if you still had contacts at the radio station who could get tickets to the MusicFest."

"I didn't know that. And no, I don't have those connections any longer," explained a smiling Georgie, his freckles no longer such a prominent fixture on his face. "Sorry, but after you called, I immediately thought about the old gang back at St. John's and decided I'd try to find Teddy and Willie. And voila! Here we are."

"I'm amazed!" said Dylan. "So, you guys haven't stayed in touch either?"

"No, other than getting here a little early and catching up," said Willie, smiling and shaking his head. "It's like most people who leave high school. It's on to college and then the working world. Other than Teddy here, I really don't know anyone who goes back to St. John's that often."

"Well, they love him there," said Georgie, exhibiting his pride in his pal Teddy. "He's always helping out, kicking in dough when they need it. Puts us all to shame!"

"Yeah, it's no secret Teddy's keeping St. John's afloat and remains the big man on campus," said Willie, laughing, then quickly changed the subject. "So Georgie, did you really go into radio?"

Although Georgie was quite proud of his two years at WXRT, it already seemed like ancient history to him. He was now ensconced in the banking world, making so much more money with a bright future staring him in the face.

"Even with the degree from South Bend, as well as four years of experience at the student radio station, I started out as an assistant producer," Georgie explained to his pals, who were enamored by the thought of him working for the popular radio station. "Within the first year, I had been promoted three times and became the lead producer on the Afternoon Drive Show. You know, Mikey Leonard's show. But after two years, I realized that I was just chasing a dream that may not be quite as fulfilling as it may have seemed when I was younger.

"I met with the station manager and asked him point blank what my chances were for getting an on-air slot in the next year. I felt like his answer really helped me make my decision."

"What did he say?" asked Willie. "What were your chances?"

"'Slim and none' was his response," Georgie laughed with a wide smile. "Even better, when I said I would have to move on, he offered to walk me to the door and gave me some parting advice saying, 'Don't let the door hit me in the ass on the way out!' Yeah, he loved me."

"You were fired?" Dylan asked.

"Fired, quit, tie goes to the runner, right?" he laughed loudly, and his three high school pals right along with him. "But it's all good, I've been working as an accountant at Stewart Savings & Loan for the past few years, doing well, just waiting for my next opportunity to come riding up to my front door."

"That's great, Georgie!" said Dylan. "At least you took your shot, right?"

"Yep, but then I did what I was supposed to be doing, and my parents haven't stopped smiling ever since. How about you, Willie?" Georgie asked his once-close friend.

"I went to Northwestern University and graduated with a business degree, then went to work with my father at his company, making a wide variety of electronic components," said Willie, exhibiting a certain pride in working for the family business. "There's quite a bit to it, and staying ahead of competitors and the newest trends in technology is a constant battle. I wasn't really sure how I'd like it, but I love it. I absolutely love it! And, it gave me an entirely new perspective about my dad. I took him for granted when I was growing up, that's for sure."

"Beautiful!" said Georgie. "I think a few of us could admit to taking our parents for granted when we were younger. I know I have told them how much I appreciate them several times since. How about you, Teddy?"

"Well to your comment earlier, I do go back to help out at the high school," Teddy said in his always measured and respectable manner and tone, always the politician, just like in high school.

"Yeah, Teddy makes a boatload of money now as 'Lawyer Boy,'" interrupted Willie, smiling at the success of his good friend.

"Ah, no kidding!" said Dylan. "So you went on to become a prosecutor to put the bad guys behind bars, just like you said you would in high school. Beautiful! But I didn't think prosecuting attorneys made that much, but maybe...."

"Well, no, Teddy didn't become a prosecuting attorney," Willie interrupted, laughing a bit, having received a quick update from Teddy before Dylan's arrival, followed by a Google search for the full story.

"Really?" Dylan said.

"Yes, he joined Slagle & Sharp, a firm that defends major corporations and big shots representing their business interests, and in some cases, keeping them out of jail," said Willie, laughing at the change in direction his old friend made in his career path.

"Now, wait a minute," interrupted Teddy. "Everyone and every entity is entitled representation in court. That's the law. That's America."

"Yeah, and the entities you represent just happen to pay a whole lot more than other entities, isn't that right?" Willie laughed.

"I take great pride in my work, Willie," Teddy said quite seriously in his measured tone, as if at a press conference addressing the media. "I work hard and make sure I represent our clients to the best of my abilities. And yes, I do go back to St. John's and make donations because I am in a position to do so. I've always believed those who can help out should help out. Isn't that what they taught us?"

"But you haven't told Dylan about one of your big cases at Slagle & Sharp, not the one they use to promote you on their website, the one that was in the news," said Willie with a look in his eye like he was dropping some information on his pals that would really shock them. "Make sure you're sitting down for this!"

"Ah, that's boring lawyer stuff that nobody wants to hear about," said Teddy, looking at his menu again. "Hey, let's go ahead and order. Hey, Georgie, do you still go for the grilled cheese sandwiches?"

"Oh, I do, Teddy, love 'em. But nice try changing the subject," Georgie laughed, slapping his successful lawyer pal on the back.

"Yeah that's right, Georgie," Willie continued. "So, Teddy, why don't you tell Dylan and Georgie about that case. It was in the national news. Did you guys read about it?"

Dylan and Georgie obviously missed the story and felt embarrassed to admit it.

"Yes, I think I'm going to break my diet a bit and have some fries with that grilled cheese Georgie," Teddy said, once again attempting to change the subject. "You know wearing these skinny-styled suits is no picnic, but sometimes I'll splurge with an order of fries every now and then."

"It was in the *Tribune*, too," Willie interrupted, not being set off course by the fascinating fries-and-grilled-cheese conversation. "Teddy defended a client who genetically altered soybeans using a gene that kills insects that bore into the soybean plants. The soybeans were approved to feed cattle but were put into products that were sold to consumers who got really sick!"

"Hah! That's funny, Willie," Dylan laughed, believing it was a joke, given Teddy's integrity, which would never allow him to get involved in such a terrible case.

"No joke, Dylan," said Willie with not a hint of humor to be read in the look on his tanned face.

Georgie and Dylan just looked at him and knew he was serious. Then, Georgie turned toward his former hockey teammate and friend, asking, "Teddy, he's kidding right?"

Teddy paused for a moment, "Well, this isn't quite how I saw this reunion going. Maybe we should order and put this conversation behind us, eh, fellows?"

Silence.

"You have to understand, it's the law," Teddy explained, his three former high school pals waiting for a clue about how he could get involved with such a case, hoping their friend was still the guy they all admired a decade earlier.

"And…?" Georgie said in an ascending tone.

"And we lost an eight-million-dollar settlement due to our client's negligence, public nuisance, and failure to provide a warning about the soybeans," said Teddy. "But I did my job, represented the points of their defense. They were negligent and put the public in harm, and there was no getting around it."

Silence.

"Okay, so the grilled cheese sandwich looks great. Miss!" Willie called out, getting the waitress' attention. A young brunette approached the table, her long ponytail bouncing across the back of her pink restaurant uniform with each step.

"Are you gentlemen ready to order?" she asked.

"Yes, I'd like the grilled cheese sandwich," said Teddy quickly, happy to shift the discussion off of his legal work. His three friends then ordered, and after Dylan made the final order of a Caesar salad, Teddy said, "Hey, a toast to our courageous friend and teammate, Joe Doyle. I wish he could have joined us today."

That stopped the momentum of the conversation and all four young professionals raised their glasses of water, clinked them together, and took a sip, thinking of their fallen friend and hero.

"Nine years fellows, nine years!" said Dylan, stating how long it had been since their friend had been shot and killed by a sniper in Afghanistan. "I really think we have to do something to remember him more, honor him. He had more courage than all of us put together."

"He sure did," said Teddy, sincerely believing that sentiment, but also relieved the conversation had moved off him.

"Any of you guys ever make it back to Washington, D.C. to visit his grave?" asked Georgie, referring to Joe's eternal resting place of honor in Arlington National Cemetery.

"I've been by there a few times, when I had cases in D.C.," said Teddy. "It's hard to look at that white marble stone, but it also makes me proud that Joe will spend the rest of eternity with the bravest Americans, who, like him, made the ultimate sacrifice for their country."

"That's great, Teddy!" said Dylan. "I wish I could have gotten back there since the funeral. Nine years! Might be a good idea if maybe we all plan something, go together sometime."

"I'm in," said Willie.

"Me too!" said Georgie.

"Great idea, Dylan," Teddy said. "I'll get my admin in touch with all of you and we can figure out a time to go."

The waitress came out with their meals, placing them on the table, as a silence fell upon the group, thinking about Joe and how one decision can change the course of a person's life forever.

"You know, I know when Joe decided to join the Marines, I really think he believed he could go over there and do some real damage against those terrorists," Willie said.

"I know he did," Georgie said. "He was going to kill all of them, all by himself."

"In his mind, I really don't think he ever believed he would be hurt, let alone killed," Willie said.

"Yeah, just six months in Afghanistan and gone," added Georgie with a frown.

"Bravest guy I ever knew," Dylan said. "Given how passionate he felt about going after the terrorists, there was truly no other choice for him. I really wish he could have lived and, well...no point...."

The memory raised a lull in the discussion, when Georgie said, "Hey, Teddy, we are sorry about prying into your business. That's how you make your living, so no problem."

Teddy put the remnants of his sandwich down, wiped his hands with his paper napkin, and looked at his three pals.

"Look fellas, I'm sorry if this offends you, but you have to understand, we live in a country that is governed by laws, and whether people like it or not, lawyers have to defend clients in cases that can be quite controversial," Teddy said, taking a quick sip of water, and then looked up at his three friends, whom he knew were more than a little surprised. "I don't have my own firm where I have the luxury of picking and choosing the cases I want to take on. The partners at the firm assigned me to that case, litigation that I wouldn't agree with on the outside, but as a lawyer, I have to represent and defend. I hope you understand that."

Quiet fell over the table of once close friends, a full plate of disappointment had been served.

"If it makes you feel any better, after that case, I asked off of that client's work," Teddy continued. "Yes, I knew morally it was wrong, but I was living up to my oath as a lawyer to follow the ethical rules. And that's exactly what I did. Regardless, I couldn't sleep at night, and it actually became a major issue between my wife and I."

"Sorry, Teddy," said Willie.

There was a long pause at the table, and Dylan hoped this issue wouldn't drive a wedge between the longtime friends. This took the four friends back to their high school days and the long gray Formica tables in the cafeteria at St. John's when they would often get into debates, but the stakes were never this personal and this high. Back then, they all believed Teddy to be a leader, a member of the student council, an assistant captain on the hockey team, an altar boy, and a good Catholic.

"Hey Teddy, don't worry about it, okay?" Dylan said, maintaining a polite decorum, while he tried to get the conversation back to lighthearted jibber jabber of which they were all experts during their high school years. "We are all grown-ups now, so you don't have to explain yourself to us."

Silence.

"So, how about those Bears, guys?" Dylan said, intent on changing the subject.

"Oh, they should be better this year, I hope," Willie said, eager to join in on the new topic of discussion.

"Yeah, their new coach Marc Trestman was .500 last season, so they should be better this year, right?" added Georgie, who knew little about football but had heard the news about the Bears coach.

Teddy raised his hands up to stop the conversation, "Just one more thing, okay?" he said, taking the floor once again. "The client they assigned me to now is a big real estate developer. Anyone have any problems with construction companies?"

"Oh no, no. No problem!" the three friends blurted out in unison, it seemed.

"Real estate developers are great!" Willie said.

"Build all those beautiful buildings in our city, great!" Georgie said.

"Congratulations, Teddy, I hope it all works out for you," added Dylan.

Teddy, smiling for the first time in five minutes, felt so relieved, like his friends had let him back into the club. "Yeah LLJ Skyscrapers," he said. "It's an impressive company. They have built a lot of beautiful buildings."

And the conversation continued, all four friends jabbering away about the skyline of Chicago, their favorite buildings, how wonderful it was to live in a city with such a long and glorious history of architecture.

Willie raised his glass of water, "Here's to Chicago!"

"Chicago!" they all said, clinking their glasses together, friends forever.

CHAPTER FOURTEEN

*D*arlene and Dylan stood in the middle of a large crowd of young music fans, dressed in warm summer apparel. Many wore T-shirts with logos and symbols of one of the dozens of bands that would be performing on this hot muggy Saturday afternoon in August of 2014.

The young Reilly couple had a one-day ticket to MusicFest in Chicago's Grant Park. Luckily, it was for Day Two, which turned out to be the only day that rain was not in the forecast for the ultra-popular outdoor concert, which drew music lovers from throughout the country. Although they would have loved to see two of their favorite bands, Kings of Leon and Young the Giant, who were scheduled to perform on Day Three, they steered away from the risk of rain, believing they were too old to get soaked and slosh through the mud just to see live music.

They had watched the five o'clock news on that Saturday in August of 2012 when pouring rain and high winds forced sixty thousand MusicFest-goers to evacuate Grant Park. Many of the evacuees made their way to nearby taverns to drink away the time until they were allowed back into the massive event. After a few hours, when the mob of drunk and soaked young adults were allowed back into the park, they each seemed to wear their individual canvass of body mud-art with great pride as a symbol of their dedication to see great musical artists, no matter what Mother Nature dealt out to dissuade them.

Darlene and her husband wanted no part of that artistic chaos. No, at twenty-eight years old, they had both reached a point when their priority was pursuing as positive experience as humanly possible at the annual festival, enjoying the music, food, and atmosphere. Enduring wind and rain would be reserved for attendance at White Sox or Bears games.

Despite the blue skies and encouraging weather report, Dylan had prepared for the worst, packing his black backpack with two rain ponchos, sunscreen, plenty of water, bug spray, gauze, medical tape, and Band-Aids, just as the MusicFest Guide recommended.

After clearing security at the main entrance, they shuffled their way through the silver metal barricades up Balbo Street toward the Lake Stage. The couple knew patience would be one of the requirements when maneuvering through large crowds of young, exuberant kids. They were tested early when one long-haired, shirtless, teenage boy in knee-length, bright orange shorts, who was walking right behind them, began screaming at the top of his lungs, "MusicFest! MusicFest!" Ten consecutive times he announced his love for the concert event, directly into Dylan's ears.

"Oh, this is fun!" Dylan sarcastically quipped to his smiling bride. "Yeah, I can't get enough of that! Got any earplugs?"

The couple took a detour to escape the sound intrusion, and a few hundred yards later, walked right into one young lady in blue-jean short-shorts and tall, black leather boots who felt it necessary to rip off her bright pink tube top, exposing her very large bosom as she danced in circles to the beat of a young rock band performing on the Cherry Stage. This flower-child display, reminiscent of 1969 Woodstock, quickly drew the attention of several inebriated young men as well as the Chicago Police. Two cops quickly covered the dancing, half-naked young lady with a leather police jacket and hauled her off to jail for indecent exposure. As they walked her to the Chicago Police paddy wagon, two of her newfound admirers yelled out marriage proposals to their damsel in no dress, which drew a look back over her shoulder and a wide smile from the city's newest criminal.

On this beautiful late Saturday afternoon with blue skies and eighty-three-degree temps, they found a very good opening on the trampled yellowing grass next to third base on the tan dirt softball diamond. They were just a few hundred feet from the stage, a perfect spot to lay their favorite large White-Sox-logoed blanket.

While Darlene got comfortable, Dylan was off to the Fest's Food-Town to fetch them something to eat. Soon, they were sitting on their blanket together, snacking on very delicious barbeque chicken sandwiches and sipping from plastic cups filled with pinot noir. They planned to later munch on the cheese and crackers Darlene had packed in her large, beige leather carrying bag. With more sips of pinot noir, of course.

As they enjoyed their meal, Dylan couldn't help but admire his wife and appreciate just how lucky he was to be married to Darlene. She was looking as beautiful as ever that evening, wearing a pretty mid-length light blue summer dress, new light brown sandals, straw sunhat, and sunglasses. Dylan, who would never be confused for a fashion expert and always depended on Darlene for apparel direction, was wearing tan cargo shorts and a loose-fitting navy blue crew neck T-shirt, his favorite white Nike athletic shoes with sneaker socks, and sunglasses sitting atop his long neatly combed wavy brown locks.

The headliner that night was Outkast, who was sure to draw a massive crowd to the Orbit Stage. Regardless, Dylan and Darlene wanted to first see The Head and the Heart, a really talented and soulful group they had found by listening to WXRT Radio, Georgie's former employer, which often played the band's songs. As the performance began at 7:15 p.m., there was still plenty of room for the three hundred or so in attendance to sit on blankets in front of the Lake Stage and watch the performance with no obstructions. The opportunity to sit and watch the band in comfort was a great treat, since standing was required at so many of the concerts due to the extremely large crowds.

Dylan had found a terrific spot to view the band while looking directly at the Chicago skyline along Michigan Avenue. The Hilton and Towers, Blackstone Hotel, and Harrison Hotel were most prominent with the famed Willis Tower in the background to the right. Although partially blocked by the trees to their right, Dylan pointed out the Blue Cross/Blue Shield Building that had coordinated lighting so a large message halfway up the skyscraper read #RockEnroll, obviously promoting enrollment into health insurance. Pretty smart, Dylan thought, and found out later how the lights on certain floors were left on and specific shades drawn in order to have that message spelled out to the massive crowd at MusicFest.

"Here's to a wonderful evening with the woman who means more to me than anything in the world," toasted Dylan, raising his plastic cup of pinot noir and touching cups with his smiling and happy bride, something he really appreciated given the turmoil they had experienced over the past few months.

"This was a really great idea, Dylie," said Darlene, making Dylan smile with the pet name. "Only good thoughts, good food, good wine, and good music on this incredibly beautiful night."

They touched glasses once again, sipped their wine, then sat back to watch The Head and the Heart perform "Lost in my Mind" which drew the full attention of the crowd, appreciating the wonderful melody and lyrics of the group's most popular tune. They followed that with "Shake" and had the crowd rocking, some jumping up to dance, but thankfully keeping their clothes on.

"I love you, honey," said Dylan to his effervescent wife, leaning in to kiss her, with all the love and passion he felt for her.

"I love you too, Dylie," Darlene whispered, kissing her husband. As she pulled back, she looked into his eyes, and Dylan found himself hoping they would enjoy a long, loving life together, praying for children to cement the union, and days of joy and happiness, growing old together and never losing the shared love he had felt since the day they met at the University of Chicago.

As the band began to play their next tune, loud screams could be heard coming from the Cherry Stage area, more than a full block away. All at once, it seemed, everyone turned to see what was happening when the air became filled with bursts of short, quick explosions.

"Oh no!" said Dylan, jumping up and taking Darlene by the hand to help her up. "Not again!"

Darlene stood with a frightful look on her face as the short bursts continued. They were rapid. They were loud.

"It sounds like a machine gun or something," said Darlene, grabbing her large handbag.

"C'mon, we've got to get out of here," said Dylan, picking up his backpack with his left hand and leading his wife as fast as he could, running together toward the slope behind them and past the hedges toward the thick elm trees along Lake Shore Drive where they could get cover.

As they ran, they could hear the gunfire. Pop, pop, pop! Pop, pop, pop! Screams of horror grew. People ran in every direction, trying to find safety in the pure mayhem. A young woman on their left, running up the slope, bellowed out, "Ahhh!!" Then she fell hard to the ground.

Dylan stopped and saw a red mark on the back of her white top.

"C'mon, honey, we have to keep running," pleaded Darlene, near the top of the slope.

"She's been shot!" exclaimed Dylan, who as always, ran over to help, picked the woman up and kept running toward the street, his wife about five yards in front of him.

Pop, pop, pop! Pop, pop, pop! Dylan could feel his adrenaline spike upon hearing the bullets whizzing by him.

"Keep running, Darlene, I'm right behind you," he yelled to her. Just as she crossed the paved walking path, she looked back for a moment, "Okay, okay, c'mon we're almost there!" she said.

Pop, pop, pop! Pop, pop, pop!

Dylan made it to the top of the slope, veering to the right, running past the hedges, looking directly at Darlene. He felt a whoosh sail past his right ear and saw his wife abruptly jolted. Darlene flew several feet to her right and down to the ground.

"No! No!" Dylan screamed. He lay down the injured woman he was carrying.

"Someone please help this woman!" he yelled out, then sprinted to his wife, who was moaning in great pain. A bullet struck her on her left side above the waist. Dylan quickly picked her up and carried her the final few feet, laying her down behind the thick brown elm tree, protecting her from any more stray bullets. Dozens of people began lining up behind the row of elm trees along Lake Shore Drive. In just a few seconds, the Reillys were surrounded by frightened, crying people. Everyone was hoping the large tree would protect them.

Darlene moaned out in pain, the blood flowing out of her side, growing a dark wet circle on the side of her blue dress.

"Give me room here!" Dylan yelled at the people crowding in on his injured wife. He unzipped his backpack, grabbed gauze and medical tape, ripped open two gauze packages, and applied them onto his wife's wound.

Pop, pop pop! Pop, pop, pop! The shots continued. People ran, screaming.

"Don't worry, Darlene, you'll be alright," Dylan assured her, looking around for a policeman, anyone who could help get her to a hospital. He took the several strips of the white medical tape and wrapped it across the gauze to hold it in place.

"Help me, Dylie, help me!" she cried out to him with a wide-eyed look of panic in her eyes.

"I'll be right back, I've got to get someone to take us to the hospital," he said, then turned and stepped out into the safety lane along the curb of Lake Shore Drive, waving his arms at the cars moving by quickly.

"Please stop! It's an emergency!" he yelled out. Car after car passed him, the drivers seemingly aware of the shootings going on, as people were running and screaming everywhere.

"Please stop! God, please help! Please stop!"

Just then, a green Dodge minivan pulled up to the curb, and the young man inside opened the passenger window. "What happened?" said the thirty-something man.

"I need to get my wife to the emergency room. Can you please help us?!" Dylan begged him.

"Yes, c'mon, get her in here," he said, pressing the button to open the automatic passenger gate, while Dylan ran back, picked up Darlene, and carried her to the van. He gently placed her on the green leather bench-seat in the second row, then ran back to scoop up their bags and heard it again.

Pop, pop, pop! Pop, pop, pop!

He ran back to the van, jumped in kneeling next to his wife. The young driver sped off, the tires burning rubber as he heard more shots.

"What's the closest hospital?" the good Samaritan asked.

"Northwestern Hospital! You will have to make a U-turn though," said Dylan, who held onto his wife as the driver, waving his left arm frantically out of his window, worked his way to the far left lane. Then, he made a quick U-turn at Roosevelt Road and accelerated. He blew through the red traffic light at Balbo, then Jackson, then Monroe, weaving through the traffic wherever he saw an opening.

"Northwestern Hospital!" said the driver to his GPS, which quickly showed the map to the hospital when Siri said, "In five blocks, turn left at Ontario."

Dylan held his wife tight, looking at her tear-covered face as she moaned in pain, "God, why?! God, why?!"

"Hold on, Darlene, we will be there in just a few minutes," said Dylan, wiping the stream of tears pouring down her cheeks. "You will be okay!"

The good Samaritan had an intense look across his face, understanding the great need to get the bleeding lady in his back seat to the hospital. He sped through the heavy traffic, laying on his horn, weaving in and out of lanes, around the Lake Shore Drive S-curve, over the river, and through a red light at Illinois Street. Then a few blocks ahead, he made a daring hard left turn around the traffic stopped in the turning lane at Ontario. He sped through a small gap in the traffic and raced toward McClurg Court, then to Huron, and pulled up to Northwestern's ER, screeching to a halt.

As he climbed out of the van, he pressed the button to open the passenger gate. He ran toward the electric glass double doors yelling, "Help! We have a gunshot victim! Help!"

Two young, athletic-looking ER staffers emerged from the opening doors with a rolling gurney. They were at the side of the minivan in seconds. Dylan lifted his severely injured wife onto the bed and followed them into the hospital with the good Samaritan at his side holding his backpack and wife's bag.

"Sir, what is your name?" Dylan asked as he walked quickly.

"Josiah!" he said, walking next to Dylan, as they were led through the emergency department. One of the ER staffers turned to the two men and said, "You will have to wait out here."

"I need to go in there with her," pleaded Dylan. "I have to be there."

"I'll check with the ER docs, but it's against our policy," the young man advised him.

"Okay, I'll be right here, but I have to be with her," he repeated.

"Okay," said the staffer and disappeared through the swinging beige metal doors leading to the ER.

"Do you want me to stay?" Josiah asked Dylan, handing him the two bags.

"Thank you so much, Josiah, for picking us up and getting us here so quickly," said Dylan, shaking the good Samaritan's hand. "Thank you. No, we are good now."

"Okay, but here is my number in case I can help any further," Josiah said, handing him a white business card with blue lettering that read, 'Josiah Josephson, Carpenter.' "Please, if you need help, just call."

"Thanks, Josiah, I will."

"I'll pray for you both. God help her," he said, then turned and exited back to his minivan. Dylan found an empty chair in the half-filled ER waiting room in front of the television. WGN News coverage of the shootings in Grant Park showed several people lying on the ground with medical personnel attending to them. The sound of police and ambulance sirens blared in the background. Groups of people stood in twos, threes, tens, crying and trying to console one and other. Some of the colorfully dressed kids Dylan had seen that day were sitting together on the Michigan Avenue curb crying and talking, obviously trying to make sense of this tragic event.

"We now go to Brad Bentley, one of our reporters at Grant Park, for an update. Brad," said the news desk anchor Steve Landers, the television screen showing Bentley standing with a Chicago Police officer.

"Thanks, Steve, I'm here with Captain Phil Parlick of the Chicago Police. Thank you, Captain Parlick, for joining us."

The stern-looking veteran policeman just nodded.

"Can you tell us if the shooter has been caught yet?" Bentley asked.

"Yes. At 7:15 p.m., as the shooting was taking place, we identified the shots coming from the 20th floor of a hotel on Michigan Avenue. We were prepared for just such an incident. We had our sniper get in position while all of our police on the scene worked to help those in the park take cover as quickly as possible. Once our sniper was ready, he was given the green light to shoot. He hit the target on the first shot."

"So, is the shooter dead?" said Bentley.

"Yes," replied Parlick

"Do you have the identity?"

"Yes, but our police commissioner, Jerry McAdams, will be announcing that shortly, once they have all of the information in order."

"Do you know at this time what the casualty numbers are?"

"We are still working on that, as you can see behind us here, with emergency personnel attending to the victims," Captain Parlick explained. "But we hope to have that information by the time the police commissioner addresses the media."

"Okay, thank you, Captain Parlick," Bentley said, concluding the interview. "So just to recap, the shooter has been killed and specific information will be provided by Police Commissioner Jerry McAdams at a press conference sometime tonight. In addition, the casualty numbers will be provided at that time. Although as I look around, I can tell you that there are dozens of injured people on the ground. The emergency rooms at area hospitals will be busy tonight. This is Brad Bentley reporting from Grant Park."

Upon hearing that the ER would soon be packed, Dylan knew that he had better make a more assertive effort to see his wife. As he walked toward the doors that she had been taken through a few minutes earlier, he glanced over at the front desk where three middle-aged women behind the desk were busy talking on their phones. No doubt, they were answering questions about victims from the shooting.

Dylan ducked through the double doors and found himself in a blue-walled hallway with green curtained-off attendance rooms on each side, where patients were being treated. As he walked past them, he could hear the moans and loud cries for help.

He checked each makeshift room, hoping to find Darlene. Not the first one, not the second, third. He had walked all the way to the final treatment room and did not see her. He saw a set of doors with a sign next to it reading, "Emergency Surgery."

Once through the doors, he could see a series of surgery rooms. He stood outside hoping someone would come out. Before he could consider walking in, one of the young staffers who had taken Darlene into the ER came out into the hallway.

"Sir, you are not supposed to be here," he sternly informed Dylan.

"I have to see my wife," Dylan said. "There will be dozens of gunshot victims coming in here shortly. I have to see her."

Just then, another man came through the door, wearing a surgical mask and scrubs.

"Jamal, can you find out if she has any family members here?" said the man.

"Yes, Doctor Jones," said the ER staffer. "It's this man right here, her husband."

A look of surprise crossed the physician's face. "Sir, can you come with me for a moment?"

As Dylan followed the doctor down the hall to a small room, he felt a buzzing in his head. Squinting in the brightly lit room, he started feeling nauseous. His wife Darlene was his whole world. She had to be okay. He had hoped this would be good news but feared the worst. Why would the doctor take him to a separate room? Perhaps he just wanted to give him an update and that needed to be stated to him in a private setting.

"Mister uh…" the doctor paused.

"Reilly," said Dylan. "But please call me Dylan."

"Dylan, I'm Doctor Jones. I performed the emergency surgery on your wife and I'm afraid I have some bad news for you…"

"No! No! No!" begged Dylan, hoping it wasn't as bad as the doctor indicated.

"The gunshot hit her in the left side, the kidney," Dr. Jones said. "And even though you obviously did a good job taping the gauze on the wound to stop most of the bleeding, the damage to her internal organs resulted in trauma that she just wasn't able to overcome. We tried everything to save her, but there was just too much damage. I'm so very sorry."

The doctor stood back and just watched the pain overwhelm Dylan, who turned to lean on the bright white wall, slapping his hand against it hard several times yelling out in anguish, "Please, no! No! No! No!"

The doctor just stood back, apparently having been the deliverer of bad news like this more than a few times. There was no way around this pain. No options. A new and unpleasant journey through agony and depression confronted Dylan who was unprepared and unwilling to accept that fate. Dylan was ready to punch the hospital walls, table, anything that would stop the pain and bring back Darlene. He fell to his knees, holding his head between his hands, sobbing uncontrollably.

"Dylan, would you like to come into the operating room before they take her?" the physician asked, waiting a few seconds before seeing the new widower nod his head.

The physician helped him up and led him to the operating room, where a white sheet covered a figure on the table.

"Are you sure you are okay to see her?" asked the doctor, while tears poured down Dylan's cheeks, as he nodded. They approached the table and Dr. Jones pulled back the top of the sheet.

Dylan walked up to see his loving wife's beautiful face, even in death. Her eyes were closed, no expression on her face. He loved her so much. He just stared down at her face, wishing he could do something to return her to life. Wishing somehow they could spend all of their days together, just as they had talked about only an hour earlier. He bent down and kissed her forehead, a final farewell, his tears landing on her cheeks. He felt the doctor's hand on his right shoulder and stood upright, watching the sheet placed over her.

As the familiar ER staffer entered the room to take Darlene's body away, suddenly the energy and sadness that had filled his heart and head dissipated. It was replaced by an anger and furor that could not be contained. Thoughts filled his mind, his heart. Thoughts he never believed he was capable of considering. Nonetheless, there they were, not to be denied.

And his life would never be the same.

CHAPTER FIFTEEN

The tension between the Persian Warriors and MG's Boys had all but disappeared during sophomore year. Arman and his four friends no longer felt threatened. They attended high school like any normal student, focusing on their studies, sports, and extracurricular activities.

Thankfully, the truce was maintained into Arman's junior year. During the second semester, he felt so comfortable at Southwest that, besides his participation on the soccer team, he thought he would join one of the other clubs that seemed to embrace one of the school's mission statements of inclusion and diversity.

He attended a meeting of the International Club. Upon entering the classroom where the meeting was being held, he looked around the room to see a couple of MG's Boys, Gould and Nowicki, seated in the back. Glares were exchanged, and Arman walked right back out the door. There was most certainly a truce, but that didn't mean hard feelings didn't continue to exist.

The next day, he went to the Unity Club, not really familiar with the organization, but the title sounded inviting. Upon entering the classroom, he noticed some of the students had nose rings, tattoos, and a variety of colored hairstyles. It turned out the club was for lesbian and gay students. Out the door he went.

But when March finally arrived, it was soccer season. After stellar freshman and sophomore seasons on the junior varsity team, leading the conference in scoring both years, he went out for the varsity squad.

Over the previous summer, Arman had a growth spurt and was now six-foot tall and weighed 170 pounds, a good size for any high school athlete. He was quick. He was skilled, smart, flexible, and a very talented soccer player. After the tryouts and only a few practices, he realized he was clearly one of the best players on the field, excelling at each practice.

It was apparent to everyone on the team that Arman, a junior, was the second best player behind a very talented senior. However, by the fifth game of the season, he was seeing minimal playing time. That's when Arman found out that the coach, Jack Waller, was a racist who hated anyone with black or brown skin, but especially Middle Eastern students. This was well-known among the players on the varsity for more than a decade, but no one would report it to the athletic director or principal for fear they would be cut.

The senior players warned the underclassman to keep their distance from him, because there was a litany of horrific stories about the coach and how he physically abused players. Arman didn't say a word to the coach. He watched Waller play favorites with some of the boys, who were at best, only mediocre athletes. This beady-eyed, prominent-nosed, goatee-bearded, creepy coach with the bulbous bald head, obviously cared little about winning.

Arman had always thought that in high school the best players would be played. Not at Southwest High under Coach Waller, where apparently the coach played the white boys who kissed his ass. It was so well-known and so ridiculous that many of the parents of those mediocre players consistently brought the coach coffee and snacks, telling him how lucky their sons were to play for such a great coach. Their sons were average soccer players at best. And, if they had to kiss the coach's backside by supplying coffee and snacks to get their boys playing time, then coffee and snacks they would bring. And it worked.

Arman now understood why the varsity team always had a terrible losing record, while his JV team went undefeated both years. He didn't care to address this unfairness. And most certainly, Arman did not want to play for Coach Jack Waller after watching him choke a black kid at practice in front of the entire team.

So he sadly walked away from the team and the sport he loved since he was four years old. Disappointed by an issue he didn't see coming, he talked to his parents about transferring and even shadowed at one of the private high schools that had expressed great interest in him.

Given that it was late into the second semester of his junior year, he decided against making the change. It was a terrible position to be in. He loved soccer. He was one of the best players at the school. Without the sport in his life, he started feeling somewhat lost without his anchor of confidence, his identity as a soccer star.

That's when the ribbing about his failure on the soccer team was launched at him by Rick Mazel, who didn't have an ounce of athletic ability in his body. Mazel was well aware of Arman's stellar reputation as a soccer star. Once word spread that he left the team, Mazel couldn't hold back the insults and attacks.

Arman knew it was time to call an emergency meeting with his pals, the Persian Warriors. Arman had always been a leader on the soccer field, a team captain until his ill-fated varsity experience.

Organizing the Persian Warriors during freshman year was the first time he took a leadership role off the athletic field. It all felt so natural to him, when he began scheduling meetings each Tuesday afternoon at the JavaPlace, which was not far from their school. It helped solidify his position with his new friends. Yes, with soccer out of his life, it became the avenue that provided the young Persian American with great confidence.

Walking into JavaPlace that Friday, he really wished he was back on the soccer field but knew he had to move on mentally. He couldn't play for such a sick-minded and incompetent coach. When ordering the coffee for himself and his four friends, he recognized some of the students from school who were working behind the counter. He had seen several of them the day he mistakenly walked into the Unity Club meeting.

Jahan put together two tables in the far corner, near the window of the coffee house, to accommodate the five Persian Warriors. Arman set the coffee down, knowing the drink orders by memory, since it never changed each week.

Arman ran each meeting. His pals relied on him, looked up to him. As a junior now, Arman could appreciate how holding these meetings turned out to be one of his best ideas. It created solidarity, unity, and a sense of belonging for each of the boys. After three years at Southwest High, they were growing weary of prejudiced looks and attitudes.

Normally, Arman prepared beforehand with subjects to address, in addition to the questions and concerns to be raised. But on this Friday, there was one lone subject. The MG's Boys had become belligerent again, and they needed a plan to be ready for an attack. As the boys leaned over the table discussing the issue, Arman just looked at them, feeling lucky to have them as friends. He realized how close they had all grown together over the past three years. They were so tight that he believed they would always stand together despite the challenges that came their way. That was a great feeling after his middle school friends had all abandoned him at the beginning of freshman year.

Leaving JavaPlace that afternoon, Arman and his pals decided they had better make sure they all walk the halls together again, just as they had done freshman year. The plan was to stick together, look out for each other, have each other's backs. Their strategy worked before, ending the verbal abuse from Mazel and his big-mouth bullies. They were counting on it to work again.

When they returned to school on Monday, the second week of April, the Persian Warriors passed by all five of Mazel's gang, plus three new recruits following behind them.

Arman sneered at the pathetic group of dim-witted kids, posing as high school students, wondering what they were plotting. He knew Mazel's gang would never accept them. Apparently being in the same building with students of a different color, different heritage, different race, religion, just ate away at Mazel and his thugs.

Park Hills was nothing like the region in Europe from where Mazel, Gould, and Nowicki had emigrated. They grew up on mean streets with mean gangs. Fighting was a constant. Survival was a question. Instead of adjusting to a new country, they continued conducting themselves as if they were still living in Sarajevo, where the growing Arab population was unwelcome by native Bosnians and resulted in great hatred and sometimes violent attacks.

Arman was certain that they were just biding their time, waiting for their opportunity to strike, catching the Persian Warriors off guard. The question was, when? When will they strike?

The answer came the next day, on Tuesday afternoon, about half an hour after the final bell. Arman and his group suddenly found themselves cornered near the gymnasium by all five of MG's Boys plus their three new recruits. Each was holding an aluminum baseball bat. The high school baseball season was already underway so no one thought anything about these bullies walking through the halls with baseball bats sticking out of their backpacks. They must be on the baseball team, right?

"What are you doing, Mazel?" Arman asked the leader, feeling adrenaline pump through his veins, his heart racing, knowing this could turn into a dangerous situation very quickly. He and his friends didn't seem to have any good options.

The ugly, pale, pimple-faced leader just laughed knowing he had the numbers and the weapons to win this battle.

"We're trying out for the baseball team, and we need a little batting practice," said Mazel, who was looking for any excuse to beat up on anyone with dark skin. "Get 'em!"

The eight bullies charged at the Persian Warriors, raising their bats up high, as the four brown-faced students sprinted as fast as they could behind their leader. They darted through the only opening left to them, into the gym.

As they fled onto the shiny-wooden gymnasium floor, Arman searched for anything he could use as weapons to defend himself. He could hear and feel MG's Boys right behind him. He was their number one target since he was the Persian Warriors well-known leader. As he ran past the half-court circle in the middle of the gym, he spotted a stack of brown metal poles in the far corner, used for the stanchions of the volleyball nets.

"There! Over there!" he directed his friends, who sprinted toward the corner.

Arman slid into the poles, feet first, like a baseball player. He grabbed one of the four-foot long brown metal poles and popped back up, ready to fight. The sight of him making such an impressive athletic move resulted in three of the eight bullies stopping in their tracks. They looked at each other, realizing that they were now confronted by an opponent who had a weapon and was really angry.

Each of the Persian Warriors was now armed with a pole and walked behind their leader as he strode with great confidence and anger toward his attackers. Arman was ready to do serious damage to each of their pale heads, hoping to bloody them the way they had cut, bruised, and bloodied him in the past. The three new recruits retreated back out the door.

"Get 'em!" yelled Mazel. "Get 'em!"

His four remaining boys just stood there holding their bats, uncertain of what to do next. They looked at the angry Persian Warriors, then looked at each other. Mazel, realizing the fight was now even at five and everyone was armed with a weapon, started walking backward like the coward he had always been his entire life, "Okay, boys. We'll take our batting practice some other time."

"Well, we'll take ours now!" shouted Arman. "Get 'em guys!"

Arman sprinted straight at his attackers with his loyal band of revenge-filled Persian Warriors right behind him, shouting loudly.

Mazel, and what was left of his army, dropped their bats and ran as fast as they could toward the door. The bullies' leader could hear Arman's Nikes pelting against the wooden gym floor, sounding closer with each thud, in the dimly lit gym. It was the moment he heard Arman breathing heavily right behind him that he felt the pain of a metal pole as it cracked across the back of his head, sending him hurtling toward the floor near the free throw line. Four more hard whacks to his back echoed off the walls of the empty gym.

Out of the corner of his right eye, Arman could see his four loyal friends sprinting right past him, hoping to dish out the same to Mazel's buddies. By the time they reached the hallway, they caught up with the four misguided Boys, hitting them as hard as they could on whatever body part was easiest to reach.

The sound of the vicious whacks from the brown metal volleyball stanchion poles emanated through the hallway, followed by even louder screams of pain, reverberating off the old dull green-tiled walls. Hard, quick thwacks were delivered across the faces, heads, backs, and bellies of the now-bloodied bullies.

One of the cowardly punks was hit so hard across his face that bright red blood streamed from his nose and splattered across the tiled wall, the boy falling hard to the multicolored squared floor. He was out cold with his enraged young attacker standing above him, wearing a look of extreme anger that melted into a smile of accomplishment. He had carried out his revenge, beating the boy who had harassed and injured him so many times since he arrived at the high school.

He turned just in time to see Gabe Toma, the smallest, quietest boy in their group, swinging his weapon across the right kneecap of Stosh Gould, the meanest, most vicious of MG's Boys.

Well, the tables had been turned on Southwest High's cruelest bully who was now squirming on the floor, begging for Gabe to stop hitting him. He wouldn't. This was an eye for an eye, just as Gabe had been taught at the gold-domed mosque he attended with his family. And it felt good.

Within the next few minutes, each of the Persian Warriors had whacked, smacked, and injured Mazel's four bullies and left them on the floor, bleeding and crying. The proud first-generation American kids could feel the surge of the victory fill their bodies, their chests moving up and down rapidly as they worked to catch their breath. After all the beatings they had taken, this was a moment they would relish. They walked back into the gym together, seeing their leader standing over a bloodied and crying Rick Mazel, who was now receiving a final warning from Arman.

"If you ever attack us again…any of us! I promise you, we will kill you all!" said Arman, who had never in his life ever threatened anyone. "Just leave us alone from now on and we will leave you alone. Do you hear me?"

"I hear you," said Mazel, wincing in pain, hoping the beating was over. "We won't bother you again."

Arman walked back to the far corner of the gym, tossed his now blood-stained pole back where he had found it, then looked up at his friends. "C'mon fellas, let's go."

CHAPTER SIXTEEN

The skies shouldn't have been blue—so blue! The sun shouldn't have been bright—so bright, so warming! The temperatures shouldn't have been pleasant—so pleasant, so inviting that Thursday morning!

And the soft breeze blowing shouldn't have felt so refreshing, sweeping across Dylan's face. He stood on the fringe of the large shadow that was cast across the bright green grass by the very tall, gray, metal statue of the Good Shepherd in the center of the cemetery. All around this devastated and mourning man were headstones, brown and gray and black. It was a scene of sadness and death, lit by a heavenly sky and bright sun.

Dylan brushed aside his long brown locks, staring at the casket of his wife, set upon the mechanism that would lower her into the grave where she would sleep forever.

No, this day should have been cold and cloudy with terrible winds and pouring rain. There should have been thunder and lightning. Mourners should have struggled to attend, because it was such a rotten day. But they knew they had to be there; had to stand in the wind and the rain. The sorrowful gathering needed to pay their respects to such a wonderful woman, so beloved by all.

But no, this would not be a day that mirrored the anguish that Dylan felt for his murdered wife. Perhaps God wanted the day to reflect the soul of Darlene, so beautiful. That's how Dylan justified it, and accepted the ironic conditions, so bright and beautiful, just like Darlene.

As Darlene's favorite song, "The Sound of Silence," played over the Sonos speaker, Dylan, his family, friends, and relatives stood around the gravesite. Several dozen mourners gazed at the coffin with Darlene's mother crying uncontrollably at the forefront. Her father stood beside her, struggling to stay strong with a look of bitter anger and sadness across his face. Behind them, so many others stood with a collective look of pain, feeling numb and depressed by the loss of such a lovely young lady, taken in the prime of her life when she was doing so much good for so many.

Why? Why? A crazy man! That's why!

The tragic reality of the unwelcomed, unplanned incident plagued Dylan's mind since leaving Northwestern Hospital on Saturday. Over five heart-wrenching and lonely days, his sorrow grew and mind raced toward an unquenched, unfulfilled anger he had never felt before.

A crazy person is just a crazy person, he thought, until someone provides a gun. Then they become a dangerous crazy person.

Dylan couldn't stop focusing on those who were to blame for the killing of his wife. It wasn't just Peter Stephens' ill-willed mission to randomly kill innocents. No one would ever know his motive since he was gunned down by the Chicago Police SWAT specialists. No one would ever know what drove him to such horror. But what did that really matter? He was a disturbed individual.

The blame fell directly on the low-life, bought-and-paid-for-politicians who allowed those types of automatic weapons to be placed into society. They gladly take the large contributions in return for their political support and the freedom to sell those guns filled with bullets of life-altering depression. How do they sleep at night? How do they justify being the gatekeepers that open the door to the murder of so many innocents?

Why? Why? Money! That's why!

Up until this point, Dylan was like so many other Americans, outraged that U.S. politicians would allow these automatic weapons to be sold. These were the weapons that killed all of those young people in schools across America, even the twenty third graders, innocents, shot down at Sandy Hook Elementary.

Up until that point, Dylan felt a general feeling of outrage. But now it was more than that for him, far more. Now it was more personal, far more personal. It cut right to his heart and soul. He was filled with an incredible anger he knew wasn't going to leave him for many years, if ever.

As he stood there with a river of tears flowing down his cheeks, staring at the opening in the ground, Simon & Garfunkel's beautiful song played in the background.

Dylan had finally reached the point where he realized his choices. He would either accept living in a country where deadly weapons would continue to be sold. Or, he would have to move to another country, a safer country—perhaps back to his family's homeland in beautiful Ireland where gun control was far more stringent.

But what would be the point of moving out of America? The greatest love of his life, the woman he lived for and thought of day and night, was gone.

He would never forget the moment he lost her. The sight of Darlene running just a few feet in front of him, turning back toward him, their eyes meeting, fear filling her face, then shot in her left side, and down.

Oh how he wished it had been him instead. He knew she was the better person, the one who should have been spared by God. But as the madman Stephens stood on the twentieth floor of the hotel, he sprayed his bullets far and wide, killing so many, killing Darlene.

Oh how Dylan wished Stephens had sprayed a little to the right and hit him instead. But no, he had not, and as a result, Darlene's grieving loved ones stood in Good Shepherd, sobbing, angry and numb.

Father William Stenzel, the beloved and respected priest who married them only a few years earlier at Providence Church, prayed over the casket while sprinkling holy water onto Darlene's eternal bed. Dylan watched the beads of faith run down the rounded top of the Argive gold-finished casket, dripping down to the concrete grave liner below.

"Ashes to ashes, dust to dust." How many times had Dylan heard those fateful words recited in Catholic churches across Chicago? Now he was living it, feeling it, dreading the thought that he would have to face the reality that life presented to all who walked the planet for so short a time—Darlene far too short. When God decides to take us, Dylan reflected, it is His choice, not ours.

How many people across the Earth have had to face that reality throughout history? How many have felt the overwhelming sadness fill their beings after swallowing such a bitter pill?

"Thy will be done. Thy will be done," Dylan kept repeating in his mind as he looked across the crowd filled with pain and sorrow, then up to the clear blue heaven above.

He would never blame God. He would accept the sinful nature of mankind. He would loathe the sinful nature of mankind, curse it. He knew the reason he was filled with such ill will, such dread, such anger, such hate.

Why? Why? Crazy men with deadly guns! That was why!

CHAPTER SEVENTEEN

It was nearly 4:30 on a Tuesday afternoon when Arman and his pals walked into their headquarters, the JavaPlace, which was fairly empty. The smell of fresh-roasted coffee and sound of specialty drinks being blended filled the air. The five boys made their way to the familiar corner table, their group's conference room.

As they sat down, Arman looked over behind the counter and saw Jenny Sullivan, the art student who was in the LGBT group he mistakenly walked into at the start of the second semester.

Jenny had become familiar with them from their weekly meetings, always held at the same table. Knowing what time they would arrive each Tuesday, she would even reserve the table to ensure they would have their favorite meeting spot.

Arman, still feeling the energy from the battle, looked intensely at his band of Persian Warriors seated around the rectangular table. To him, they looked too relaxed, too comfortable, like the war had ended.

"Okay look, we may have won our fight today, but it's not over," he said, slamming his fist on the table. "It's just starting!"

"What do you mean?" asked Omar. "We just beat them. They're not going to bother us anymore."

"That's wishful thinking, Omar," laughed Arman, sitting straight up in his wooden chair. "You don't know those guys. Yeah, Mazel's a punk, a coward. But I was told that Stosh Gould and Nathan Nowicki are right off the boat. They came from a horrible situation in Sarajevo, living in a very rough area filled with gangs and crime. Guys like that don't back off. We won today, but do you really think they are going to let it go?"

"They come at us again and we will do the same thing to them," said Jahan, slamming his fist on the table.

"It won't be bats, Jahan," explained Arman, his friend since second grade at Park Hills Elementary. "They now know that we can fight. And bullies don't like fair fights. That's why three of them ran out the door. No, if it's fists, they won't fight. If they have bats and we have poles, they'll run. They'll be looking to get weapons where they can win for sure!"

"Chains?" asked Gabe.

"Tasers?" Dabney wondered. "What about tasers?"

"We have to be prepared for the absolute worst," said Arman. "They may get a gun."

"A gun?" questioned Gabe incredulously. "How are they going to get a gun? They're not twenty-one."

"I realize that, Gabe, but we can't discount that they may know how to get a gun, somehow," Arman said, not side-stepping the realities of the situation that he and his pals were now deeply involved in. "We have no choice, guys. We have to be prepared to protect ourselves from anything. I can buy a BB gun."

Arman could see this was an escalation that his friends were not eager to experience.

"A BB gun? What's that going to do against a real gun?" asked Dabney, who, Arman knew, just wanted all of the fighting to end. "The minute you get a gun, even a BB gun, you're committing yourself to shooting it at someone. And they'll be shooting back at you. Some of us may get hurt. Some of us may die. I'd rather leave the school."

"It's just an insurance policy against them coming at us with a gun," said Arman. "If we've got a gun, a BB gun that looks like a real gun, they'll back down. They backed down when we had poles. They'll back down if we have a gun."

"I don't know, Arman. This is not something I want to get involved with," said Gabe, now feeling nervous about going back to school.

"Look, if any of us leave the school, don't you think they'll find us?" asked Arman. "They know where you live, Dabney. They know where we all live. They'll find us. Look at the situation right now. Yes, they're physically injured, hurting, but they're more embarrassed about what happened. That embarrassment will last and eat away at them."

"No one at school knows about the fight, so what do they have to be embarrassed about?" offered Omar.

"The MG's know about it, Omar," said Arman. "And that's what will really eat away at them. But to your point, they may think we will come back and brag about it, making them feel worse, embarrassing them further."

Just then, Jenny approached their table. "Hello, Arman, I don't mean to interrupt your meeting, but can I get everyone your usual drinks?"

"Oh, hi, Jenny," he said, noticing her looking at their blood-stained shirts. "I'm sorry. We should have come up to the counter."

"It's fine," she assured him. "I can get them."

"Well thank you," he said, now smiling at the considerate gesture. "Yes, that would be great! We just got done playing a football game so I apologize for how messy we look."

"I can see that," she said, chuckling. "It must have been a pretty rough game. You've got blood on your shirt."

"Yeah, no one here got hurt, but yes, we were hitting pretty hard out there today," said Arman, watching Omar, Jahan, Dabney, and Gabe laugh at the comment.

"Oh, I'm glad no one got hurt," she said, smiling.

"Yeah, someone got hurt alright!" interrupted Jahan, still feeling the bravado and adrenaline from the battle. "And they'd better keep their mouths shut, or they'll get hurt a lot worse!"

"What?" Jenny said, confused by Jahan's comment.

"He's just playing with you," said Arman, giving Jahan a stern look, hoping to shut him up. "We will all have a venti dark roast. No grande vanilla latte for Jahan today. And thank you, Jenny. That's very nice of you."

Jenny just smiled and returned to the counter to get their coffee. Arman continued watching her, believing Jahan may have set off an alarm that would be announced to the entire school.

She took out her iPhone and looked to be texting someone. She obviously didn't believe the story about the game and was probably aware of the conflict with MG's Boys. The entire school was well aware of that rivalry.

Arman worried that she might be starting a chain of social media inquiries among the student body at Southwest High that could become a big problem for him and his friends.

"Arman! Arman!" said Dabney, trying to snap his friend's focus back to the table. "She'll get our coffee, don't worry."

"Yeah, yeah," Arman nodded.

"Okay, I get that we should be prepared for MG's Boys getting a gun," said Dabney. "But before we go to that extreme, can't we at least call for a sit-down to see if we can reach a peace agreement? No one knows about the fight at school, so they have nothing to be embarrassed about. They're injured so I'm sure some, if not all of them, want to end this. Remember, they ran the second we picked up those poles. This whole problem could have been cooked up by just one guy, Rick Mazel. So we should try to talk to all of them, not just him."

Arman looked back at Jenny preparing the drinks and then at his concerned friend. "Well, I hope you're right, Dabney, and no one finds out about the fight. If that's the case, we can try for a peace agreement. And if they live up to it, we're done, right? But if they agree to peace and then ambush us again, then what?"

Jahan nodded, "Yes, that could happen. So we work toward the peace agreement but prepare for an ambush."

Omar agreed, "We always carry knives, every one of us. And if we are attacked, we fight back knowing the next step for us is to get a BB gun."

"And if we are attacked, we record it with our phones," said Gabe. "Let the entire school see what these bullies are doing. They'll be thrown out. Hell, we should have done that today!"

Arman smiled, knowing his friends were developing some great strategies, some great solutions to this major problem. "I like it! We stay in packs all the time and have our phones and knives at the ready in case they jump us. Agreed?"

"Agreed!!" said his four friends.

CHAPTER EIGHTEEN

*I*n such a large school, perhaps it shouldn't be surprising that no one in the Southwest High School administration was aware of the fight that took place between MG's Boys and the Persian Warriors the previous week.

Whereas word of the bloody battle spread throughout the student body quickly via social media, only a few teachers heard the whisperings in the hallways. It wasn't enough to set off any alarms. When business teacher and head football coach, Mr. Neal Michaels, heard a few of his athletes laughing about it, he was determined to get to the bottom of the matter.

"What's going on, fellas?" said the tall, smiling Irishman in his low, powerful tone of voice. "What's this I keep hearing about a fight that took place here last week?"

His quarterback, Mickey Hern, and fullback, Rob O'Halloran, just looked up at their coach, feeling like they were now on the hot-seat.

"Oh, it's nothing, coach, we were just kidding around," said the stiff-necked, perfectly-postured, light brown-haired high school superstar quarterback, laughing off his nervousness.

"Really? Because apparently about a dozen students in my classroom have been kidding around about the same subject for the past few days," said Michaels, now looking a bit more serious about the matter. "So I guess the 'nothing' that didn't happen is well known by several students, all of whom are kidding around about it simultaneously. Even though by all accounts, nothing happened! Is that right?"

"I guess," said Hern, wishing not to reveal the news, but at the same time, not wanting to get in trouble with the coach who would determine his playing time and future success at the school.

"Well you know, Mickey, I'd love to have you starting at quarterback for me again next year as a senior, but if our wonderful principal, Mr. Leonard, learns that you and Rob have been holding back information about a criminal matter, that's jail time, boys. And Mickey, as much as I'd like to have you at QB and Rob at fullback, you can't do it from a jail cell."

"Wait, coach," said O'Halloran, a big strong 235-pound fullback, who was weighing offers from the University of Michigan and Ohio State, and didn't need to have his future threatened twice. "It was Mazel and his group. You know that gang that goes around here calling themselves MG's Boys. They went after Arman Farzan and his buddies after school last week. The Arab kids stood up to them though and apparently beat the hell out of 'em."

"What?" said a somewhat stunned Michaels. "Where did this happen?"

"Right here in the school," Hern chimed in, suddenly completely unafraid to provide his testimony now that the door had been opened wide. "Last Tuesday after everyone had left the school. What I heard is that Mazel knew the Arab kids get together every Tuesday after school, so he and his gang waited for them by the gym."

"Yeah," said O'Halloran. "And they were standing there holding baseball bats, like they were on the baseball team."

"That's a joke!" quipped Hern.

"So they went after them!" O'Halloran said, now excited to tell the amazing story that apparently every student at the high school had heard by then.

"Chased them into the gym…" Hern interjected.

"And the Arab kids out-ran them into the corner of the gym, grabbed the poles from the volleyball stanchions, and turned to fight," said a wide-eyed O'Halloran.

"That's when some of them MG's turned chicken and ran back out of the door leaving Mazel, Stosh Gould, Mike Felder, Benny Kowal, and Nathan Nowicki standing there to face the five really pissed off Arab kids…"

"You know them, Arman Farzan, Omar Abadi, and that group," said O'Halloran.

"Five on five! Mazel's gang ran, but the Arabs caught up with them and beat the living shit out of them."

"Blood everywhere!" exclaimed O'Halloran. "At least that's what they said."

"Who said?" asked Michaels, now more than a little perturbed that a war had taken place in the school and no one in administration had been told about it.

"Well, we first heard about it from Sally Butarski, but she said she couldn't tell us who she had heard it from," said Hern, raising his hands indicating that was all the information he had been given.

"But it's all over Twitter and Facebook!" added O'Halloran.

"Oh yeah, I don't really know much about that," said the forty-five-year-old coach who had previously vowed to reject social media due to the trouble it causes. "Okay, well listen, fellas, I didn't hear it from you, so don't worry. But I am going to get to the bottom of this situation. You know with all the craziness going on in this country, shootings and all, these are the types of incidents that need to be headed off. I just need to find out if there is any truth to it, that's all."

The two football players nodded.

"Thanks fellas, you may have saved lives today by telling me this," said the big lumbering coach, who turned and walked quickly toward the administrative offices to talk with the principal, Ben Leonard.

CHAPTER NINETEEN

Even into his seventies, former U.S. Marine Sergeant James Henry went to the Chicago Gun Range in downtown Chicago weekly to keep his skills sharp. He also enjoyed watching others exhibit their skills and experience, and some shooters, their obvious lack of training.

On this beautiful, sunny, seventy-two-degree Thursday, August 14, 2014, each of the six lanes were filled with shooters working to improve their marksmanship.

On the right side of the range, two older men in green U.S. army camouflage jungle jackets practiced with M-1 carbine rifles. Each was a Vietnam War veteran, as was proudly displayed in gold letters on the front of their black military baseball caps.

On the left side, two women in their thirties, who looked like identical twin sisters wearing matching pink range sweatshirts, were practicing with Glock 43 handguns.

Next to the sisters, in the middle, was a shooter practicing with an M-14 rifle, who stood out from the others. He had long, blond hair and was wearing old denim jeans, black combat boots, and an American flag shirt.

Sergeant Henry sat watching the man from the other side of the soundproof glass, wondering if the Guinness Book of World Records had a category for worst shooter in history. The veteran wanted to personally award that honor to the American flag shirt-wearing freak in front of him.

Henry continued to watch in total disbelief as the strange-looking man aimed and fired. He missed the target to the left. Henry cringed. He adjusted his feet, obviously hoping for better accuracy, then aimed and fired again. He missed the target to the right.

Frustration filled his face and he shouted out four-letter words in anger, which drew the attention of those around him, despite the loud noise from the gunfire.

Long-Hair lifted his right hand in apology to the other shooters then continued his exhibition of no talent or skill with a gun.

The sergeant watched in total dismay as the frustrated Long-Hair continued to shoot, but apparently couldn't hit the broadside of a barn with his M-14 rifle, even if he were standing five feet away.

Shaking his head at the awful display, he wondered just how stupid someone had to be to wear a disrespectful American flag shirt to a gun range filled with ex-U.S. military men. If they eyeballed that shirt, there was a good chance they might just miss the gun range target on purpose, preferring to shoot the hippie dipshit in the middle lane of the range. The old Marine just turned away from the numbskull with the M-14, shifting his attention to the shooter to his right.

Bang! Bang! Bang! The gunfire echoed off the walls of the indoor shooting range. The bullets passed through the circular target, two directly through the center, the third just a few centimeters above it. Bang! Bang! Bang! This time all three were dead on through the center.

This young, twenty-something shooter got the old Marine's full attention, watching a pure exhibition of talent. A smile grew on his face, curious about this fellow, whom he had never seen at the range.

Bang! Bang! Bang! He was dead on, once again. The old man had to find out. Was he a trained military sniper just looking to get some prac-tice? Had he been in the Marines? Or perhaps he was a Navy Seal. This was talent the old man rarely saw at the shooting range.

He put on a pair of electronic earmuffs, pulled open the heavy metal green door, and was suddenly engulfed in the muffled sound of exploding gunfire. Loud noise was no issue for the old vet, a sharpshooting sniper himself, who had served two tours of duty in Vietnam. He was one of America's bravest men, having earned the Medal of Honor for conspicu-ous gallantry and intrepidity at the risk of his life above and beyond the call of duty.

As he strode past the two Vietnam veteran shooters, whom he knew well from his weekly visits to the range, his eyes were focused on the unfamiliar young man wearing a navy blue hooded sweatshirt. On the back was displayed a logo of a ferocious looking wolf with lettering underneath that read, GO WOLFPACK. He leaned over as far as possible, but was unable to see the name on the front.

The young man didn't see him walk up behind him. His earmuffs kept the sound of the gunfire from damaging his ears, but also the sound of footsteps. The old Marine knew better than to walk up to a man with a gun and tap him on the shoulder, having witnessed too many incidents in his day where an ex-military man suffering from post-traumatic stress syndrome overreacted and mistakenly fired his weapon at the person approaching him. No, he would just wait until the young man turned around.

Bang! Bang! Bang! He shot three more, right through the center. Boy, this kid was good, thought the old man, smiling and shaking his head at the remarkable shooting. That's when he noticed the young shooter was using a vintage Smith & Wesson .38 Special, pearl-handled six-shooter.

Now he was doubly curious. Who the hell could shoot like that with an old gun? The young man with long wavy brown hair set his gun down, lifted off the green earmuffs, and hung them up on the hook to his right. Then he turned and saw the old man staring at him.

"Hello!" said the old Marine reaching his hand out to shake. "My name's James Henry, Sergeant James Henry, retired U.S. Marines."

"Oh, hello, Sergeant," said the young shooter. "Very pleased to meet you. I'm Dylan Reilly. And thank you for your service."

"Well, thank you. That was some shooting exhibition you just put on there, young fellow," said the Marine. "I have never seen you here before and just wanted to introduce myself."

"Oh, thank you, Sergeant Henry," said the Dylan, reaching out to shake hands. "Yes, this is just my fourth time here."

"So I have to assume that you are military and a trained sniper, like myself," said Sergeant Henry, who courageously fought and saved several men in his platoon, battling the Viet Cong in Phuoc Long Province in August of 1969.

"No, no sir," said Dylan, who began walking toward the green door with his new admirer walking beside him. "I'm actually a high school history teacher at Watson College Prep. Never been in the military."

"You've never been in the military?" asked the war hero, who abruptly stopped walking. "Are you kidding me?"

"No sir, as a matter of fact, this is only my fourth time ever shooting a gun, all right here at this range."

A look of pure amazement filled the old man's face, walking quickly now to catch up with Dylan. "Please tell me you're joking!"

"No, sir," said Dylan, pushing open the heavy green metal door. "Up until just over a week ago, I had never touched a gun or imagined myself ever using one."

The old man's eyes opened wider and his jaw dropped as he followed Dylan out the door and the loud gunfire was silenced, allowing for a clearer conversation.

"I'm sorry, son, I don't think I heard you correctly with all of that noise," he said. "Did you just say you had never touched a gun until a week ago?"

"That's right," Dylan said, walking over to the soda machine and placing a dollar bill and two quarters into the automatic pay slot, then pushed the Coke button. The loud thud of a cold can of Cola-Cola landed in the catch tray.

"Honestly, I never thought I had the courage to pick up a gun. But in just the past few months, my wife and I were unfortunately on the scene at the Freedom Tower when a terrorist attack occurred..."

"I heard about that..."

"And then near Water Tower Place when that terrorist started shooting people on Michigan Avenue," said Dylan.

"Heard about that too. Wow! At both of them, my goodness..."

"Then we were at MusicFest in Grant Park," Dylan continued, anger and sadness welling up through is eyes, his jaw beginning to quiver. "When that piece of shit...when that damn crazy man, Peter Stephens, started firing an AK-15 from the twentieth floor of a hotel, killing dozens of innocent people, including my wife. My wife!"

Tears poured from Dylan's eyes, uncontrollably, down his cheeks. He quickly wiped them away with the bottom of his blue sweatshirt.

"Oh, God, I am so sorry to hear that," said Sergeant Henry, who was all too familiar with stories of friends and loved ones being shot and killed.

"I had to face facts," Dylan said, sniffling heavily and continuing to wipe his face. "Forced to face facts, whether I liked it or not. They're never going to get rid of assault weapons in this country. Never! So I came to the conclusion that either I had to move to a country with stricter gun laws or learn how to use a gun to protect myself.

"I'm an American and not leaving. And, I'm not going to run from the problem. I'm not a coward! And after what has happened to me, I don't only want to defend myself, I want to be there to defend others from those terrorists and lunatics who can just walk out in the middle of crowd and start randomly shooting people.

"They have no idea the pain they bring into people's lives. Or worse perhaps, they know exactly how much pain they bring into people's lives and just don't care. Well I'm going to stand up to them, fight back! I don't care if I get killed while I'm trying. I've got nothing to lose. They killed my wife! Those bastards! They killed my wife!"

The old man just looked at the distraught young man in front of him, who was struggling mightily to maintain his composure. He had seen this type of anger before, many times after bloody battles in Vietnam. This was a common reaction of a soldier who had just seen his buddy right next to him get killed in combat. Sergeant Henry had seen overwhelming anger fill the hearts and souls of those soldiers, determined to strike back at the enemy with everything they had available to them.

That was during a war on foreign soil, where those men were putting their lives on the line for a country that didn't return the respect they deserved through their bravery and commitment. Sergeant Henry always said blame the political leaders, but don't blame the boys who were willing to make the greatest sacrifice. After all, these were the boys who were willing to fight and die for their country when they were called upon, courageous men, true patriots.

The old Marine just put his hand on Dylan's shoulder and said, "Son, if you want to stand up to the terrorists, I'll help you. I'll train you. I'll show how to use a gun and use it so no one can sneak up on you. I'll train you so no one can fire on you without having you return fire on them and take them out."

Dylan's face lit up as he looked directly at his newfound friend, "Seriously?"

"Yes, Dylan," he said. "This is what this world has come to. We live in a dangerous world, where if you don't carry a weapon and aren't able to protect yourself, you may not survive. I was specialist in the Marines. There was no one like me, before or since. I was given special training by an old cowboy when I was a kid. He taught me some things that made me a dangerous soldier for the Viet Cong, or any enemy. He helped me become very quick, very accurate, very dangerous. You have special talent, and I can show you, if you wish."

"Yes sir, yes sir, I wish. I most definitely wish!" responded Dylan, a desperate gleam in his eye.

Sergeant Henry smiled, knowing he could help this young man who had a natural gift for shooting guns accurately. The decorated U.S. Marine specialist was certain that his special training would greatly improve Dylan's skills and make him a fierce opponent for any enemy combatant.

"Just one thing I have been perplexed about though since watching you on the range," said the Marine. "You were hitting that bullseye nearly every time you shot. Dead center nearly every time. Are you telling me that in just four sessions, you were able to achieve that level of accuracy on your own?"

"Yes sir," said Dylan. "I researched and read as much information as I could about using a gun and how to shoot with accuracy. All of the research said it would take some time, weeks, months, and maybe longer to become accurate. But my third time out, two days ago, I started hitting that bullseye. And today, I barely missed."

"I saw that," said the Marine. "And believe me, I was amazed to see you do it! But now I'm absolutely blown away that you were able to do that on your own after only four sessions. Son, you have a natural gift. I have never met any man or woman who could do that, not one! Teaching you these skills is going to be a great pleasure."

As the two new friends walked toward the exit, the long-haired man from earlier scurried past them, holding his brown rifle bag and muttering to himself.

"I suck! Never coming back here! Terrible!" And out the door he went, still berating himself as he walked toward his beat-up old black 1968 Ford Mustang with a broken exhaust pipe hanging down to the pavement.

A few seconds later, Dylan and Sergeant Henry walked out of the front door of the Chicago Gun Range, only to witness the strange angry man starting his old beater, fumes of black exhaust shooting out across the parking lot. They then watched in amazement as he drove away with sparks flying from the dragging exhaust pipe of the old Mustang.

"You know, I think that fellow has more than a few screws loose," said Sergeant Henry, only half-kidding. "I swear, wearing that American flag shirt, he must be an admirer of that hippie Andy Huff. Oh, but you're too young to know who that is, right?"

"Actually, I do," said Dylan. "Remember, I teach U.S. history, so we have covered your war and the protestors, all of it. I don't suppose you were too fond of Andy Huff."

"He was lucky one of us didn't shoot that son of a bitch back then!" the Sergeant expressed quite clearly, his face filling with a shade of red. "We are over there putting our lives on the line for our country, and that coward is telling everyone to burn their draft cards. I get mad all over again thinking about it. Then, we come home, and we are treated like the bad guys!"

"It was a terrible time," Dylan said, nodding sympathetically.

"I'm proud of my service, Dylan, and so are all the guys I knew who went over there," said the old heroic Marine. "They may not have respected Johnson or Nixon, but the draft dodgers didn't see what we saw. And we saw plenty of bad things! Plenty! I just think those hippies, yippies, and draft dodgers were all a bunch of cowards, every last one of them. Wish they all would have gone to Canada and stayed there. And to Hell with Jimmy Carter for letting them back in. Worst president in the history of the United States! He spit in the face of all the guys who had the guts to go over there, died over there."

A few minutes later, after Sergeant Henry calmed down, he traded phone numbers with Dylan and set a date to start the training. The two men shook hands, and the Marine veteran smiled, nodded, and walked back inside.

OOO

Dylan stood at the entrance for a moment, collecting his thoughts. He felt so blessed. A smile grew on his face. He actually began feeling good again, happy.

Dylan walked out toward his red Jeep Cherokee, the bright warm sun upon his head, shoulders, and back. It felt so good.

He looked up to the sky, pointing to the heavens, and said out loud, "We're going to stop those terrorists, Darlene. We're going to stop 'em!"

Then, he climbed into his Jeep, backed out of his parking place, and turned on WXRT Radio only to hear the Strumbellas singing their hit song, "Spirits." Dylan just smiled as he drove away listening to the lyrics, so fitting on this day, about guns in his head and they won't go.

CHAPTER TWENTY

A sea of white mist hung over the still suburban forest preserve lake. Arman sat on an old, wet, gray wooden bench this Saturday morning in August of 2014, listening to the wailing screams of toads and crickets chirping. He breathed in the wonderful smell of fresh rain, while watching droplets of dew fall from the maple trees.

A father and son, a few hundred yards away in an open field, were flying a remote control plane, having a wonderful time together. Arman smiled seeing them have so much fun.

The sun had barely been up two hours, yet some early picnickers were already entering the park preparing for a fun day of cooking out, playing catch with a football, or fishing in the large pond for blue gills or crappies.

This forest preserve was close to Arman's home but wasn't used by many of the local residents. He noticed how those who did frequent the wide open park off LaGrange Road always seemed to be enjoying themselves, while spending very little money, if any, to do so.

The Park Hills Forest Preserve most certainly offered a good deal of inexpensive fun and adventure for families, couples, and especially fathers and sons who loved spending time together flying their remote control airplanes.

On this particular morning, a mix of anxiety and excitement permeated Arman's heart and mind. He never expected to purchase a real gun in his life, although it was only a BB gun, considered a toy by some. He had researched about a dozen websites with ads run by private gun owners.

He decided to purchase a Smith & Wesson MP40 BB gun, which he found surprisingly easy to buy on the web. Certainly, this wasn't a real gun, but Arman felt it would do the trick to defend against Rick Mazel and his group of derelicts.

Arman and his Persian Warriors were able to avoid any further conflict during the last few months of their junior year when the football coach and principal found out about the fight with Mazel's gang and took control.

All of the MG's Boys parents were once again called in for a meeting. This time however, they not only met with Principal Leonard and Coach Neal Michaels, but Park Hills Police officers Donnie Joy and Matt Durkin were in attendance. They wanted to make certain the parents understood that if their boys were to start another fight, it wasn't only expulsion from the high school they would be facing, but potential jail time.

That meeting shut down any vengeful thoughts Mazel and his group may have had at that time. In the hallways, they wouldn't even glance at Arman and his buddies, who became quite confident that the remainder of junior year would be peaceful.

However, entering senior year, Arman reverted back to the lesson learned from his sophomore year when the punishment rules presented to the MG's during freshman year seemed to disappear. So beginning on this Saturday morning in August, Arman would begin preparing for the worst and hoping for the best during his senior year.

When the old, red Dodge pickup truck entered the parking lot of the Park Hills Forest Preserve, Arman knew his trainer had arrived. Out of the truck stepped a large, bearded, middle-aged man, dressed in a green and brown camouflage coat and matching hat, old beat-up blue jeans and hiking boots. He looked like someone who'd fallen out of the Outdoor Channel.

Arman approached Grizzly Adams' truck, a name he quickly related to this man.

"Hello, are you Mr. Jaworski?" he asked, politely, having no wish to be a wise guy at such an important meeting.

"Yes, Arman?" the large man asked and Arman nodded. "Can I see your BB gun?"

Arman reached into his duffle bag and pulled out his black Smith & Wesson.

"Nice, very nice," said Grizzly Adams, holding the gun up and looking it over.

"I know this is just a BB gun, but I thought I had better get some training on how to use it correctly," said Arman, making his intentions clear.

"Have you used this gun, son?" asked the man and Arman nodded again.

"Yes, sir," lied Arman, who had never seen or held any type of weapon other than a squirt gun. All of a sudden, he began feeling nervous, knowing he purchased the BB gun and then lied to an adult about it. He made a mental note to attend the three o'clock reconciliation at St. Michael's. "Sir, I read that you were a sharpshooter, so I thought you might be able to help me."

Grizzly Adams laughed. "Well, I can most certainly do that. But after today, you will need to practice to get good. You have two choices. You can either go to a firing range, and there is one fairly close in Tinley Park. Or, you can drive out to the middle of nowhere and practice."

Over the next hour, the teacher and student found an open area with no one in sight to conduct the training. Arman watched his six-foot-tall trainer nail a round white wooden target with the four red circles drawn across the front onto a large maple tree.

Then the work began. Grizzly Adams demonstrated all the correct technique, best tips, and most efficient use of the weapon. Arman repeated them. They practiced and practiced some more, drawing and shooting. Over and over, the trainer showed him how to draw and shoot correctly, quicker, faster. Arman was quite shocked to see how fast the large man was able to pull the gun from the holster and shoot so accurately. It was impressive.

After finishing the lesson, Grizzly Adams gave Arman a fifteen-minute lecture on gun safety. Even though it was just a BB gun, he believed strongly that anyone using any type of gun should understand the dangers, as well as how to safely carry, store, and fire a weapon.

Arman paid his skilled gun-trainer fifty dollars and thanked him profusely for his help. He then watched Grizzly Adams climb into his old Dodge truck and waved to him as he pulled away.

So excited by the experience, he didn't want to waste any time and was eager to practice. Seeing that the forest preserve was beginning to fill up with picnickers, remote control plane hobbyists, and Frisbee players, he decided he had better drive to a remote location for his practice.

It was close to noon by the time he parked his black Toyota Forerunner along the side of the road next to the vast forest in LaSalle County, where he had camped once during his one year in the Boy Scouts. Having spent four days there, he knew the landscape pretty well and how dense the forest was in certain areas. It was most certainly thick enough to provide plenty of privacy to practice shooting his new Smith & Wesson MP40. Given there wasn't a home or building within miles, it would serve his purpose.

The young Persian-American was dressed in a brown poncho. He had purchased it online because it looked like the poncho Clint Eastwood wore in one of his favorite movies, *Fistful of Dollars*. Arman finally found the clearing in the forest that he had remembered from his scouting days. He set up the round white wooden target provided by his trainer. His hour-long lesson made him quite confident, and comfortable, loading and shooting his BB gun.

After emptying his chamber of round copperhead balls, he walked up to the target to see his results. There were new marks inside the smallest circle. Arman smiled, feeling some sense of accomplishment, hitting the bullseye more than a few times.

Arman kept shooting, practicing, improving. As his hand grew steadier and aim sharper, he began hitting the middle of the target more and more. Clink! Bullseye! Clink! Bullseye! This was starting to really appeal to him, a lot of fun.

He strapped on his leather holster, placed his MP40 inside it and then practiced drawing. From Grizzly Adams' excellent direction, Arman was fairly quick on the draw. Over the next ten minutes, he became even quicker.

Then he stood with arms at his sides, looking directly at the wooden target.

"Okay Mazel, I'm not going to tell you again," said Arman, preparing himself for the day when he would be confronted by MG's Boys. "Leave us alone and there won't be any trouble…. Oh, you want there to be trouble…? I don't' think that's what you want, Mazel…. Oh, you have a gun, huh…?"

With his right hand, Arman pulled back his brown poncho, revealing the gun he had in his holster. "Me too!…. Now again, you need to leave us alone. Just walk away…. No, you don't want to…? Okay then…."

Arman stood for a moment, looking like the gunfighters he had watched so many times in his favorite Westerns, but especially Clint Eastwood. Then, he drew the gun from his holster. He pulled it out quickly and cleanly and clink! Bullseye! Clink! Bullseye!

His heart raced from the excitement of his new ability with a BB gun.

He was positive the MG's would be confronting him and his friends again at school. And he was fairly certain they would be coming after them with some sort of weapon. The worst case would be a gun, and probably a BB gun, he hoped.

Arman believed that whether it was a real gun or BB gun, he would outdraw Mazel and stop him with his MP40. He knew he was much faster than the incredibly non-athletic bully. He was convinced he would win.

By 2 p.m., he felt like he was prepared, and so he drove home.

CHAPTER TWENTY-ONE

A stream of colorfully attired workers, business professionals, lawyers, journalists, students, poured out of Chicago's downtown train stations on this bright and sunny Thursday morning. Thousands, dressed appropriately for the lovely weather, emerged from Union Station and Northwestern Station over the Jackson Street Bridge, Adams Street Bridge, and Washington Street Bridge.

This was the typical scene on any weekday morning in Chicago. Swarms of people crossed the many bridges over the Chicago River and into the Loop for the employment or education that was awaiting them.

Past the bridges and into the Loop, the army of workers dispersed in various directions, walking quickly—always walking quickly—to ensure they arrived at their destination on time. "Can't be late, never late," was the universal thought running through their collective minds.

This was Chicago, the city of hard-working people. They were on time. They did their job to the best of their abilities, accepting nothing less. And most often, most always, they out-performed and out-delivered, because that's who they were. The job needed to be done right. For the workers of the biggest city in Midwest America, the City of Big Shoulders, they would always work toward that objective.

They took great pride in their work, greater pride in how hard they worked. This was a blue-collar, lunch-bucket mentality that carried over from the hard-working construction workers on the street to the white-collar office workers in the buildings throughout the Loop and into the suburbs.

Professionals flooded out of LaSalle Street Station, walking quickly through the Midwest Trade Building corridor and past the two Greek goddess sculptures, salvaged from the old, long-gone Chicago Trade Building.

It was Thursday, September 11, 2014. The black iron minute hand of the large round clock above the fast-moving pedestrians snapped forward to 8:45 am. Can't be late! They walked even quicker, some turning left onto Jackson Street. One minute later, the minute hand moved again, to 8:46 a.m., when a massive explosion occurred on the twenty-second floor of the Midwest Trade Building. Brick, glass, mortar, and steel burst out over LaSalle Street, crashing down onto the pavement below.

Everyone ran, but some of the pedestrians running on the sidewalk directly below the explosion were unable to avoid the falling building material. Shouts and screams filled the twenty-second floor halls, people running, panicked by the loud explosion.

Word spread quickly, and the evacuation alarm was sounded. The unfortunate early-birds in the historic building ran for the exits as quickly as possible. There were only two employees in the Baily Investment Group's office where the seven sticks of bundled TNT exploded. Both were killed instantly.

Police sirens were heard in the distance with every squad car in the area receiving an all-points bulletin about the unexplained explosion. Out the front door of the building exited Ziad Haznawi, ecstatic that he had accomplished his task on the thirteenth anniversary of 9/11. The explosion was triggered at the exact same time that the first hijacked plane hit the North Tower in New York.

Ziad felt no remorse about killing innocent civilians, Americans. He smiled, looking up to see a blazing fire coming out of the blown out windows. Haznawi was dressed in a black cargo jacket, black jeans, and combat boots with a black ski mask to protect his identity from street cameras. He slung his backpack over his left shoulder then raised his right arm high, preparing to give his two conspirators a signal.

Just fifty yards north on LaSalle Street, positioned inside the squared off, protected doorway of the Trust First Bank Building, Hassan Bahar and Fayez Hanjour were dressed identically to their leader. They intently watched Ziad.

Then Ziad dropped his right arm and sprinted east. As he ran, he could hear the distinctive sound from the launch of a rocket propelled grenade echoing off the surrounding buildings. Hassan Bahar had fired the highly explosive antitank weapon and smiled as he watched it fly directly toward the Midwest Trade Building. It struck just below the fire blazing from the massive hole on the twenty-second floor.

Feeling the adrenaline fill his body, Ziad sprinted farther away from the loud explosion behind him. The sound reverberated off the buildings. Chunks of brick, mortar, and steel were once again sent flying downward. A large section of the building smashed the roof of a blue and white Chicago Police squad car which had just arrived on Jackson, west of LaSalle.

As some of the debris flew toward Ziad, he made a quick right turn, avoiding the metal and mortar, as he ran past the two Goddess sculptures. He sprinted directly toward his black motorcycle, which he had parked along the side of the building for a quick escape.

The policeman in the severely damaged squad car was able to crawl out of the passenger side window. But once out, the sound of gunfire filled the famed Chicago business corridor. Several bullets struck the graying, middle-aged cop in the right shoulder and back, jolting him to the ground behind his car, where he lay bleeding but still alive.

Meanwhile Ziad was on his motorcycle speeding toward Clark Street and the narrow lane in Federal Plaza, which was protected by barriers that only a bike or motorcycle could drive through. Ziad zipped down that lane, past Calder's Flamingo, and north down Dearborn Street. He slowed down just for a moment to fold his mask up to look like a wool hat, so as not to attract any further attention.

On LaSalle Street, his two associates were firing their AK-47s at anyone moving. Screams, shouts, and panic rang through the street. Citizens ran for cover into the closest building they could find. They ducked into retail stores, banks, anywhere to escape the flying bullets which smashed windows and pelted cars.

Screams, shouting, police sirens, loud cries of anguish, horns honking; chaos filled the street. A man in a gray Brooks Brothers suit was running as fast as his legs would carry him toward the Bank Reserve Building but stopped to help a middle-aged woman who had fallen directly in front of him. As he reached down, he heard a zipping sound, and then felt a stinging sensation in his left leg. He fell but crawled quickly toward the entrance of the bank, bullets hitting the pavement behind him as he scurried to safety.

The older women he tried to help wasn't so lucky, taking a direct hit in the shoulder. She lay bleeding on the sidewalk. The man, now safely inside the doorway, turned to see her lying prone and helpless. Two security guards ran up to him intent on pulling him away from the door. He refused to go. He would wait until the shooting stopped, then go out and pull the injured woman inside. He looked down at his leg, which was bleeding from the bullet that pierced his left ankle.

"C'mon, they'll kill you!" pleaded one of the security guards, hoping to get the man safely inside.

"No sir," said the brave Brooks Brothers man, a former U.S. Marine, who served four tours of duty in Iraq. "I'm going to get her out of there!"

Above, a police helicopter buzzed the area trying to spot the location of the shooters. As it hovered, the sound of the sweeping blades filled the sky above and street below. Just then, an RPG was fired toward the chopper. It was a direct hit! A huge ball of fire above sent the remnants of the helicopter onto the roof of the Cookery Building and then bounced down to the pavement along LaSalle Street. Hearing the explosion, the man hobbled out the door of the Bank Reserve Building, lifted up the injured and sobbing woman, and carried her inside.

"Thank you, thank you," she repeated to the brave young man, who made it safely into the building. The two security guards helped him, taking the bleeding woman, and laid her on the floor to provide medical attention.

It seemed that within moments, a dozen black Chicago Police squad cars sped down Adams Street, producing a chorus of sirens. The parade of vehicles screeched up to the intersection just west of LaSalle Street, where they remained hidden from the terrorists now known to be at the opening of the Trust First Bank Building.

Each pair of bullet-proof vested police officers jumped out of their squad cars, taking cover behind their vehicles. Each aimed their Glock 22 handguns in the direction of the assailants, nearly a full block away. Two more Police SUVs pulled up on Quincy, a narrow, single lane street that runs next to the Trust First Bank Building. Anxious police officers jumped out and immediately took cover. A few second later, a large black

Chicago PD SWAT truck came bouncing up the debris-filled intersection of Jackson Boulevard. The massive armored assault vehicle barreled over chunks of mortar, turning left onto LaSalle, where they had a full view of the bank where the terrorists were hiding.

Rat-a-tat-tat! Rat-a-tat-tat! Bullets bounced off the SWAT truck, while six fully-outfitted members of the SWAT team disembarked. They quickly and safely exited from the rear with their MP5/10 submachine guns at the ready. Sirens could be heard blaring from the other side of the building, coming from the hook-and-ladder Chicago Fire Department trucks pulling up on the south side of the building on Van Buren Street. Dozens of firefighters wearing protective helmets, coats, and boots jumped from their trucks and began the challenging process of putting out a fire in the forty-four-story building.

From the scant cover of the nook in the Trust First Bank Building, Hassan Bahar looked up at the burning landmark, hoping the building would implode at any moment, just as the World Trade Center had done thirteen years earlier. The two terrorist assailants were counting on it as a distraction to provide them with an opportunity to escape.

As planned, they knew Ziad had already fled the scene, but as they stood inside that doorway, completely surrounded, they began to wonder about the logic of Ziad's plan. They could see what looked like hundreds of Chicago cops and a SWAT team in front of them. Police sirens were coming from every direction, letting them know they were now surrounded.

All at once, the police opened fire on the two terrorists, the bullets hitting the building and pavement all around them. The glass doors and windows were instantly blown out from the gunfire. The SWAT team shot tear gas bombs on the street directly in front of them. It was at this point, the terrorists knew they only had one other option, because the Midwest Trade Building did not come crashing down.

"Plan B," said Bahar to his young compatriot. "Plan B, let's go!"

They laid their assault rifles on the pavement and quickly ducked into the building. They both stripped off their ski masks and black leather jackets, throwing them into a large metal trash receptacle. Then, they sprinted down the empty white marble-floored hallway, past the escalators and the evacuated security desk.

Once they passed the golden-doored elevator bank, Fayez spotted a half-dozen people inside a café standing in front of a television mounted on the wall. They were watching the news coverage of the terrorist attack, apparently not aware that the killers were in the same building as them.

As the two scowling American-hating extremists entered the café, they watched the WLS-TV news anchor, Katie Block, report, "The helicopter was shot down by a rocket propelled grenade, exploding in mid-air with debris landing on the Cookery Building. However, before being shot down, the pilot was able to identify and report the location of the terrorists. They are wedged in a nook at the entrance of the Trust First Bank Building."

One of the women watching the report screamed, "We have to get out of here!" She turned to see the two dark-skinned men, holding handguns. The young woman let out an even louder scream, then fainted. The other five in the café—three men and two women—stood frozen, staring at the two black-outfitted men, praying they wouldn't kill them.

"What do you want from us?" asked a tall, blond-haired, twenty-something man with a strong athletic build and look that indicated no fear.

"You are going to be our hostages," Hassan said sternly with a mean snarl across his face. His conviction was based on the knowledge that taking hostages was their last chance to stay alive, since the agreed upon Plan C was to strap on the explosive belt and blow themselves up in the biggest crowd they could find. He and Fayez led the five hostages back to the bank entrance from where they had just fled.

"Just do what you are told and you won't be hurt," Fayez instructed them. "Do something stupid, and we will kill you."

As they walked toward the entrance, past the security desk and escalator, a loud voice could be heard on a megaphone outside. "This is the Chicago Police. We have you surrounded. Come out with your hands in the air."

Hassan laughed, "I guess they don't understand what this is all about, eh, Fayez?"

"No, I guess not," said his concerned young friend, who really didn't want to die and was running all types of options through his head, hoping to escape.

When they reached the entrance, the floor was covered with shredded glass from the blown out windows and door. Hassan stood far enough inside to avoid being shot by the snipers they knew would be positioned in the building across the street. He then selected one of the five hostages to go outside and give the police instructions on how they were to proceed.

"Don't shoot! Please don't shoot!" yelled Perry Ostrowski, a thin, balding, middle-aged man, holding his hands high as he walked out of the entrance and into the middle of the street. "I work for the bank. I'm a hostage. I'm supposed to pass along instructions."

"Are you the only hostage?" asked Special Agent Harold Roberts over the megaphone.

Ostrowski looked over toward the terrorists, not knowing if he was allowed to answer the question. Bahar nodded.

"No, there are five of us," said Ostrowski. "They want a helicopter to land right here to take them to Midway with a private jet ready for them on the runway. If the helicopter isn't here in fifteen minutes, they will start shooting us one at a time, every ten minutes. Please, sir, please do it! They will kill us! I'm certain of it."

Then the terrified fifty-something year-old man, who was having cravings for one of his cigarettes at that moment, walked back toward the entrance. Watching him intently was Bahar, who stood against the north wall behind the gold metal frame, previously the door to enter the bank.

The terrorist kept his gun pointed at Ostrowski, whose eyes danced back and forth, uncertain if he should walk back into the building, which could mean certain death. As he drew closer to the door, all of a sudden, he darted off running as fast as he could away from death's door. He sprinted north toward Quincy Street hoping not to be shot in the back.

Bahar took two steps toward the opening to shoot him, but the second he stepped outside the nook, shots rang off the pavement in front of him. The snipers shots landed just short of their target. The shooters were overcompensating so they wouldn't hit the hostages inside. Bahar quickly ducked back inside.

"That infidel! That infidel!" shouted Bahar.

"We still have four," said Fayez. "It's no loss."

"Yes it is! They'll think we aren't serious," said Bahar, grabbing the right arm of the young athletic man. "I'm going to send him out into the middle of the street and shoot him. That will send the message."

"You can't do that," said Fayez. "You need all of them in case we have to shoot them one at time. You shoot one of them now, and we lose a bargaining chip. We have to walk out of here with at least one hostage, if not two. C'mon let's get inside. Those snipers can pick us off in here."

They turned and walked back into the hallway, when all of a sudden, a twenty-something year-old man, dressed in a black gabardine overcoat, gray turtleneck shirt, blue jeans, and brown Chukka boots, stepped out into the middle of the hallway. He stopped about fifty feet in front of them. Startled, Bahar and Fayez quickly lifted their guns toward him.

"Okay, good! Now we have our fifth hostage back. Get over here."

"I don't think so," said the stern-looking man with long thick wavy brown hair, pulling back the right side of his coat, revealing a holster with a pearl-handled Smith & Wesson six-shooter. "You're going to need to let them go."

Bahar and Fayez looked at each other and laughed.

"We will kill you right now, you American swine!" Bahar said, pointing his gun directly at the man. "Are you with the police?"

"No," said the man.

"FBI?"

"No."

"Then who the hell are you?"

"My name is Dylan, and I'm the guy who's going to kill you if you don't put those guns down right now. We clear?"

The two terrorists just looked at Dylan.

"Drop that gun on the floor right now," ordered Bahar, who still thought he could take Dylan as a hostage. "We have killed dozens of Americans today. You won't get another chance."

"Or maybe *you* won't get another chance," threatened Dylan, watching Bahar's eyes grow wide, about to pull the trigger. Before he could squeeze, Dylan, with lightning-fast speed, drew his gun and fired a shot. Blam! Right through Bahar's forehead.

Then just as quickly, he turned toward Fayez. Two more shots. Blam! Blam! Right through Fayez's heart. Both fell to the ground, blood pouring out of them, running on the once-pristine white marble floor in the elegant hallway.

"Wow!" said the athletic young man, walking quickly up to Dylan. "Wow! That was incredible! You did it. You shot them. My God, you're fast!"

The woman Bahar was going to shoot ran up to Dylan and hugged him. "Thank you! Thank you! Thank you!"

Before Dylan knew it, he was surrounded by all four ex-hostages hugging him, thanking him, shaking his hand. He had saved their lives.

"Where did you learn to shoot like that?" asked the athletic young man.

"A former U.S. Marine taught me," Dylan said, smiling. Just then, the sound of a helicopter was heard and became louder, landing on the street right outside the Trust First Bank Building.

"Well, I guess they won't need that any longer," said one of the thirty-something year-old women, who had tears pouring down her cheeks, the stress emptying after such a dangerous confrontation.

"Hey, look, this isn't over yet," said Dylan. "We need to make sure the police know that we have taken care of these two. I'll go out there and tell them."

"That's okay," said the athletic man. "It's my turn to do something. I'll do it."

They all agreed. Then the twenty-something man walked through the gold-framed entrance, the sound of the glass crackling under his black wingtip shoes. With his hands held high in the air, he walked toward the middle of the street. Sweat began pouring down his face at the sight of an army of police, SWAT team members, and plain-clothes officers, all with their guns pointed directly at him. The sound of the helicopter, ten yards behind him, diminished as the blades slowed down.

"The terrorists are dead! They've been killed!" said Drew Jeffries as his blond hair was being blown by the rotating helicopter blades, winding down with each passing second.

"What?" yelled FBI Special Agent, Harold Roberts, struggling to hear over the noise of the chopper.

"A man came in here and shot both the terrorists! They're dead! We are safe!"

"Okay, son, we are going to take this slow," said Roberts, thinking this may be a trick, but couldn't understand why since the helicopter had arrived.

"Can I bring them all out safely now?" asked Jeffries.

"Okay, no one shoot!" Roberts said through the megaphone so all of the police, SWAT teams, and snipers could clearly hear him. "I repeat, do not shoot. We are going to bring out the hostages."

Jeffries turned toward the bank and waved for the others to come out. Each walked out with their hands in the air, except for Dylan, who disappeared up the elevator bank to hide out in an office where Jeffries worked until it all blew over.

Within the next hour, every media outlet in the country, and many across the world, reported on the terrorist incident.

"The two terrorists who were holding four hostages in the Trust First Bank Building this morning were shot and killed by a concerned citizen, who we do not have the identity of at this time," said the beautiful brunette WLS-TV anchor, Katie Block. "Our reporter, Stacey Rocco, is on the scene with one of the hostages. Stacey."

"Thanks, Katie," said the young reporter, with long auburn hair, wearing a tan trench coat, and a very serious look. "Yes, we are here with Drew Jeffries, the hostage who came out of the bank to alert the police and FBI that the terrorists had been killed and the hostages were safe. Drew, what can you tell us about this hero who shot the two terrorists today, saving all of you, and possibly many others?"

"I can tell you he is the most amazing man I have ever seen," said a wide-eyed Jeffries, the adrenaline still pumping through him, so excited to be alive. "The only thing he said is that his name is Dylan. But you have never seen anyone draw a gun as fast as this man. He is lightning quick! It was unbelievable!

"The two terrorists were pointing their guns right at him. And he pulled back his long coat to show them that he had a gun in his holster, just like a cowboy. And then he asked them to drop their guns, but they wouldn't. They laughed at him. He gave them one more chance. Then when it looked like they were going to shoot him, he drew his gun and shot them so fast. I mean it was unbelievable! He has to be the fastest gun in the world. Really fast!"

"I'm sure the police will be sending an artist to draw a rendering from your description," said Rocco. "Do you think that will help identify him?"

"No, he definitely doesn't want to be identified," Jeffries insisted, now feeling the weight of protecting the man who had protected him and the other hostages.

Rocco thanked Jeffries, then stepped over to the middle-aged man, who was also one of the hostages. "Sir, what is your name and what can you tell us about the man who saved your life in there this morning?"

"Bob Fry," said the man in a blue business suit. "He said his name was Dylan."

"Dylan, yes, but did he give a last name or can you describe him?" asked Rocco.

"No, just Dylan. He's good looking, has brown hair, not too long, but wavy, and was wearing a long black coat, blue jeans, brown boots. Honestly, I thought he looked a lot like that actor. You know, what's the guy's name? That famous actor in those movies."

"Movie star?" asked Rocco.

"Yeah, you know, he's in those action movies. Looks kind of like him."

"Our hero is a movie star?"

"Well, he looks like the actor, real tough guy. It's not him though. But you know, he sort of looks like him. But my eyesight isn't very good. It was twenty/eighty last checkup, so...."

"Do you have any idea of how he got out of here unseen?" asked Rocco, looking intently at Mr. Fry hoping for some insight on where the hero went. "No one saw him come out of the front door."

"After seeing what he did in there, he probably jumped out of a window and flew home," chuckled Fry, thinking he was now getting his fifteen minutes of fame.

"Thank you very much, Mr. Fry," said Rocco, trying to hold back a laugh during such a serious crisis, where nothing could be accepted as funny. All around her, she saw critically injured victims being taken away in ambulances.

She turned to the camera. "So, Katie, all we know about the hero who killed these two terrorists and ended this crisis is his name is Dylan, and he sort of looks like a famous action movie star, we think. This is Stacey Rocco at the Trust First Bank Building."

CHAPTER TWENTY-TWO

After his entrance into the world of BB gun owners, Arman entered his senior year at Southwest High with great confidence. He was ready for any attack by Mazel and his thugs.

The first day, he called his group of friends together in the cafeteria to prepare them for a potential attack. The five boys, the Persian Warriors, huddled around the table and spoke in whispers, hoping not to draw attention to themselves.

"It's a new year, and we all know that means the rules and understanding from junior year go right out the window," Arman told his trusted group of loyal friends. "When they come at us, and have no doubt that they will come after us, we have to be smart!

"If they just try to fight us with fists, we'll fight them with fists. If they come after us with bats, or chains, or knives, they will most likely try to attack us outside of school. So we have to stick together. Don't ever walk out of this school alone. Do you understand?"

The four seniors nodded.

"Yes, Arman, but what if they catch one of us in the school alone, then what?" asked Omar, who had been on the wrong end of that experience more than a few times.

"None of us can let that happen," instructed their confident leader, who had no intention of letting them know he now owned a BB gun. "Go from class to class, stick together. If you see any of them in the hall, avoid them at all costs. Go into a classroom with a teacher until they pass. Do whatever it takes. Do you understand?"

"But what if Mazel brings a real gun into the school?" said Dabney, who was absorbed with that thought, really wishing he could just transfer out of the school. "You know he's just crazy enough to do that."

"And angry enough," said Jahan, who felt certain something was going to go down during senior year and was really glad Arman had called everyone together to discuss a strategy.

"Don't worry about that," said Arman. "I'm prepared for that."

"What do you mean, you're prepared for that?" asked Gabe.

Arman knew Gabe had talked to his parents, letting them know about the bad situation at school. They'd assured their son that if anything else happened at the school, they would transfer him to St. John's Academy for the remainder of the year.

"Don't worry about it," said Arman, not concerned in the least. "Just know that I've got that scenario covered if he tries to pull a gun on us."

The five boys felt better after the impromptu meeting, and together walked toward their first class, scanning the hall in front of them for any of MG's Boys. Then out of the bookstore to their right, an imposing figure stepped in front of them.

"How is it going, boys?" asked the six-foot-six head football coach, Neal Michaels, who had taken steps the previous spring with the principal and police to address the conflict. Like Arman and his friends, he hoped senior year would be peaceful.

"Oh, hello, Mr. Michaels. Everything is good, thank you," said Arman, always polite.

"Well boys, I just want you to know that we are closely monitoring Rick Mazel and his group," said Coach Michaels. "Principal Leonard and the Park Hills Police are actively involved with this situation. If Mazel threatens you, or tries to attack you again, I want you to come right to me. Understood?"

"Mr. Michaels, we think they might come after us with knives or even a gun," said Dabney, obviously not wishing to hold back on this information any longer. He too had talked to his parents, letting them know how anxious he was all summer about returning to Southwest High.

"Dabney!" scolded Arman.

"Well, we do! And Mr. Michaels said he'll help us," said Dabney.

"I agree," said Gabe. "The whole school needs to know about this. There's no reason to hold back on it."

"Arman, I will help you," assured Coach Michaels. "Here, all six of you, type my cell into your phones. And text me if anything happens again. I'm here all day, either in school or on the football field. So I'm here to help and will also alert the authorities."

"Coach Michaels, we appreciate it, but if we are standing in an empty hallway and Mazel pulls a gun on us, what are we supposed to do?" asked Arman, trying to bring to light the worst case scenario, which he fully expected to occur.

"As you know, after that brawl last spring, we addressed the seriousness of this situation with their parents directly," said the coach. "Our hope is that they finally got the message. But I understand your concern. I'll talk with Principal Leonard. I think it would be a good idea if Mazel and his group came into the front office for a talk, just as a reminder. This is the kind of thing that we have to stay in front of, so no one gets hurt."

The five boys looked at each other, trying to read the reaction to this level of support from Mr. Michaels and the school's administration. Slight smiles appeared, each beginning to feel much better about the situation, knowing they had a real supporter in Mr. Michaels. They felt confident he would deal with the issue, support them, not let this conflict get out of hand and become truly dangerous.

Regardless, Arman still carried his BB gun with him each day to school, just in case one of MG's Boys became so angry and so desperate that they didn't care if they were sent to jail for assault and battery.

The offer of support from Mr. Michaels was quite welcome, and timely, since in only a few weeks, the calendar would turn to Thursday, September 11—the day that many Americans of Middle Eastern heritage tried to avoid each year by calling in sick, staying at home, anything to stay out of sight. The annual news coverage of 9/11 often resulted in anger directed toward young men who resembled, or could potentially be, a Muslim.

They didn't have to be a Muslim extremist to receive glares. No, they just had to look like the Al-Qaeda terrorists who flew United Airlines Flight 175 or American Airlines Flight 11 into the twin towers of the World Trade Center, killing 2,977 innocent people and injuring more than 6,000. They just had to resemble the five hijackers who flew American Airlines Flight 77 into the Pentagon, killing fifty-nine innocent passengers and crew on-board plus 125 Americans inside the building. Observers just had to believe they could be relatives, friends, or supporters of the four Al-Qaeda who hijacked United Airlines Flight 92, resulting in forty-four more deaths after the plane crashed, when brave American passengers and crew fought back. Thirteen years after the tragic incident, Arman, his family, and friends all had to continue dealing with the fallout from those evil men who had no connection to them.

Fortunately for Arman and his family, the hatred toward those of Middle Eastern dissent seemed to fade a bit with each passing year. When the infamous anniversary arrived in 2014, Arman was sitting at his desk in the back row of the history class, avoiding eye contact with two of Mazel's gang. Nathan Nowicki and Benny Kowal were seated at the front of the class, glancing back at Arman every few minutes. At 9 a.m. sharp, Arman watched the popular teacher, Mr. Brian Hanley, enter the classroom and turn on the television mounted to the wall above the green-board at the front of the class.

NBC's Today Show came on the screen showing the network's coverage from that fateful day. Mr. Hanley wanted to share an important history lesson, an event everyone in the classroom had lived through at a young age. However, at 9:25 a.m., the coverage was interrupted by breaking news.

"There was a terrorist attack at the Midwest Trade Building in Chicago this morning where a bomb exploded and terrorists shot more than twenty-five people in the street," said WLS-TV news anchor, Katie Block. "This was followed by a hostage situation in the Trust First Bank Building. The terrorists held five hostages and threatened to shoot them all unless a helicopter was delivered to take them to Midway Airport where a plane would be waiting for them. As the Chicago Police, Homeland Security, and the FBI managed the hostage situation, suddenly and without warning, one of the hostages came out of the building to let them know they were safe.

"A man, identified as Dylan, had somehow gotten into the building and confronted the terrorists. This man was carrying a Smith & Wesson gun, an old heritage six-shooter. One of the hostages, a Mr. Drew Jeffries, said the next thing that happened looked like a gunfight out of a Western movie. The terrorists would not back down and not drop their weapons as the man, Dylan, had requested. When they went to shoot him, Dylan drew his gun incredibly fast and shot both of the terrorists, killing them, and saving the hostages."

Applause exploded across Mr. Hanley's classroom with students jumping up and down and cheering for the hero known as Dylan. Even the always stoic Hanley was smiling from ear-to-ear, shaking his balding head in amazement at the news.

"Wow! That's amazing!" yelled out one student from the back of the room. "Just like a cowboy! Shot those damn Muslims!"

"Shoot 'em all!" yelled Nowicki, turning back to look at Arman.

"Yeah, they should run all of those damn Muslims out of the country," agreed Kowal, pumping his fist in the air.

"Settle down! Settle down everyone!" said Mr. Hanley, hoping to restore order to his classroom. "First of all, I don't want to hear another derogatory word about Muslims in this classroom again. Anyone who breaks that rule, well, that's a trip to the principal's office for certain. Second, I'm sure that account she just described has been misreported. People don't show up at hostage scenes with a gun in a holster like in a cowboy movie. It just doesn't happen. This is 2014! Not 1814. So let's just wait until all of the facts are in before we get too crazy here. Now sit down. Got it?"

Many of the students felt like Mr. Hanley had just thrown a bucket of cold water onto their enthusiasm for an incredibly heroic and unique moment. Smiles turned to frowns and cheering jubilation muted to dead silence.

Arman sat at his desk with a huge smile growing on his face. If the story were true, then there was another cowboy out there, someone just like him. He knew the heroic Dylan had to love Clint Eastwood movies, just like him. He knew Dylan had to be passionate about the principle of good guys going after the bad guys and defeating them, just like him. Oh, how he wished he could meet this hero, Dylan.

When the bell rang and class ended, the hallways were filled with exuberant students who passed the word about the story reported on the news. The buzz filled every hall, every wing of Southwest High. Within minutes, every student at the high school became aware of the heroic story.

Unfortunately for Arman and his friends, however, there was another response to the story—it inspired a renewed hate toward anyone who was

Arab, Middle Eastern, or Muslim. This wasn't like other years where ugly looks were directed their way. These were intense, hateful scowls.

Two terrorists attacked their city, Chicago. Now the battle was on their turf. And they would fight back against every identifiable enemy, anyone who resembled a terrorist.

By the final period of the day, Arman and each of his five friends believed transferring out of the school was the only answer to this new onslaught of negative energy directed toward them. It also enlivened Rick Mazel, who told his gang of evil racists that they were definitely going to get even with those Arab punks that day.

Arman texted Coach Michaels to alert him that he and his four buddies were sitting in his classroom and they needed his help. They were nervous about the overwhelming negative vibe they were getting since the news broke about the terrorist attack downtown. They wanted protection to leave the school safely.

It was approximately 3 p.m. when the 2,300 students poured out the doors toward the yellow buses, parked cars, or parents in the pickup line at the front of the school. Fifteen minutes had passed and Arman had not received a response from Coach Michaels, which completely frustrated him as the seconds ticked away. With no response from Mr. Michaels, Arman and his Persian Warriors did not want to be left alone in the school. They thought the best and safest option was to go out with the crowd.

Once outside, surrounded by other students, they believed witnesses would dissuade MG's Boys from attacking them. They just needed to get to Jahan's car, parked in his space at the back of the lot, along the fence near the football field. They hoped they would see Coach Michaels on the field. But they had to get to Jahan's car first. Then they would be home free, probably never returning to the school where their lives now felt threatened after the student body's overwhelming reaction to the Midwest Trade Building attack.

"Okay, we're going out to your car, Jahan," Arman directed his friends, who wondered why he was wearing a brown cloth poncho. They had never seen him wear it before. "Stick together and keep your eyes open. If you spot Mazel or any of his thugs, call it out. Once we get to the car, we will be fine. We just have to get to the car. Does everyone have their knives?"

They each nodded with a universal look of seriousness and fear, eyes wide, jaws stiff.

"Get them out!" Arman ordered. "Don't open them, but just cup them in your hand, just in case. Hopefully it won't come to that."

Arman quickly checked the hallway where a few students were still making their way toward the exit.

"We've got to go now, before it's too late," said Arman, leading them out of Mr. Michael's classroom door. "C'mon, let's move!"

Out the door, the five boys ran, trying to catch up to the large crowd they knew would be exiting out the back doors. Arman was in front, searching each hallway they ran past for their enemies. As they reached the bookstore, he started to feel excited that they may be able to get out without a problem. Ahead, he saw hundreds of students flooding out the exit. All of a sudden, a tall boy came running at him from the right. Arman stopped. He held his arm up to stop his friends. The tall boy ran right past them, obviously just trying to get to his bus before it left. Nonetheless, it made the over-anxious group of boys even more nervous for a brief moment.

"C'mon!" said Arman, running again. They reached the crowd of coatless, backpacked students. The five boys wormed their way into the crowd, so no one could spot them on the fringes. The bright sun blinded Arman as he exited the school. He quickly pulled out his sunglasses to be sure he could see anything, or anyone around him, or coming at him.

"Get your sunglasses on, fellows," instructed the only student at the school wearing any type of overcoat, a poncho in his case. "And keep your eyes open. Stick together!"

Once outside, hundreds of students dispersed in various directions, thinning out the crowd, as they made their way to their rides, exposing the Persian Warriors. The five friends, altogether, moved fast in unison. Arman's instincts took over, as he now felt the threat of being out in the open. They were an easy target for Mazel, if he were waiting for them in the parking lot. But there was no sign of MG's Boys. None.

"C'mon!" said Arman, who started to run, his four loyal pals right behind him, looking like a track team heading toward the finish line. Jahan's black KIA Sorento was now only fifty yards away.

With each stride, Arman searched the area, and it looked like a clear path to the car. Mazel was nowhere in sight. As the running boys drew closer to the KIA, smiles appeared on their young faces. They felt safe for the first time since the news of the Midwest Trade Building attack was reported that morning, which turned so many of their classmates against them.

"We made it!" said a happy Arman, who turned around to see his friends, but didn't see the back doors of the orange-white-and-blue Chevy van, parked next to Jahan's KIA, open wide.

Mazel and eight of his thugs, knives in hand, stepped out onto the parking lot pavement.

"Where do you terrorists think you're going?" asked the incredibly ugly, pale-faced leader, as his group walked in front of the KIA to block them from their escape vehicle.

"Back off, Mazel!" the courageous leader of the Persian Warriors said in no uncertain terms. "Mr. Michaels is on the football field and heading over right now."

Arman looked over at the field and yelled out, "Coach Michaels! Over here! Coach Michaels!"

Everyone looked over at the football field. No Coach Michaels.

"Coach Michaels! We're over here, where you told us to meet you," said Arman, waving his arm in the air.

Everyone looked toward the field again. No Coach Michaels.

Then Mazel turned back toward his prey. He didn't bat an eye, directing his gang, "Knives boys!" And with that order, each lifted their right hands and snapped out the blades, the sounds of eight knives flicking open all at once.

"Yeah, we figured that's what you would try, Mazel. Knives, fellas!" said Arman, the sound of five more knives heard snapping open. "Omar, record this. I'm not going to let this be our word against theirs."

"Oh real smart, you fuckin' terrorist piece of shit!" snarled Mazel, who reached in his jeans coat and pulled out a Glock gun. "Did you figure on this?"

"A gun! That's a real gun!" yelled Gabe, as the four Persian Warriors behind Arman gasped, their hearts pounding, heads feeling like they would explode. They only wanted to go home. Gabe wondered why this had to happen. It felt like a terrible nightmare!

MG's Boys watched the reaction with great delight. Obnoxious smiles appeared. Cockiness presented itself fully. Given that they had more soldiers and better tools, a Glock gun, they were quite confident about how this battle was going to end.

"Yes, I did," said Arman, standing with his arms to his sides, then pulling back his poncho with his right hand, exposing his holster and gun. The MG smiles disappeared quickly, and Mazel's eyes grew wide. Real fear! No more safe options!

They thought it was a real gun.

"Now put your weapons away and get the hell out of here before you get hurt," ordered Arman, his arms straight down, right hand next to his holster, like a gunfighter ready to draw. Mazel could see and feel the courage of the Persian Warrior's leader, the same boy that beat the hell out of him in the gym.

"C'mon, Rick, let's go," said Mike Felder. "I'm not getting shot over this."

"Hey, I've got a gun too!" said Mazel, holding his Glock in his right hand, hoping he could bluff Arman. "Now toss that gun on the ground, or I'll be forced to use mine."

"You move that gun toward me and I'll kill you right where you stand, Mazel," warned Arman, bluffing him, knowing his BB gun would only hurt him but certainly not kill him. "I'm not just going to shoot you. I'm not just going to wound you. I'm going to kill you! Now this is the last time I'm going to tell you. Get out of here. Now!"

A long pause. Silence filled the air. The wide eyes of the thirteen high school seniors, faced off in a duel of ethnicities, that should never happen in the Twenty-First Century.

This was not a scene incited by two decades of hate, ignited by three airplanes crashing into targeted U.S. buildings, followed by two wars—Afghanistan and Iraq. This was not a scene fueled by ISIS and Al-Qaeda's spread of terrorism globally with brutal beheadings, and misrepresentation of a peaceful religion. This was not a scene birthed from a saga of hate and misguided choices and actions, spreading more hate, more terrorism via the propaganda broadcast on YouTube and promoted on the Internet.

No, this was a scene of ignorance and stupidity. A misguided group of youths used the terrorist events of the day to justify their own evil actions. So there they stood, thirteen students, in the back of their high school parking lot, trying to settle a score.

"Okay, we'll let you live to fight another day," Mazel chuckled, trying to cover his cowardice with a false laugh. "C'mon, boys, put your knives away. We'll have our day."

Stosh Gould looked reluctant, as the other seven closed their knives, some trying to maintain a tough look. It was clear however, that they were backing down again from a force of five, who had just seemingly matched them in weaponry, but far exceeded them in courage.

"C'mon, Stosh!" Mazel barked at his general. "We'll be back."

Gould, sneering hate at Arman, closed his knife, and walked with the others toward the multi-colored van. Arman's four loyalists closed their knives. A collective sigh could be heard and felt.

"Keep recording, Omar," ordered Arman. "Until they're gone."

"Yeah, keep recording, Omar," said Mazel, a smirk crossing his face as he turned to walk toward the van, all the while continuing to watch Arman. "In case he shoots me in the back."

Mazel turned completely away from Arman and walked directly toward the van. The four Persian Warriors felt relieved. Jahan, Gabe, and Dabney started walking toward the car. Omar stayed behind Arman, recording every movement.

Arman was fully focused on Mazel as he walked away, but then suddenly turned very quickly with his gun pointed directly at Arman, who with lighting speed, drew his Smith & Wesson from the holster and fired off one shot. It was a direct hit, knocking the gun out of the sneaky punk's hand, into the air, and onto the pavement, spinning behind the stunned MG leader. Mazel, clutched his right hand and then looked up in horror at his enemy. He had no idea it was just a BB that hit his Glock gun. He thought it was an actual bullet.

"Don't shoot!" Mazel begged him. His gang of seven stood behind him, awestruck and horrified all at the same time by the skill of Arman Farzan. Shouts of victory exploded from the KIA, his three friends jumping out of the car again.

"Yeah, Arman!" yelled Omar from behind him, still recording.

"Wow!" Gabe exclaimed. "Wow!"

"Unbelievable!" said Jahan

"That was fast, man. Really fast!" said Dabney.

"Jahan, get that gun," ordered Arman, watching his friend run over and pick up the Glock, handing it to Arman, who was still focused on his enemy.

"Mazel!" he shouted.

"Yes," said the fallen leader with as much politeness as he could feign.

"That's the end of it. Agree?"

"Yeah, that's it. We're done," he said, then slowly stood, walked toward the van, and climbed into the back, feeling lucky to be alive. His bully cowardice was fully quelled by what he thought was a life-threatening incident.

Arman stood there, arms still to his sides, staring at the driver of the orange-white-and-blue van, hoping the visual impression would be cemented in his enemy's minds, never to be challenged again.

The old Chevy vehicle rattled away, the motor running noticeably loud, smoke emanating from the tailpipe. Arman finally felt a calm relaxation fill his entire body for the first time that day. At that moment, he heard running footsteps coming from his right. He unhinged his poncho, letting it fall back over his gun, and then turned quickly. It was Coach Michaels.

"Arman! I just got your text," said his strongest advocate at the school. The coach glanced around while he worked to catch his breath. He saw Arman's four smiling friends standing behind the KIA, obviously waiting for their leader. "I'm so sorry. I was in a conference with the principal which ran late. The text didn't come through until I was outside the office. I'm so sorry! Is everything okay?"

Arman just smiled, "Yes, sir. Everything's fine."

"Well, I feel terrible," said Mr. Michaels. "I promised you that I would be there for you, and the first time you message me, I get it too late. Maybe we should figure out a backup plan."

"Oh no, that's okay, Mr. Michaels," said Arman, looking down and laughing at the irony of the moment. "I think we did figure one out. It's all good!"

"Well, okay, but if for some reason you can't get ahold of me right away in the future, I want you to call 911, okay?" he instructed the young man.

"911, that's ironic," smiled Arman. "Yes, sir, I will."

"You know, our conference was called at the last minute to discuss the terrorist attack downtown this morning and how some of our students might react," said Michaels with a look of great concern. "We think some of them may start harassing some of the Arab students like you."

"Is that right?" said Arman, not wishing to correct the coach about mistakenly referring to him as an Arab.

"Well, we hope not, but based on the reaction by many students to the news coverage today, it's a possibility."

"I see, well, don't worry about us, Mr. Michaels. I think we'll be okay," Arman assured him with great confidence, which was evident to the coach.

Michaels looked as though he was struck by those comments. "Did something happen?" he asked.

"Well, let's just say, we met with Mazel and his buddies and worked it out with them. That's all! I promise you, it's all good and no one is hurt."

"Do I need to call their parents back into school?" Michaels asked, determined to make sure he covered this issue fully.

"No, sir. There's no problem," smiled Arman.

"Okay, well thank you, Arman," said Michaels. "I have to say, I am impressed with you. You are quite a leader. Had you ever thought of running for Student Council President?"

Arman just laughed, "Thank you, coach. But no, that's not something I'm interested in."

"Well, if you do, let me know. I think your voice, confidence, and leadership would be a great asset to the school, especially now with so much turmoil after the attack."

As Coach Michaels was about to walk away, Arman said, "Oh, coach, just one thing." Then he looked over at his friends, "Jahan."

Jahan, leaning against his KIA, walked over and handed Arman Mazel's Glock gun.

"Here you go, coach," Arman smiled, handing the gun to the tall, now stunned-looking educator. "We took this away from Mazel a few minutes ago, so he wouldn't do anything stupid."

"Did he fire it?" asked Michaels with a great look of concern.

"No, he just dropped it on the ground and Jahan picked it up," explained Arman, leaving Coach Michaels convinced that he was not getting the full story. "We got to go, sir. Thanks again for your support."

The five happy Persian Warriors drove off in Jahan's KIA Sorento, headed for JavaPlace. Once there, they would celebrate their victory with their favorite coffee drinks, while viewing the entire incident on Omar's phone.

An incredibly bad day turned into quite a remarkable day for five boys. Their friendship was cemented forever by that moment when they stood together facing serious danger and possibly death. But thanks to their leader, Arman, they sat in JavaPlace unharmed and happy, reliving the moment none of them would ever forget.

CHAPTER TWENTY-THREE

An ever-present cloud of dust filled the air. The sounds of jackhammers hammering, chainsaws buzzing, large yellow cranes moaning, and powerful truck motors revving up dominated the intersection of Jackson Boulevard and LaSalle Street. Dozens of strong, burly construction workers in bright green safety vests, blue helmets, and leather boots performed their union specialty to repair the extensive damage to the Midwest Trade Building.

Just a few blocks away that morning, Dylan Reilly walked quickly, holding the palm of his right hand over his mouth to avoid breathing in the pervasive dust. He escaped the sounds, smells, and polluted air, ducking into Stewart Savings & Loan in the Financial District of Chicago.

Once inside the revolving doors, he felt like he had stepped out of a war zone and into the heavenly look, feel, and smell of a luxury office building. It felt so good, so safe, and so comfortable.

At first glance, he couldn't help but be impressed with this magnificent building. This was the workplace of his pal Georgie, who had walked away from his dream job in radio to pursue a more realistic and lucrative career in investment banking.

Everything about the bank seemed so buttoned up. Dylan couldn't help but observe the new carpets, security guards dressed perfectly, shined marble floors, and impressive round marble pillars ascending to the roof.

Checking in at the security desk at the front entrance, he was greeted by a strong-looking African American security guard named Lawrence Lavelle. Dylan was quite surprised by the lax screening process, which amounted to Lavelle giving Dylan the once over, then checking his identification via his driver's license. The guard seemed a bit curious about Dylan's black overcoat, most likely from all the news reports about the terrorist attack at the Midwest Trade Building. But there was no metal detector to pass through, which was fortunate for Dylan, since he always carried his gun.

After being handed a nametag sticker, Dylan proceeded through the bank, walking past a row of windowed offices. He glanced inside to see expensive and sleek mahogany desks complete with professional bankers typing on their computer keyboards, apparently making the bank money and earning their keep.

The white sticky nametag Dylan placed onto the front of his coat was already beginning to peel, so he yanked it off and placed it in his pocket, in the event anyone needed to see it.

As instructed, Dylan walked down a private corridor where he found the office with the sign on the front stating, "Investments." He had already texted Georgie to let him know he had arrived, so when he entered the door, there was his old high school pal waiting for him.

"Hey, Georgie boy!" said Dylan, reaching out to shake hands with his always-smiling friend.

"Dylan! Great to see you!" said Georgie, shaking hands and moving in for the now traditional semi-embrace. "Thanks for coming down on such late notice. I didn't want to say anything at the funeral. You had enough on your mind. But I just felt bad about our lunch meeting and hoped we could grab a cup of coffee."

"No worries, Georgie. Coffee would be great," said the long brown-haired history teacher, who had taken a leave of absence from Watson College Prep following Darlene's death. "I've got plenty of time now, and it does my heart good to see you again."

"Well, day at a time, right, Dylan? Day at a time," said Georgie with an encouraging smile.

After a quick tour of the department, which was empty because his co-workers were meeting in the conference room down the hall, it was back out the door. Georgie provided a top-notch guided tour of the bank, complete with its history as well as a description of his job.

"I was just promoted to working in an investment group, searching for good bets for the bank to generate long-term revenue," he explained.

"It may not sound like the most exciting work in the world, but believe me, when we make a big deal and later I receive a check bigger than any amount of money I have ever made or seen before, I get pretty excited about it," said Georgie, his dry sense of humor on full display.

"I'll bet you do," laughed Dylan, happy for his friend.

"It would have taken me a decade to make that kind of money working at the radio station. So bottom line, if we are working for the money, this seems to be the quickest route to success."

Dylan couldn't help but be incredibly impressed with his friend. He was amazed at how quickly he had turned his life in a new and better direction. He seemed really happy.

"Plus, your parents have to be quite happy about your profession," Dylan added.

"Oh, I wouldn't be able to wipe the smiles off their faces with a sandblaster," joked Georgie. "I'm sending them both down to Florida next month to spend the winter there, stay out of the cold, and really enjoy themselves."

"That's great!" said Dylan, as they reached the large square foyer with about a dozen tellers stationed behind impressive shimmering wooden booths, servicing the banking customers lined up to transact their business. The sound of Georgie's expensive black wing-tipped shoes echoed off the walls of the great corridor as they walked. He stopped abruptly to point out the intricate architecture and design of the magnificent-looking interior.

"And right there, Dylan, that inscription was done in 1922 by..." said Georgie, who stopped when a loud blast was heard coming from the entrance, about two hundred feet away. He looked over and saw three figures dressed in black, carrying guns and running right at them, obviously destined for the teller windows.

"Oh no!" said Georgie, quickly looking at Dylan, who had a look of anger and determination on his face. "C'mon, this way, Dylan. Let's get out of here."

Georgie started running for the door, but Dylan didn't move. "C'mon, Dylan!"

"Go ahead, I'm staying here," he told his friend, who froze in his tracks when he heard one of the bank thieves yell out, "Stop right there! Nobody move! Nobody move! Or I'll kill you all!"

Shrieks of fear filled the large hall, screams, crying, as those in the massive marbled foyer became aware that they were under attack. An older woman fell, apparently having fainted. Thankfully, the man next to her caught her before she hit the hard marble floor and seriously injured herself.

Georgie was only fifteen feet from Dylan and watched as he pulled back his long black coat, revealing a pearl-handled Smith & Wesson in a brown leather holster.

"Oh my God!" said Georgie, in somewhat of a whisper. "You're the guy?"

"I'm the guy, Georgie," said Dylan, full of confidence and courage. "And those three punks are going to wish they had picked a different bank to rob today."

A proud smile grew on Georgie's face.

The three men, each wearing a black sweatshirt, with hoods pulled over their heads, and black pants and athletic shoes, entered into the large main hall of the bank. That's when the leader spotted Dylan standing with his arms to his sides and the now famous white pearl-handled gun exposed for all to see. He immediately stopped and raised his right arm to halt his two co-assailants. "Hold it! Hold it!"

Dylan looked directly at him, no fear in his eyes, just strong confident determination, which the three thieves could readily see through the small holes in the black wool stocking hats covering their respective faces.

"Now you boys picked the wrong bank to rob today. But you don't have to make this your final destination," said Dylan, his low powerful voice bouncing off the walls of the bank, the three dozen customers and employees behind him now less fearful knowing America's new hero was on the scene to help them. "It would be a good idea right now to put your guns down."

One of the two men, standing behind the leader, looked panicky as he rocked back and forth in place, his shoes squeaked as he swayed, not knowing what to do. Then he said, "Jaquez, we put our guns down and we are definitely going to jail. And that security guard…"

"I know," said the leader, Jacquez, staring at Dylan. "Are you that guy…?"

"Yeah, I'm the guy," said Dylan, staring directly at the leader, looking for any movement that would require him to draw his six-shooter.

"Shit!" Jacquez cried out. "Look, we haven't done anything, we just want to back up and leave, okay?"

"Nope!"

"Nope?"

"You shot that security guard at the entrance," said Dylan, watching the leader look over at his big-mouthed co-conspirator, who realized their options for escape were just nullified.

Silence filled the hall. Then, the big-mouth, knowing there was no way out, made a snap decision and jerked his gun up toward Dylan. Georgie's eyes grew wide, as did everyone else in the bank watching this scene.

Before the loud-mouth thief could squeeze the trigger on his Magnum 357 handgun, Dylan quickly drew his pearl-handled six-shooter and fired off two shots. One hit the Magnum, sending it flying. The other struck the right hand of the assailant, who screamed out and fell to the floor, clutching his right hand, and curling up in pain.

Seeing their friend get shot, his two buddies became infuriated. Jacquez yelled out, "Shoot him!"

The two black-garbed assailants turned toward Dylan with a vengeance. They fired their Magnums repeatedly at him, the bullets passing just inches over his flying brown locks as he dropped to the floor while firing off four shots, two bullets directly into the chest of each assailant. Both were jolted backwards by the impact, falling onto the marble floor. Jacquez's head bounced off the unforgiving ground, which quickly turned into a canvass of red extending further and further, the blood flowing from the chests and backs of those shot.

Their wounded friend, curled in pain, could only watch in anguish, too injured to retaliate. His eyes filled with water and hate, knowing his two friends had just had their lives ended by his stupid spur of the moment decision.

Within seconds, the murmur of voices from those in the bank was heard throughout the hall. The thrill of witnessing the heroic moment became apparent as smiles appeared everywhere. People in the bank were so happy. Georgie hurried over to Dylan, who quickly popped up from the floor.

"Damn, Dylan! That was unbelievable!" said Georgie. "Absolutely incredible!"

"Thanks, Georgie," Dylan replied, spinning his gun forward, then quickly backward and into his holster. That's when they heard the police sirens and saw police officers coming through the front doors of the bank.

"I've got to get out of here," Dylan said, looking for an exit.

Georgie quickly understood the situation and said, "C'mon, follow me!"

He began running toward a side exit, Dylan right behind him, as several customers in the bank walked toward them, hoping to meet Dylan and thank him for saving their lives.

"Thank you, sir! Thank you!" yelled out a young dark-haired man in his early thirties, dressed in a blue suit and holding a briefcase. His voice could be heard clearly. All eyes were on Dylan. A loud cheer arose from the three dozen customers, tellers, and bank managers who had witnessed this incredible moment.

Six Chicago Police officers entered the main hall of the bank. Within minutes, it seemed, the two dead men were being taken away on stretchers. The lone survivor, still clutching his injured right hand, was placed on a rolling gurney and loaded into an ambulance destined for Stroger Hospital, only a few miles away.

Georgie and Dylan both jumped into a cab on Clark Street and were driven to Georgie's three-bedroom high rise condo on South Lake Shore Drive. Fifteen minutes later, the two friends were sitting on Georgie Hanlon's brand new leather sofa in his spacious condo on the thirty-ninth floor, overlooking the expansive blue water of Lake Michigan.

The sights of the lakeshore would have to wait, though, while the two men's focus was directed toward the large screen television centered on the beige wall, decorated with expensive historical photos from the 1960s.

"We have breaking news this morning from Stewart Savings & Loan on Clark Street, where there was an attempted robbery," said popular WGN-TV news anchor Gina Clare. "Our reporter, Brad Bentley, is at the bank with a live report. Brad."

"Thanks, Gina. Yes, we are outside of the Stewart Savings & Loan where the Chicago Police have cordoned off the area while they examine the crime scene," reported Bentley, a graying, middle-aged, veteran reporter with a serious and purposeful demeanor. "We can tell you that there were three robbers who entered the bank with large handguns. We are told they were 357 Magnums, although we haven't confirmed that information with the police yet.

"Upon entering the bank, the three men wearing black hooded sweatshirts with their faces covered immediately shot the security guard at the entrance. The guard, Lawrence Lavelle, has been taken to Northwestern Hospital to be treated.

"We were told by one of the police officers, who arrived on the scene immediately after the shooting, that Lavelle was alive but suffered a gunshot wound to his right shoulder. That same officer told me that a full report will be provided by the Police Commissioner, Jerry McAdams, regarding the status of the three bank robbers and how they were shot.

"Early indications are that two of the three thieves were shot and killed, with the third assailant injured and taken to Stroger Hospital to be treated. But we haven't been able to confirm that yet. What we have been able to confirm, however, is the shooter of these three criminals. We have an eyewitness, one of the people inside the bank, when all of this occurred. Sir, can you please state your name and what you saw here today."

"Yes, sir, my name is Bob Murphy," said the dark curly-haired young man in a blue suit, white dress shirt, and blue and white patterned tie. "I went into the bank to cash a check and was in line at one of the teller's windows when I heard a loud bang come from the entrance of the bank, which is not that close. I mean, it was loud though. Very loud!

"When I looked toward the entrance, I saw three people, all dressed in black and their faces were covered up by one of those knit hats with the holes in them, you know. And then, I saw them run into the bank, right toward the area I was standing.

"Like everyone else, I looked for a door to escape, but as I ran toward a side exit, one of them yelled out, "Stop! Or I'll kill you all!" I did stop, as did everyone else. And that's when we saw the man standing in the middle of the floor. You know the hero guy. And he does sort of look like that one movie star."

"Which one?" asked Bentley, hoping he had the big scoop all America wanted to hear.

"I'm not sure of his name, but you'd know him if you saw him," continued the eyewitness. "But he had his coat open showing that pearl handled gun we have all been hearing about on the news. I'm pretty sure everyone had the same reaction. Everyone saw the reports last week.

"Oh man, I can't tell you how excited I was to see him. And I could see the fear on the robbers' faces. Everyone has heard the story. Everyone knows this is the guy who is lightning fast on the draw, whose name is Dylan.

"He tried to give them a chance to put their guns down and wait for the police, but one of them panicked and tried to shoot him. Tried to shoot the fastest gun! That's what they should call him, because he drew his gun so fast, so fast! I mean, it was amazing!

"It was like, before you even knew what happened, it was boom, boom! And the bad guy was down. Then his two pals tried to shoot Dylan, but he was too quick for them. Way too quick! And just like that, it was over.

"I tried to thank him, but Dylan and another guy, in a gray suit, a nice one, ran out the door together. Well we all started cheering for him. We were so happy to be alive, no one hurt. Except I heard the security guard was shot. Is he okay?"

"We're not sure, but we think it may just be a shoulder wound," said Bentley. "So there you have it, Gina. An eyewitness account, and thankfully our brown-haired, long-coated hero from last week, Dylan, just happened to be in the bank when this occurred or who knows what could have happened. Or how many more innocent people could have been hurt?"

"One question for Bob Murphy there," Gina Clare interjected. "Does anyone know who the other man was that ran out the door with him?"

"Good question, Gina," said Bentley. "Mr. Murphy, does anyone know the other man in the gray suit that ran out the door with Dylan?"

"I don't know," said Murphy. "I'm sure that is something the police will be trying to find out, because you would have to think he knew Dylan, since they ran out together."

"Well, we hope so, if we are ever going to find out the full name and identity of this unknown hero who has saved so many lives in the past week. Then maybe we can finally figure out which movie star he looks like, since no one seems to know."

Dylan turned off the TV and set his glass of water down on the coffee table in front of him.

"I never thought you looked like that movie star," said Georgie, laughing at his pal's new identity.

"Me neither, Georgie," laughed Dylan. "Which movie star?"

"Well, I'm not sure," said Georgie. "But whoever he is, you don't look like him."

"I agree completely," laughed Dylan. "I really wasn't looking to become some celebrity hero here. It's just amazing that I was visiting you at the bank today."

"Amazing and really lucky for everyone at the bank," said Georgie. "Dylan, I thought you would never use a gun."

"Well, that was the plan, but after Darlene's murder, I made the decision to arm and prepare to defend myself and others."

"But Dylan, you're a guy who never owned or fired a gun before! How in the hell did you become so good, so fast?" asked Georgie. "I mean, I heard those news reports about you and the terrorists last week. But watching you today, it was unbelievable! You are really fast!"

"I met a war hero who trained me," said Dylan. "He said I was a natural with a gun and blessed with quickness."

"He had that right! You were always really quick on the hockey rink too, so maybe I shouldn't be surprised at how quick you are with a gun."

"I'd rather be shooting pucks than shooting people," said Dylan.

"Bad people, though," Georgie smiled, watching his pal nod in agreement. "And you're right, if they find out who you are, you'll be all over the news. I wouldn't be surprised if Hollywood came after you to be in the movies."

"Yeah, that's not for me," Dylan laughed. "You heard that Murphy fellow. Will anyone know that was you going out the door with me?"

"That's what I'm afraid of. They'll get the video from the bank cameras. We will both be on there, going all the way back to when we walked out into the main hall together. I'm just going to have to tell them that you were a customer I was working with."

"Well that's not true."

"It could be. If you open up an account, you'll save me a trip to the confessional."

Dylan just nodded and realized he needed to make a trip to the confessional. "Okay, a bank account I shall open, but it may be a few weeks until things calm down."

"And while you're there, can I talk you into purchasing some mutual bonds?" laughed Georgie, just to get a laugh. He did, Dylan wagging his finger back and forth at his banker friend and smiling.

It was a good day. They were both still alive.

CHAPTER TWENTY-FOUR

ylan stood on the curb, safe from the speeding parade of cars streaming down Madison Street. He gazed up the magnificent art deco brown stone sculpture of Christ on the cross, centered inside the large window of St. Peter's Catholic Church in downtown Chicago.

How many times he had walked past the cathedral-like sanctuary and never noticed the incredible sculpture on the facing of St. Peter's, called "Christ of the Loop." But there it was, right in front of him. He couldn't take his eyes off the lifeless, yet ever-compelling face of the crucified Jesus Christ. He stood across the street mesmerized by the beauty of the intricate and impressive sculpture, designed by Arvid Strauss and executed by Chicago artist, J. Watts. So sad, yet so powerful!

He crossed the street and walked up the two steps, pulled open the long heavy golden center door, leading into St. Peter's. Once inside, the sound of the hustle and bustle of downtown Chicago faded and the robust melody of the organ took focus, playing for the late morning mass.

A wonderful feeling always filled Dylan's heart, mind, and soul every time he entered St. Peter's, a unique church that conducted mass several times a day and offered confession from 7:30 a.m. until 6 p.m. It most certainly gave Catholics who lived or worked in the downtown area every opportunity to practice the sacrament that cleansed the soul of sin. And that was most certainly the purpose of Dylan's visit on this Friday morning, the day after his visit to Georgie's bank.

For the twenty-eight year-old high school teacher, the anonymous hero, Dylan, knew he had to confess his gravest sin. "Thou Shalt Not Kill."

The Fifth Commandment has been debated for two thousand years, given the never-ending wars and right of self-defense against attackers. The question for Christians remains: Do they have to stand mildly by while attackers hit them, shoot them, and kill them? A Christian purist would say yes. So many early Christians during the time of the demented Roman Emperor Nero died horrible deaths following that teaching, torn apart by dogs, fed to the Lions, burned alive, hacked apart.

As a history teacher, Dylan was well aware of those stories, but wondered how the priest would address his acts of courage. Would it fall under the Catholic Church's teaching of "Just Defense"? Dylan thought so but nonetheless felt strongly that he had better take his case to a priest in the confessional, because proactively ending another human being's life was a mortal sin.

As he approached the glass doors to enter the church, he stopped for a moment to look at the Catholic newspaper on the table along a guard rail. Then he looked over to his right to see a security guard staring at him with a curious look on his face. Everyone knew the hero had wavy brown hair and wore a long black coat with a gray turtleneck. And those identifying markers were on full display as he entered the church.

This was not the time to consider the guard's thoughts. Dylan quickly entered the sanctuary, walking to the left side of the church behind the last pew and watched the late morning mass being celebrated by a middle-aged white-haired priest, who moved to the lectern to read the Gospel.

Dylan took a Reconciliation Preparation pamphlet from the plastic holder mounted on the large marble column butted up to the left side of the last pew. Then he walked a few rows up and kneeled down in the pew next to the confessional. He prayed and reviewed the recommended steps for a thorough examination of conscience. He mentally prepared himself for his testimony to the priest, who would be sitting behind the screen, which would protect Dylan's identity.

As he carefully thought through his sins, his attention became diverted by the priest at the lectern, reading the Gospel of St. Luke.

"He said to them, 'But now let the one who has a moneybag take it, and likewise a knapsack. And let the one who has no sword sell his cloak and buy one,'" read Father Patrick O'Malley, closing the Bible and saying, "The Word of the Lord."

"Thanks be to God," said Dylan in unison with the few hundred others in the church that morning. Standing for the Gospel, they all sat down to listen to the priest's homily.

Hearing Father O'Malley read the Gospel of Luke seemed like a sign to Dylan, who had printed out a copy of that specific section of the New Testament in order to address his actions with the priest in the confessional. Given that reading, he realized it would be very important to hear the priest's analysis of St. Luke's Gospel. Still kneeling, he made the sign of the cross and sat back on the old wooden pew, which creaked from several decades of use.

"The reading today from Saint Luke is one of the more controversial excerpts from the Gospels," said Father O'Malley, who Dylan recognized, having heard him speak in the past. He well knew that this was an intelligent priest. "If you recall, previously Jesus told his Apostles they didn't need any provisions, food, and money when they went out to spread the Good News. That's when it was all new to them.

"But here, just before the Jewish soldiers are to take Jesus away, he tells the Apostles to take a money bag, and likewise, a knapsack with food and supplies. And even a sword. A sword! Why would Jesus tell them to take a sword? Because he knew from that time forward, when the Apostles travelled to various regions of Africa and Europe to share the Good News, that many people in the towns visited would not welcome them.

"As a matter of fact, he knew that in many places they would not be cared for at all. They would not be provided with food and shelter. No, they would be attacked and required to defend themselves, if they were to survive. The sword might be needed for that defense. Defense! This is important. We can never attack with the sword, but we may defend with it, even if it means severely injuring our attackers.

"As the Catechism of the Catholic faith states, 'Legitimate defense can be not only a right but a grave duty for one who is responsible for the lives of others. The defense of the common good requires that an unjust aggressor be rendered unable to cause harm. Love toward oneself remains a fundamental principle of morality. Therefore, it is legitimate to insist on respect for one's own right to life. Someone who defends his life is not guilty of murder, even if he is forced to deal his aggressor a lethal blow.'"

As Dylan listened to those words from the priest, a spine-tingling sensation filled his body. This was an overwhelming feeling he would always credit to an inspiration from the Holy Spirit. It was the same sensation that ran through him during the terrorist attack, giving him the ultimate courage to defend the hostages and himself. It was the same feeling he felt in the bank, trying to encourage the thieves to drop their guns, but once that option was exhausted, he knew his only choice was to deal his aggressors a lethal blow.

The light above the confessional door turned from red to white, signaling it was time to enter the holy compartment of faith. As he stood to approach the door, he glanced over toward the entrance, and there was the security guard looking directly at him again. He quickly turned his head and ducked into the confessional, closing the door to the small dark absolution booth.

Dylan genuflected onto the old wooden red-padded kneeler, which creaked loudly and felt like it would break. The square framed opening in front of him slid open, producing a light through the white fabric screen.

"Bless me Father, for I have sinned, my last confession was two months ago," Dylan said, while making the Sign of the Cross.

"Yes, my son," spoke a gravelly older voice from the other side of the screen. "What have you done in that time?"

"Father, I have to tell you that I have just listened to Father O'Malley's homily, talking about self-defense as a legitimate action to protect oneself and the others around you, if the aggressor is attacking with the intent of serious harm."

"That is true, and it comes from Saint Augustine," said the priest confessor.

"Yes, and the Gospel of Mark as well, correct?"

"Yes, chapter 22: 35-38. Very good. I see you have come prepared. But this sounds serious."

"Yes, Father, it is very serious. Over the past ten days, I have shot and killed four men in two separate incidents," said Dylan, hearing the priest's breath expelled in surprise of the admission. "In the first attack, two terrorists had taken several hostages, and I went down there for the sole purpose of stopping them from killing anyone else. They had already killed more than twenty people on LaSalle Street."

"Yes, I saw this on the news. You were there?"

"I was close to the Trust First Bank when the news broke and was able to get in through a side door that I saw a janitor running out of that morning. I grabbed the door before it closed and walked toward the main hallway near the entrance. I surprised them. They had four hostages. When they raised their guns toward me, I had to shoot them. I had no choice."

"You're the guy?" the priest said with great excitement, sounding less like a priest confessor and more like a fan.

"Yes Father, I'm the guy," Dylan admitted. "But with you behind the screen, you have to understand that I am intent on protecting my identity. If people find out who I am, I will become a target for so many terrorists, tough guys, and those who view themselves as the fastest gun."

"They say you're really fast!" said the priest, continuing to veer off from his confessional duties.

"Father, each time I'm filled with a sensation, and courage, which I believe is the Holy Spirit."

"The Holy Spirit is guiding you?" voiced the priest.

"I believe it with all my heart, Father. Because when I was visiting my friend at the bank yesterday, and the three thieves came running at us, ready to shoot us, I felt it again. I did plead for them to throw their guns down, but they wouldn't listen."

"I heard that. That was an amazing story!" the priest said in what was becoming a very unusual reconciliation experience.

"I was able to deter the first thief and shot the gun out of his hand. But the other two became enraged and started firing at me. I had to shoot them, Father. I'm sorry. I'm not sorry I shot them. But I'm sorry it came to that. It was absolutely self-defense!" Dylan said, pleading his case.

"Yes, it was, my son. Yes it was," acknowledged the priest. "You have not sinned through your actions. And as a matter of fact, I believe from what you have told me today that perhaps you have been chosen to save those innocent lives which would have been lost had you not been there. This is an important sign."

"That's what I thought, but I just wanted to be sure, to make certain my soul was clean."

"Well, have you done anything else that…."

"No Father, I can't think of anything, but just to be sure. If I have misled anyone, or lied or offended anyone, I ask for God's forgiveness."

"Yes, very good. For your penance, I want you to say five Our Fathers for all the souls of those who died in that tragic attack last week, on

LaSalle Street, as well as the terrorists and thieves," the priest said, administering his penance of forgiveness.

"The terrorists and thieves?" Dylan questioned, challenging the priest's guidance. "I'll pray for those they killed."

"Love thy enemies," the priest stated, citing Jesus' teaching during the Sermon on the Mount.

"I'll pray for those they killed," Dylan insisted, making his position clear on the murderers who ended the lives of so many innocent people, negatively impacting the lives of each of their families forever.

"I understand, now please say the Act of Contrition," the priest stated in an understanding tone.

After Dylan finished reciting the Act of Contrition, the priest said, "I absolve you from your sins in the name of the Father, and of the Son, and the Holy Spirit, Amen. Now go in peace and may the Holy Spirit continue to guide you."

"Thank you, Father," said Dylan, then stood, as the kneeler creaked loudly again. He opened the door, seeing another Franciscan priest dressed in the order's brown cassock, sitting in the pew outside of the confessional. Dylan glanced away quickly, not allowing the priest to see his face.

As he retraced his steps around the back of the pews, he heard the confessional door open. He didn't want to turn around, exposing his identity. He realized the priest in the pew was waiting to relieve the one in the confessional.

As he walked toward the middle of the church, he knew that his coat and hair, the description the news media used for him, would help identify him. He turned slightly to glance over his shoulder toward the priest, who was standing outside the confessional, looking directly at him. Dylan got a good look at the Franciscan but didn't give the priest a full view of his face.

Instead of praying his penance in the pews, Dylan turned right and exited out the glass doors, taking a quick peek to his left where the security guard was once again eyeballing him. He ducked his head down and walked quickly through the center door, down the two steps and back onto the Madison Street sidewalk, melding in with fast-paced pedestrians going East in downtown Chicago.

Fifteen minutes later, he was kneeling in the pews on the right side of Holy Name Cathedral, saying his prayers of penance, while the large pipe organ bellowed the entrance hymn "Holy, Holy, Holy" to begin the noon mass. He prayed for the victims, their families, and to God, thanking the Lord for helping him save the lives of others. He thanked God for filling him with the Holy Spirit and asked for the guidance to stop evil if the day ever came where it confronted him again.

Somehow he knew that day would arrive.

CHAPTER TWENTY-FIVE

Sitting at the small wooden desk in his nicely decorated bedroom, the sun shone through the blue-draped window, making it difficult for Omar to view the video on his iPhone. Blocking the light with his left hand, he played the video over and over again. He couldn't help it. It was such a great moment, a moment of pride for a group of boys who had been picked on for too long.

Seventeen year-old Omar Abadi should never have done it. But he did. He couldn't help himself. He was so proud of his good friend Arman Farzan that he had to share the video of his friend's incredible heroic moment with the world.

After all, Arman, the leader of their close-knit group, just shot the Glock gun out of hand of the MG's Boys' leader, Mazel. He knew no one would ever believe the story, no matter how well he told it, even with the most precise details. They would have to see it for themselves. And Omar recorded all of it on his iPhone. He had all of it, from start to finish. It was all captured so beautifully. Not one incredibly courageous moment was missed.

When Omar posted the sensational video on YouTube at 10 a.m. that Saturday morning, he knew Arman would not be happy with him. But he credited that to his friend's humbleness. Within an hour of being posted, it went viral. By noon, the video had more than twenty-five million hits.

"What are you doing, Omar?" Arman screamed over his cellphone, late that afternoon, once he became aware of the posting. "Take that down! You'll get me killed! Take it down!"

Omar deleted the video, realizing he really hadn't understood all of the ramifications of making it public. But it was too late. Whereas the video was no longer available, the word of mouth spread even faster than the video.

At 5 p.m., two uniformed officers from the Park Hills Police Department knocked on the front door of the Farzan family's red-bricked Park Hills home, which featured a wide cement driveway leading up to their two-car garage and basketball net on the side. Arman's father, Amir, was devastated by the news passed along to him by Officer Matt Durkin, a middle-aged Irish-American policeman standing in his living room with his partner, Donnie Joy.

Both Durkin and Joy couldn't help but notice a crucifix hanging on the wall and fairly large statue of Mary on the end table next to the patterned beige sofa. The entire living room was beautifully decorated with two white armchairs on each side of the sofa, brown mahogany end tables, plush light brown carpeting, and bright white drapes. They were opened to allow the warm sunlight into the room, which exposed a nicely manicured green lawn outside.

"That's a nice statue," said Officer Durkin, raising his eyebrows in amazement, looking over toward his younger partner.

"Thank you," said Amir, with obvious disappointment filling his eyes. He then called upstairs to his son. "Arman, please come down here."

"We bought that at Saint Anne's over on LaGrange Road. They have many beautiful statues," Amir informed the two officers, forcing a smile during the tense moment. "I just wish my son would spend more time going to church with us. He will after this incident, I can promise you that."

"Oh, which church is that, Mr. Farzan?" asked Officer Joy, a late-thirty-something, dark-haired policeman, filled with curiosity about a Middle Eastern family with Christian statues in their home.

"Saint Michael's on 143rd Street," he said. "It's a wonderful parish. They are very welcoming and friendly people. Love Father Mike. He's a smart man! We went through RCIA there."

"Nice! My brother-in-law attends that church. I'll tell him we met you," said Officer Durkin. Amir nodded then saw his son coming down the steps, stopping the second he saw the two police officers.

"Is there something wrong, Father?" the nervous young man asked, having never seen—or believed he ever would see—the police in his home.

"You know what's wrong, Arman. Get the gun and bring it here," instructed his father, working with every ounce of energy to maintain his composure, so disappointed that his son would buy a gun and put himself in such danger. A few minutes later, Arman returned from the garage, where he had hidden the BB gun in a blue duffle bag, stashed in the far corner under an old orange bucket the family never used.

"Thank you Arman," said Officer Joy, taking the black Smith & Wesson MP40. "This is only a BB gun!"

"Yes, sir," said Arman.

"You shot a Glock gun out of that boy's hand with a BB gun?" asked the surprised police officer.

"Yes, sir," said Arman. "It's legal for me to own a BB gun."

"Yes, I know, but on the video, it looked like you shot a real gun."

"No, sir," said Arman. "If you noticed, there wasn't a loud noise, just the clinking noise it makes when you shoot it."

"Wow!" said Officer Joy. "Son, you were very lucky that boy didn't shoot you."

Amir looked at his son with great disappointment.

"But don't worry, Arman," Joy continued. "He will be in custody today. I don't know how you ended up in that predicament, but that boy could have killed you."

Officer Durkin interrupted, "Next time, alert your teachers. They will contact us and we will monitor the situation. As long as your school administrators are aware of this, you will be protected. Do you understand?"

"Yes, sir," said Arman, not wishing to debate the point, knowing he would get nowhere with the argument, even though he did alert Mr. Michaels, who said he was in direct contact with the police. As the two police officers walked out the front door, Arman's father closed the door behind them, turned to his son with a look of extreme anger he had never shown before.

"Are you crazy?" he scolded his youngest son. "A gun? A BB gun against a Glock? You could have been killed!"

"No, Dad, I would have been killed," he informed his father, not feeling the least bit sorry or ashamed of his decision and actions. "I didn't want to bring you and Mother into this again. It's that same gang that came after us with bats last spring. The ones the principal called you about to make sure you were aware of it."

"I thought that was all taken care of," said Amir, calming down a bit.

"It was. The principal called their parents in to alert them of the situation and suspended all six of the boys. They warned them that if it happened again, they would be expelled from the school."

"That's what we were told," said Amir. "So that should have been the end of it."

"It was the end of it last year," explained Arman. "But every year, no matter what happened the previous year, we knew that it wouldn't last. I knew for certain that their leader would go to any length to beat us, even getting a gun. So I got BB gun, just in case."

"A BB gun!" Amir exclaimed in disbelief.

"It turned out I was right," Arman continued. "Because of that attack downtown, it seemed the entire student body glared at anyone who looked like us, all my friends. When school ended, we tried to get to the car in the lot, but they were waiting for us. And that's when he pulled out the Glock gun. So see, no matter what that policeman says, I had only one choice to protect myself and my friends, and I made that choice. And it did save us."

"You shot a Glock gun out of his hand with a BB gun?" said Amir in amazement.

"Yes Father, hit him right in the hand, bullseye!" smiled Arman.

Arman's father dropped his head and sighed loudly, placing the palm of his right hand across his face, realizing his son was right and had made a wise decision. His anger turned to pride, appreciating that his young man had grown up far quicker than he expected.

"I'm sorry, Arman," he said. "You made the right choice, but I just wish you had told me about your concerns. I would have never let you go back to that school."

"I couldn't abandon my friends," said Arman with great conviction. "If I had left, they would have been sitting ducks!"

Amir held out his arms and gave his son a hug of love and support, holding him tightly, so glad he was alive and well. They agreed he would return to school, but Amir and Sofia would first have a meeting with the principal.

Outside the Farzan residence, the two police officers climbed into their black Park Hills Police SUV. Officer Durkin was in the driver's seat. As he drove away, his young partner typed into the vehicle's computer all of the details about the Farzan family and the BB gun. He wanted to know if the police database had any criminal information on the family. Nothing came up.

Two days later, early Monday morning, Amir, Sofia, and Arman sat in Principal Leonard's office. Seated next to them were Omar, Jahan, Gabe, Dabney, and their parents. They were prepared to address the dangerous circumstances.

The video was the main topic of discussion. There were dozens of angry parents outside the main office that morning, withdrawing their students from the school, moving them to one of the private schools in the area, Marist, Providence Catholic, or St. John's Academy. Some were there to demand that Arman and his friends be expelled from school.

They were all afraid for their own children, none of whom had any connection to the fight between the two groups. Bottom line for those parents was not having their children at a school where two of the students were known to have guns and had already fired one.

ooo

As all of this chaos was taking place in the front office of Southwest High in Park Hills, Ziad Haznawi, the only terrorist to escape from the Midwest Trade Building attack, exchanged messages on the Dark Web with his main terrorist contact in Afghanistan. Apparently, Arman's video came to their attention. No one knew it was just a BB gun, but that didn't matter. They knew he was fast and good with a gun.

Ziad was ordered to recruit Arman. The plan was to turn him loose with his weapon among a large crowd of Americans, where his talent would be able to kill dozens of them before being shot and martyred.

Ziad agreed and prepared a plan.

CHAPTER TWENTY-SIX

*I*t all started with a community meeting between the residents, developers, and city officials.

That didn't go well.

Despite the outcome, each resident in a four-block radius just east of Union Square received an offer from LLJ Skyscrapers to purchase their homes.

The offers were low.

For many, however, it was less about the money and more about the neighborhood. Of the 128 homes affected, only twenty-four homeowners were eager to take the offer, all fairly new to the neighborhood. The others were longtime residents, many of whom were born and raised there and had no interest in leaving the community they loved.

News reports of the big bad development company trying to push longtime residents out of their homes had received a great deal of news coverage. One of those residents, Delia Burns, was an experienced public relations professional. She saw an opportunity to use the momentum from the negative news coverage to pressure LLJ to back down and find another place in Chicago for their skyscraper.

Union Park was the perfect place to hold a rally, given the proximity and history. The park was named after federal unions in 1853 and was surrounded by union offices. It was a place to come together as a united front against powerful big-money interests.

And that was exactly what was taking place on this soggy Saturday, September 20. Groups of neighborhood residents and concerned citizens began pouring into Union Park, past the statue of Irish republican hero James Connolly, a leader of the 1920 Irish Revolution. They got up early to show their support for the call to action defined in the press release that was distributed by Burns a few weeks earlier.

Young and old, rich and poor, people of all faiths, every race, creed and color, marched purposely in twos and threes and more toward the near-Westside park. They were inspired by the numerous news stories about LLJ Skyscrapers forcing residents out of their neighborhood so they could construct a forty-story building, uprooting longtime residents.

The smell of the morning rain still filled the air in Union Park, the wet grass trampled and slippery. A mix of concerned citizens stood together in a large crowd, holding up signs, protesting LLJ's plan.

The sound of Warren Zevon's powerful voice, singing "Lawyers, Guns and Money" blared from the large speakers, arranged on each side of the wide stage which was set up at the front of the park.

Many young faces, students mostly in their late teens and early twenties, walked across the matted down turf, raising up colorful signs reading, "Support the Residents!" "Say No to LLJ!" "Stick Your Skyscraper Up Your Ass!" They pumped their fists in unity with each slogan as they shouted out, "No skyscraper! No skyscraper! No skyscraper!"

Television news vans from every station in Chicago were parked along Warren Boulevard on the south side of the park. Reporters with camera crews milled among the masses conducting interviews. Helicopters and drones buzzed overhead, filming the event.

Despite the obvious and overwhelming reaction against LLJ, the multi-million dollar corporation sent representatives to speak at the rally. Certainly, they didn't send an LLJ executive for fear of being attacked. Instead, they would be represented by an executive from their public relations firm, Reputation Builders, and lawyer from their legal firm, Slagle & Sharp.

That was the information that got Dylan's attention, knowing his former high school friend, Teddy Webb, would be there to represent his client. Like the slick-looking, gray-suited and overtly-tanned PR executive from the public relations firm, Teddy had requested a few minutes on the agenda from Delia Burns.

The accomplished young lawyer was intent on speaking about the positive aspects of building the skyscraper in the neighborhood, part of the continuing development of the West Loop. He believed that once he started speaking, he could make a strong case and win over the majority of those affected, as well as those who attended to protest against his client.

When Dylan entered the park that morning, he made a deliberate attempt to change his look just enough to place doubt in the minds of those who may give him the once-over. Attending a large public event, he wanted to deter anyone who would point at his coat, his hair, and resemblance to the movie star to whom he was so often compared. He visited a barber for a slightly shorter haircut, just enough to look a bit different. He also began growing a slight beard, the popular facial fashion of the day. Ray-Ban Classic Aviator sunglasses were the final touch on his mini-makeover, somewhat hiding his identity.

After making his confession at St. Peter's Church a week earlier, the security guard at the church did an interview with WLS-TV News. He revealed that he saw Chicago's hero at the church and had the video from the security camera to prove it. That's when the video was shown on the screen with a grainy longshot of Dylan walking down the steps of the church and out the front door. He could be seen from the side, but not his face, so his identity was still unknown.

"I believe that was him," said long-time security guard, Bob Anderson, who was standing next to the priest who had listened to Dylan's confession. "He fits the description. Looks just like that movie star. You know that Bradley guy from the Jason Bourne movies."

"You mean Matt Damon or…?" asked WLS reporter Stacey Rocco.

"No, no, not him. Cooper, you know, that Cooper guy! You know, he was in that movie where he was on the front of the boat with that lady, and then he was a sniper in the army and kills a bunch of the bad guys," said the confused security guard. "I'm not sure. He looks like one of those movie stars, though."

Rocco rolled her eyes then turned to interview the priest. Dylan felt his anger rise, believing the priest was selling him out. He then watched the priest speak to the reporter, "Look we don't know if that is the man. He fits the description, but there are thousands of young men who look just like him. I don't believe that's him."

Dylan felt relieved that the priest didn't break the sanctity of the confessional. He knew the man in the video was the hero and obviously was working to keep Dylan's identity secret. The security guard, on the other hand, was hoping to collect the $10,000 reward being offered by Trust First Bank, which wanted to publicly thank the hero that stopped the robbery at their main downtown bank. And while they were at it, Dylan was certain that they would use his image to promote their bank. $10,000 would be a small price to pay for that level of advertising.

As Rocco was signing off, the security guard jumped into the shot and said, "I know it. It was that movie, *Titanic*. And I don't want to ruin the ending, but the boat sank! Then he did those Vegas movies, you know with Andy from that show, *The Office*."

Rocco once again rolled her eyes, turned to the camera, and said, "Back to you, Katie."

Dylan walked to an opening on the fringe of the crowd to watch the event, providing himself with a quick escape if anyone started pointing him out as the hero. He took out a Virginian cigar and placed it between his lips to complete the look.

He scanned the large crowd in the park and began laughing to himself when he saw several men, dressed in long black coats. They each had long hair combed back to the right, obviously copying the look provided by the rendering from the Police sketch artist that had been shown on news programs across the world. Dylan started counting them, and there were at least eight, but two were in their mid-forties, wearing wigs, and looked absolutely ridiculous.

He didn't quite understand why they were at the rally or why they were copying him. For attention, he wondered. Then he watched young women, very attractive young women, approach a few of the more legitimate looking copycats. Big beautiful smiles and looks of admiration from the pretty ladies, giddy with delight, requesting photos and hugs with the hero-imitators. Ah, now Dylan understood. He had heard of men dressing up as U.S. Marines, Vietnam or Gulf War veterans, heroic servicemen, to elicit this type of response. Now they had a new ploy.

He watched a well-dressed, professional-looking, middle-aged lady step to the microphone. "Hello, my name is Delia Burns. I am a resident of the neighborhood and would like to thank all of you for coming out on this soggy morning."

Cheers rose in the park for the well-spoken PR expert. As Dylan listened to Burns' strong encouragement to residents to stay unified against

LLJ, he glanced over to see two young men in their twenties, one tall and thin and the other short and pudgy, pointing at him. Dylan actually felt much better about his chances of not being identified, now that the copycat heroes were spread across the park, taking photos with their new admirers.

He walked away from the two inquisitive-looking strangely-dressed men, staying on the fringe of the crowd. Chewing on his unlit stogie, he heard someone behind him say, "Who are you supposed to be? You're not the hero. You're just another copycat trying to pick up chicks. Is that it?"

Dylan turned to see the two curious young men laughing. He took his stogie out, looked at them in their short tight jeans and matching multi-colored t-shirts, and just smiled. They backed up a few steps, apparently threatened enough by the thought that Dylan might actually be the hero.

"You'd better be careful," said the tall, thin, bristle-faced nerd, in a noticeably high-pitched voice, blurting out a slight nervous laugh. "The terrorists are looking for that guy, and if they think it's you, you're dead!"

Dylan put his unlit stogie back into his mouth and just nodded at the two laughing jokesters. He walked away, now feeling confident that the changes to his look were working. Once a good distance away from his two detractors, he turned toward the stage to watch the next speaker introduced by Burns. Dylan recognized him immediately.

"Hello, my name is Drew Jeffries," said the tall, blond-haired, athletic-looking young man, who had quickly gained notoriety throughout Chicago and the nation as the hostage from the terrorist attack who had stepped out of the bank to let the police know the terrorists had been killed, ending the crisis.

A long and loud applause erupted. "I think many of you know that I was one of the hostages in the terrorist attack just nine days ago. Well, I'm a resident of this neighborhood as well. And I think LLJ should build their skyscraper somewhere else!"

The crowd erupted in applause.

"After what I went through with those terrorists, I can tell you that I was inspired by that hero to step up and help, whenever I can. Today, I believe I can help, which is why I'm here.

"Like all of you, I witnessed a horrific scene that morning. And then when I was taken hostage with the others, we were so lucky to get out of there alive! So lucky that the brown-haired man in the long coat appeared when he did. He saved all of our lives. I'm sure of it.

"Some of you have heard what took place inside the building that day from our accounts given to the news media. But I can't begin to tell you how blessed we all feel that we are alive. That man was so fast drawing his gun and killing those two terrorists. So fast! Those terrorists were bullies and Dylan stopped them. Well, I think the executives at LLJ are a bunch of bullies too! And we should stop them!"

Clapping, cheering, and whistles expressed the appreciation for that attitude that so many shared in the park that day. Dylan smiled. A few of the imitators reacted to the applause, waving to the crowd, as if acknowledging their valiant act of courage. Dylan laughed. Drew Jeffries thanked the crowd and walked off the stage as a large group of young women and girls surrounded him, asking for his autograph.

"We have promised time to representatives of LLJ," said a serious-faced Burns. "We want to be fair to the company that wants to throw you out of your longtime homes for a much lower price than you would get if you sold it yourself. Our next speaker is from the law firm of Slagle & Sharp representing LLJ. Please give a polite welcome to Ted Webb."

Boos and hisses were mixed with commentaries, "You suck!" "Skyscrapers suck!" "Leave our neighborhood alone!" were being shouted from every area of the park at the man Dylan knew as Teddy.

A smattering of loud cheers and yelps could barely be heard from the few supporters, most likely young professionals from the PR firm planted there to voice their fake support. As lawyer Webb strode up to the podium, he was completely unfazed by the negative reception. He looked like he was more than a little familiar with this type of reaction. He raised his arms to try and quiet down the crowd.

"Please settle down, everyone, settle down," he said, hoping to be able to make his statement and get off the stage as quickly as possible. "I just have a statement I would like to read."

More boos, louder boos.

"Bullies! You represent bullies!" yelled out one angry man in the crowd about fifty yards from Dylan. The livid man was standing with two other very angry men, similarly dressed. They didn't look like upset residents who attended just to voice their dissent against LLJ. Somehow, there was a distinct difference. These were hard, tough, mean-looking men who were booing aggressively to express their disdain. They were wearing military caps, army fatigues, black shirts, and black pants.

Dylan had noticed them earlier but didn't think much of it. Now they had his full attention. He wondered if they were militarists upset that big business and big money were pushing around people who seemingly had no say in the future of their homes. City Hall was behind the development, so Dylan wondered if they were there because they were anti-government, anti-establishment. That's what it looked like to him.

While Teddy prepared to speak, the anger and hate in the form of shouting was most definitely being directed toward his high school pal. The energy behind the hateful words set off Dylan's instincts. He felt that now familiar tingling run up his spine, a definite signal that something bad was about to happen.

"I just want all of you to know that we are extremely sorry for those neighborhood residents who will be displaced by the new beautiful skyscraper, which will draw major tax dollars to your area supporting schools and businesses," said Teddy with a serious but somewhat friendly look on his face. "The building will make this great neighborhood even greater!"

"Shut up and get off the stage, asshole!" yelled one of the tough-looking men in front of Dylan, receiving a smattering of applause for his foulmouthed statement.

"As you know, just twenty-five years ago, the development started in earnest on the near West Side of Chicago. The hard work and effort replaced poor housing and dilapidated buildings with big beautiful condos, restaurants, shops, and entertainment venues," Teddy continued. "What was once Skid Row on Madison Street is now an attractive and thriving destination for many. That work was done in the name of progress, economic development. Who would rather have Skid Row still there?"

"We would!" yelled another one of the militarists in front of Dylan. "Take your skyscraper and shove it up your ass!"

A loud applause followed, and Dylan watched the three men slapping high fives. That's when he noticed a gray bag on the ground in front of them. It looked like a rifle bag.

He felt his spine tingle again and started walking toward the men. The two jokester nerds jumped in front of him, both getting right up in his face, blocking his line of sight.

"What are you going to do, hero, huh?" said the short pudgy nerd. Dylan felt adrenaline shoot through him, knowing there was danger in the park. He quickly moved the two jokesters to the side, trying to see the five militarists. It was too late.

A series of loud pops shot through the air, bullets sprayed across the stage. Teddy was hit and fell backwards. The slick PR executive was shot in the head, dropping to the stage floor, dead. Delia Burns sprinted for the wings, diving for cover, the bullets just missing her. People in the crowd ran, sprinted, dove behind trees, anything to avoid being hit by bullets.

The eight Dylan pretenders all ran away. A few of them tossed off their coats so they wouldn't be mistaken for the hero and shot. The area directly in front of the stage cleared out quickly, creating a large opening.

Dylan was nearly trampled, but he could see the shooter. One of the militarists held an AR-15 assault rifle and was firing at the stage. His two comrades stood by his side holding Glock guns to protect him in case anyone charged at them. The shooter finished his clip and went to reload.

People were running and screaming. Several police officers assigned to the rally came running across the park toward the shooter, guns drawn. Dylan got there first.

"Drop the guns!" shouted Dylan at the three domestic terrorists, only ten feet in front of him. The two loyal comrades holding Glock guns, recognized him immediately, dropped their guns and ran away, leaving their AR-15 sniper alone to face the fastest gun.

The shooter, dressed in military fatigues, his head shaved, and tattoos across both arms, had his back to Dylan. He snapped his magazine into his gun and glanced over his shoulder to see Dylan standing with arms at his sides, his coat pulled back, showing his pearl-handled Smith & Wesson.

"Drop it or I'll drop you!" warned Dylan, still trying to give the crazy skinhead killer a chance to live.

A sinister smile grew on the shooter's ugly, bony, narrow face, as he turned as fast as he could to shoot. But it wasn't fast enough. With lightning speed, Dylan drew his gun, and squeezed off three shots from his six-shooter. All three bullets were direct hits to the chest of the military-fatigued man with the dark smile, sending the assailant backwards, the assault rifle flying up into the air and landing on the ground. As the shooter lay lifeless on the wet grass, three Chicago Policemen sprinted up to the scene. Dylan holstered his gun and proceeded to meet them where the shooter laid bleeding.

A short, twenty-nine-year-old, athletic-looking Italian cop, was the first one to arrive. He bent down to check the shooter, then looked up and said, "He's dead."

"Sorry, he gave me no choice," said Dylan.

"I know. We saw it," said the nodding police officer, standing up as five other blue-uniformed men from his unit arrived breathless from the two-hundred-yard sprint. "We all know. That was amazing. Are you the…?"

"Yeah," said Dylan. "I got to go check that fellow up there. He's a friend of mine."

"Yeah, yeah, go ahead," said the policeman, smiling. "We'll take care of him. But we will definitely need to talk with you to get a statement. I'm Officer Panozzo, Greg Panozzo."

Dylan just nodded then ran toward the stage where doctors and nurses were working on those who had been shot. He saw Teddy lying in the center of the stage, his blood on the stage floor. A doctor, one of the residents from the neighborhood, was working on the wound when Dylan walked up. "Is he going to be all right?"

"Yes," said the doctor. "He was shot twice in upper right shoulder, but one just grazed him."

"Teddy, it's me, Dylan," he said to his friend, who was in terrible pain. "Hang in there, Teddy. I'll stay with you."

Teddy recognized his old friend, and a smile appeared despite the pain. As he was carried toward the ambulance, Dylan glanced at the white sheet over the PR executive.

A few minutes later, he gave Officer Panozzo a statement and his contact information.

"Hey, we will work to keep this under wraps," Panozzo said, fully aware of the importance of protecting Dylan's identity. But Dylan knew better. Once it was logged into the database on the police computer, it was over. He knew someone would go to the bank with the information to collect that $10,000.

But at that moment, he really didn't care. He was more concerned about his friend Teddy. He flagged down the ambulance as it was leaving. He appealed to the two paramedics in the front seat to let him ride in the back with his friend. The two young women looked at each other, then back at Dylan, realizing they were talking to America's hero.

"Yes, absolutely you can ride with us," said the tall brunette paramedic. "Anything for you, Dylan."

Dylan smiled. Then he quickly climbed into the back of the ambulance where Teddy was being administered to by the neighborhood doctor.

"Hang in there, Teddy," said Dylan. "You've got a lot of great people working to make sure you will be okay."

Teddy looked at his pal and nodded, knowing he was lucky to be alive.

CHAPTER TWENTY-SEVEN

The familiar sound of shuffling feet meshed with young voices in energetic conversation moved through the halls of Southwest High on this sunny Tuesday morning in September.

A large crowd of backpacked students in light fall coats and sweatshirts maneuvered through the human chaos to their lockers. Freshman next to senior, sophomore next to junior, was the universal scene stretching all the way down the long corridor in each of the eight hallways of the massive school. Bleary-eyed students stood in front of their slim beige storage compartment, organizing their books, preparing for first period class before the bell rang.

When Arman entered the school with his four friends that Tuesday morning, they really didn't know what to expect. Arman's father instructed him not to let anyone goad him into an argument or a fight.

After the meeting in the principal's office the previous day, he was aware there were a host of parents who didn't want "those Arab kids!" in the school, even though those "Arab kids" were really "American kids," and just as American as their own kids.

Arman was taken home after the meeting with Ben Leonard. His father hoped that the principal could get things in order before his son returned to the school. But he also used that afternoon to meet with James Hushing, the long-time respected principal of St. John's Academy where Amir considered transferring his son.

On the tour of the Catholic college preparatory school, with a stellar reputation as one of the best high schools in the nation, several of the students recognized Arman immediately. There was no avoiding the infamy created by the YouTube video. Thomas Nolan, the assistant principal leading the tour, had heard about the famous video but hadn't seen it. The reaction of the students was the only aspect of the tour that Mr. Farzan and his son needed to see.

Driving out of the school's parking lot that morning, they knew transferring to another school, even a private Catholic school, wouldn't wipe the slate clean. And if he were to transfer, they most definitely wanted a clean slate. Without a fresh start, there was no point in transferring. Plus, it was his senior year and Arman did not want to abandon his friends. So by the time they left St. John's, the decision was easy. He was going back to Southwest High to finish his senior year.

The next day, when Arman and his four friends entered the front doors of Southwest High, they were prepared for every negative comment, or look, directed their way. They convinced themselves that the negativity would dissipate in a few weeks and things would go back to normal. At least that was their hope.

Walking quickly with the crowd of students through the foyer, they searched for the band of bullies. No sign of the thugs. Arman wanted to be hopeful and optimistic. Maybe it was all over and he could just be a student again. That was his prayer to God at St. Michael's Church each Sunday.

When the five boys turned down the hall toward their lockers, however, all of a sudden, Arman saw out of the corner of his eye a tall, muscular senior boy coming right at him. Arman turned quickly, preparing for a fight. He no longer had his BB gun, so this would have to be a fist fight.

"Hey, Arman!" said a smiling Mickey Hern, the always stiff-necked, perfectly-postured, athletic-looking, brown-haired young man.

Arman froze. He didn't know how to respond to the most popular boy at the school being nice to him.

"I know a lot of the kids here are pretty afraid of you right now, but I just want you to know, I get it," offered Hern, wearing his number eleven jersey, since there was a pep rally scheduled for later that day. "I know what Mazel and his punk friends were trying to do to you. Honestly, I'm sorry I didn't get involved. I'm supposed to be one of the student leaders at this school, and I did nothing but watch. I'm very sorry."

Mickey Hern was the quarterback of the football team and point guard on the basketball team. When he reached out his hand, Arman smiled somewhat skeptically but shook the hand of the high school's "Big Man on Campus."

"I appreciate it, Mickey," he said, stepping back to introduce his friends. "These are my pals, Omar, Jahan, Dabney, and Gabe."

"Hey fellas," said the square-jawed senior, who at six-foot-two, towered over them as he shook hands with each. "I'm Mickey. And again, I'm sorry. But one thing I can tell you that I think you will appreciate. Coach Michaels told me yesterday afternoon that Mazel and every one of his friends transferred out."

"What?" blurted Omar, the collective jaws of the five Persian Warriors dropping all at once.

"Yep, apparently once that video came out, their parents realized their boys were out of control. I don't know if it's true, but supposedly, Mazel avoided jail time by agreeing to register at a military academy in Indiana."

"Oh my goodness!" said Arman, now smiling widely. "Are you certain of this, Mickey?"

"I know for certain they transferred out, but am not certain about where they will be going," he informed them.

The five close friends, who had literally been tested in battle together, were ecstatic, giving each other high fives, yelping with joy. Mickey stood to the side watching this display of happiness, realizing he had made their day. His girlfriend, Peggy Hake, a pretty brunette who was also an honor roll student, approached them.

"Hey, Arman," she said, holding her backpack in her left hand and extending her right hand out to shake.

"Hello, Peggy," Arman said, shaking hands with her, ignoring Mickey's surprised look.

"Where did you learn to shoot a gun like that?" Peggy asked. "Everyone wants to know!"

"Well, let's just say, it's a bit of natural skill. And practice makes perfect," he laughed, seeing a puzzled look on the quarterback's face, given his girlfriend's strong interest in the real high school hero. "But I have no intention of picking one up again. And Mickey just gave us the good news that the band of bullies have all transferred out."

"Oh, well that is good news!" she said, jumping up to give her boyfriend a high five.

A few hours later, Arman and company were called into Mr. Michaels' class during the first lunch period at 11 a.m. The football coach, who had sincerely wanted to help the boys, finally had a happy look on his face.

"Boys," he said to them, each seated in a desk at the front of the classroom. "I have some really great news for you. You'll never guess what happened."

Arman chimed in quickly, "Mazel and his band of bullies transferred out!"

Mr. Michael's smile dropped, "Wait, how did you know?"

"Mickey told us," said Omar, laughing as he realized the quarterback ruined the surprise for his coach.

"Last time I tell him anything. Big mouth!" said Michaels, now laughing along with the boys. "Great news though, eh, fellas?"

"You ain't kidding, coach," said Gabe, who had barely said a word to anyone at the school the entire year.

"Wait, Gabe. You talk?" joked the coach.

"Only on the days when the bullies transfer out," he laughed.

"Hey, when did Gabe get funny?" asked Arman. "Coach Michaels, thanks for trying. I mean, we know you tried to help, and I just want you to know we appreciate it."

"Well, after seeing that video, I don't really think you need much help, Arman," laughed the tall educator with a bigger heart. "I mean, you are really quick. Do you play any sports?"

"Just soccer, and I fool around a little with basketball on my driveway at home, but that's it," said the young leader, smiling at the recognition for his skills. "And now that this is all resolved, and with Coach Waller getting fired, I'm going back out to play on the soccer team. And so are all my buddies. Right guys?"

Gabe jumped up, thrusting his right hand in the air, "Soccer!" Everyone just looked at the small, thin young man, who apparently had the weight of the world lifted off of his shoulders.

After leaving Coach Michaels' classroom and going to the cafeteria before their lunch period ended, Arman and his friends were really surprised at how many students approached them, expressing how cool it was to see them back down the bullies that everyone at the school feared and despised. It was easily their best and happiest day at Southwest High, and they all hoped it would never end.

This was the first day in three years that they didn't have to wait for each other to walk down the halls together. They didn't have to scan the halls, search the crowd of students, looking for the bullies. Finally, they were free of the anxiety that had filled their lives for too long. And it felt wonderful!

As the smiling boys walked out of the school that Tuesday, Arman called them together at the entrance doors.

"Hey, we don't have to go to JavaPlace every Tuesday afternoon any longer fellas," said Arman. "No more meetings to plan our defense against Mazel. It's over! So I got an idea. How about we meet up at the Park Hills fields and let's play some soccer?"

"Oh yeah, I'm in!" Gabe shouted out.

"Me too!" said Omar, Jahan, and Dabney, almost in unison, smiling so wide, so happy. They were high school kids again, now allowed to enjoy their youth instead of fearing for their lives. It was a new day.

As the boys broke apart to head for their bus or car, Arman asked, "Anyone need a ride?"

"Not today, Arman," said Dabney. "We can actually take the bus home for once, thank goodness."

Arman walked toward his Toyota Forerunner. As he drew closer, he noticed someone sitting in a beat-up looking blue Chevy Impala parked next to his truck. His heart dropped. Maybe this wasn't over.

Worse, he didn't have his gun any longer. He stopped thinking about it and instinctively knew that he had better run. A man stepped out of the Impala and yelled, "Arman!"

Arman had never before seen the curly haired Middle Eastern man, dressed in black shirt and black jeans. He wondered how he knew his name.

"Who are you?" Arman asked, still prepared to run.

"My name is Ziad," said the unknown man. "I would like to talk to you."

"Okay, so talk," said Arman, beginning to slowly backup toward the school, while keeping his eye on this stranger who knew his name.

"You are going to need to come with me. I need your help," said Ziad Haznawi, resting his left arm on the top of the open car door.

"Help you with what?"

"Well, I'm sure you are familiar with the term Al-Qaeda, right?"

"I'm not a terrorist!" Arman proclaimed.

"Yes, but I am," said Ziad, and watched Arman, turn and sprint away. "I have your parents!" he shouted out. Arman stopped abruptly and turned back toward the man.

"What?" he said loud enough for him to hear. "What did you say?"

"I said I have your parents, Amir and Sofia Farzan," he said, holding up his iPhone, too far away for Arman to see. "If you don't come with me, I will order them to be killed."

The young Persian American's head started spinning. His heart was pounding. He looked at the evil man who had not only ruined one of the happiest days of his life, but possibly his future.

"I saw the video," said the sick-minded Al-Qaeda terrorist. "You're good with a gun, and you're going to help me kill Americans!"

Arman just stood limp, lifeless, depressed. He looked up to Heaven, praying for help. Tears poured down his cheeks as he pleaded, "God, please help me!"

CHAPTER TWENTY-EIGHT

The traffic on South Michigan Avenue was fairly light on this Sunday evening in September. The sun was still bright, fully reflecting off the calm waters of Lake Michigan.

Pete Burns, a middle-aged Irishman wearing an old White Sox cap, continued checking the rearview mirror of his black GMC Envoy. He wondered what the long blond-haired Uber passenger in his back seat was doing, jostling around the contents of an unzipped brown canvas bag, which clanked loudly with each movement. Apparently some type of metal was inside, and Burns' instincts were on high alert. The clanking container looked like a rifle bag—he was quite familiar with bags like it from his days as a Chicago Police officer, although he was now retired and driving to help pay the bills.

His tired and anxious-looking passenger zipped up the brown canvas rifle bag then grabbed his rumpled newspaper, opened it, and began reading. Burns could easily see the *Chicago Tribune*'s front page had two large headlines, "Shootout in Union Park!" And, "Dorgan Stalker Killed!"

He pulled his 2012 Envoy up to the entrance of the famed Hilton Hotel at 720 South Michigan. The troubled-looking passenger climbed out with the crumpled *Tribune* in his right hand and clanking brown rifle bag in his left. The Irishman just watched him, his police instincts taking over, wondering what he was planning.

As he closed the door, his blue denim jacket opened up just enough for Burns to see the shirt he was wearing. He watched the strange looking fellow walk into the thick gold revolving doors of the hotel. Burns then spotted a police office, sitting in his new Chevy Tahoe SUV just a few hundred feet in front of him. Feeling a sense of urgency, he quickly pulled up next to the cop.

"Hey!" said Burns, waving his right arm, trying to get the officer's attention. The young uniformed man took a bite of his old fashioned Dunkin donut. Burns continued waving. The officer continued chewing his old and hardened baked good.

Exasperated, Burns laid on his horn. It startled the cop, who finally opened his window.

"Good evening, officer, I'm Pete Burns, retired CPD," he said, his Irish-accent quite evident.

The officer nodded his recognition. Then he took another bite of his stale donut, all the while looking directly at Burns, continuing to listen.

"I'm driving for Uber and just had a passenger that looked a bit strange," he continued. "He a had brown canvas rifle bag that may have had a weapon inside of it. Also, he was wearing an American flag shirt. It just seemed strange. Thought I'd better let you know."

The information was so incredibly important to the officer that he took another bite of his donut, sip of his large coffee, and said, "Thanks! That's good to know." Then he closed his window.

Burns drove off, shaking his head in disbelief, "Young cops! Not worth a damn! Glad I never ate donuts! Young cops!"

CHAPTER TWENTY-NINE

*A*s Haydon Huff walked to the elevators in the Hilton, his mind was filled with the *Tribune*, "Dorgan Stalker Killed." His head had been buzzing all day, since first seeing the newspaper early that morning on the floor of his apartment's reception area. He knew his best friend, Paul Cavon, must have reached a point of extreme frustration. His columns in *The Bleeder*, reporting on the corruption of the Dorgan administration, were being dismissed. The analytics showed fewer and fewer readers of his columns each week. That downward trend would have made sense to anyone in the news business, except Paul Cavon.

Jimmy Dorgan had been out of office for more than three years, and no one cared about his administration any longer. It was over, long gone. Yet, Cavon was convinced that he could expose the former mayor's corruption while in office and perhaps win a Pulitzer Prize for his investigative reporting. He hoped to become the next Mike Royko, Chicago's most legendary newspaper columnist, who had exposed the City Hall corruption of Jimmy's father, James J. Dorgan, considered the last Boss Mayor in America.

Huff was probably the only person in the country who could understand Cavon's obsession with the Dorgans, since he felt the same level of disdain, given his own father's battles with Chicago's most powerful family. However, he never imagined Cavon would show up at Dorgan's condo with a snub-nosed .38 ready to shoot him.

Huff suspected that the two security guards at the entrance were both former Chicago cops and recognized Cavon before he entered the

Lakeshore Drive condo. The *Tribune* story detailed how they unloaded nineteen rounds into him, leaving his bloody body lying on the red-stained cement walkway, where two staffers from the Coroner's Office picked him up and hauled him to the Cook County Morgue on Harrison Street.

The details in that front-page *Tribune* story, and the decision by his friend, were all the motivation Haydon needed for his new plan. Like his friend Cavon, he planned to go out in a blaze of Millippie glory!

A few hours later, just before 7:30 p.m., with the sun setting on this cool and breezy Sunday evening, Huff was positioned on the northeast corner of the roof of the Hilton.

He looked down on Michigan Avenue at the exact same spot where forty-six years earlier, on August 28, 1968, dozens of Chicago Police officers used billy clubs to beat down rioting protestors.

As a youth, Huff had watched the old television footage of that scene many times on a VCR in his father's Boston apartment. Embedded in his memory were the images of an army of Chicago cops dragging the bloodied bodies of hippies and Yippies across the black asphalt, and throwing them into the back of one of the many Chicago Police paddy wagons lined up on Balbo Street.

Huff knew his father instigated all of it, telling the protestors to put razor blades into the front of their shoes and kick the police in the shins. He told them to fill baggies full of feces and urine and throw them at the cops. Haydon heard all the stories directly from his father.

Now, he stood right above that historical landmark, holding his M-14 rifle, ready to finally pay back the pigs.

Once the sun had completely set, Huff looked through the sight of his rifle, pointed down over the cement corner of the massive red-bricked building. He waited for the next blue & white Chicago Police vehicle to pass in front of him on Michigan Avenue.

The Millipie leader of one follower, himself, had been to the gun range several times over the previous weeks and was certain he had improved his marksmanship. He was prepared to die that day but was committed to taking as many Chicago cops as he could with him.

Just then, he saw a Chicago Police SUV making an illegal U-turn from the front of the hotel and was headed north on Michigan Avenue. Huff pointed his gun and looked through the sight at what looked to be a fairly young cop.

He took aim and blam! The SUV kept moving as a flock of pigeons twenty feet away from the police vehicle suddenly flew up into the air to avoid the stray bullet that had just missed them. The cop looked around frantically after hearing the recognizable gunfire. People in front of the hotel heard the shot as well and scurried inside or away from the building.

Haydon took aim again, this time directly at the officer's thick head of black hair. Blam! He hit the front tire, which exploded, abruptly halting the Chevy SUV. The young police officer jumped out and ran around the front of the vehicle to take cover on the passenger side. He pulled out his Glock 22 and pointed it straight out, while scanning the area in front of him, looking for the shooter.

With his left hand, he called Chicago Police Dispatch for backup. That's when another shot rang out. It was Haydon's most accurate, hitting the cop in his left forearm. The jolt knocked him backwards to the ground. He screamed out in great pain. His phone landed on the pavement with the police dispatcher's voice heard, "Officer are you okay? Officer..."

In what seemed like only seconds to the lone Millippie, dozens of Chicago Police vehicles with flashing lights and sirens blaring, came speeding up to Balbo and Michigan.

Huff, now on his belly to stay out of sight, looked down. He heard the screeching of cars stopping quickly. He peeked over the top to see an army of cops jumping out of their high tech vehicles. They took cover and pointed their assault rifles upward, scanning the area for the shooter's position.

Haydon Reuben Huff, proudly wearing his father's American flag shirt, was certain these were his last few moments on Earth. As his last desperate act of revolt and revenge, he was going to shoot as many rounds as possible at the pigs behind those vehicles, hoping to kill all of them.

He loaded a new twenty-round magazine into his M-14. He then counted three and rose up over the cement to see his targets. He aimed and fired round after round, the hot empty casings flying up and over his shoulder, landing on the white cinder-covered roof.

Once his rifle emptied, he could hear the return rapid fire coming from dozens of automatic assault weapons. Bullets rained over his head, hitting the cement ledge in front of him.

Adrenaline shot through his body, creating an entirely new level of energy. He quickly crawled on his belly toward the door, hoping that he may be able to somehow escape. His courage had departed, replaced by survival instincts. He would need them. The police most certainly knew his position, so his chances of getting away weren't good.

Far enough away from the side of the building, he stood, grabbed his rifle bag, and ran toward the rooftop doorway. Only ten yards away from the door, he watched it open in front of him. He quickly stopped, dropped his rifle bag, and positioned himself on one knee, ready to shoot.

Out of the door stepped the well-known heroic twenty-something year-old man, dressed in his black gabardine overcoat, gray turtle neck, blue jeans, and brown Chukka boots. Haydon immediately recognized him from the many news reports, but also the gun range. What was he doing there?

"Haydon," said Dylan Reilly, hoping to stop the confused man he remembered well from the gun range. "I know who you are."

"I know who you are, too!" said Haydon, taking aim through his rifle sight, Dylan not flinching a bit. "What do you want? Why are you here?"

"I'm hoping to save you from being shot," shouted Dylan over the noise of gunfire in the background. "There's more than fifty police officers down there ready to shoot you."

"Yeah, I caught that. As a matter of fact, I couldn't miss it!"

"If you put down your rifle, you can walk away from this unharmed," implored Dylan.

"Unharmed, I'll be sent back to prison. I hate prison! I don't think I can spend another day there."

"Well, it's that or…"

"Escaping!" he shouted, then began to squeeze the trigger of his M-14. But before he could do so, Dylan with lighting fast speed drew his pearl-handled six-shooter. Blam! Blam! He shot the rifle right out of Huff's hands, sending it flying five feet away.

"How the hell did you…. I'm getting out of here!"

"I don't think so," said Dylan.

Haydon dove for his rifle. Dylan shot it again, sending it flying farther away from him. Haydon landed hard on his belly, grabbing a handful of cinders and face full of dust.

It was at that moment that Andy Huff's son realized he never had the courage to go out in a blaze of glory. He was never brave enough to do anything that required courage. He stood slowly, his arms held up high.

"Okay, I'll go in," he said, huffing and puffing from the exhaustion of the past few minutes. "I guess I am better off alive. Who knows, maybe some politician will pardon me."

Dylan just smirked, "You never know, but I can tell you that you are smart to surrender, because if the police had arrived here first...."

"Yeah I know," Haydon responded. "They got my friend yesterday. That's why I'm here tonight. Payback! They brought my father down! They brought my best friend down! And now I guess they are going to bring me down."

"Yes, but at least you'll still be alive."

"Yes, at least I'll still be alive!"

Just then, two police helicopters simultaneously ascended up from the north and east corners of the Hilton, snipers positioned with assault weapons aimed directly at Huff.

"Oh shit!" he said, watching them open up on him, more than four dozen rounds, hitting him at a rapid rate; Dylan ducked back inside the door to avoid the gunfire.

A few minutes later, a SWAT team arrived on the roof and found the bullet-riddled and bloodied body of Haydon Reuben Huff lying prone on the white cindered roof.

ooo

When Dylan arrived on the ground floor, the hotel was swarming with police, checking everyone in the lobby. Recognized immediately by a tall middle-aged officer posted at the entrance, he was given a respectful nod and allowed to exit through the revolving doors.

He decided to make the two-mile walk back to his apartment to clear his head. Haydon Huff! His last moments on the roof of the Hilton was all he could think about.

Earlier that evening, when he first heard his police scanner announce a shooter was on the roof of the Hilton and believed to be Haydon Huff, he certainly wasn't expecting to find the strange fellow he saw at the gun range. But now it made sense. Now he understood why the long-haired, American-flag-shirt-wearing fellow was practicing with an M-14 rifle.

Dylan was grateful that Huff's moment of vengeance didn't kill or seriously injure any police officers. He learned later that the only police officer hit was a young cop, who was bandaged up and back on the job the next day. His only other casualty was the front tire of the Chevy SUV, which was quickly replaced.

Later that evening, as Dylan Reilly sat in the living room of his west side apartment sipping a glass of William Hill chardonnay and watching the news accounts of the event, he couldn't help but feel badly for Huff. From his experience as a high school teacher, he knew all too well that kids are products of their parents. It was confirmed for him at every parent-teacher night.

He knew nothing about Haydon's mother, but was well-versed about his father, whom he had addressed in his history classes each year. Dylan could never respect Andy Huff and felt sorry for his son and the circumstances he was born into, so sad, so tragic.

Later that evening, he prayed for Haydon Reuben Huff, a lost soul living in a world of confusion, now finally at peace.

CHAPTER THIRTY

The expansive shadow from the tall silver Good Shepherd statue fell over Dylan, who was standing over Darlene's grave. He felt so frustrated, staring at the newly placed black headstone. He read the right side of the four-foot tall marble stone:

Darlene Marie Reilly (Quilty)
Loving Wife & Daughter
Dedicated Social Worker
Mary Pray for Her
May 1, 1986 – August 3, 2014

As strange and frustrating as it was to see those words, it was even more bizarre for Dylan to look at the left side of the headstone, which read:

Dylan Michael Reilly
March 17, 1986 -

One day that gap between his name and dates would be filled in with statements about his life's story. He hoped that he still had plenty of chapters to be written.

Nonetheless, his wife's life had been edited down to just twenty-eight years. She spent three decades selflessly helping others, placing everyone else first, loving her family and friends, and always trying to do the right thing.

Dylan knew there would never be a better testament to a Christian life than Darlene's time on earth. She was truly a devout Catholic.

Standing there gazing at the monument, he knew that if he were given another sixty years, he would never achieve the goodness and grace of his wife. He could no longer use her as his role model, given his latest calling to defend himself and others with a gun. That was a choice Darlene would never support, and Dylan knew it.

The newly planted grass in front of the headstone was already starting to grow, which signaled to Dylan that his wife had already been there for some time, more than six weeks. He thought of her every day, every hour of every day, nearly every minute of every hour.

How he missed her! How he wished he could have her back. How he wished they would have skipped MusicFest and gone to see a movie instead. Or perhaps gone to MusicFest on Day Three, the day they had originally planned to attend, but were deterred by rain in the forecast.

Oh how gladly Dylan would stand in that rain, pelted by thousands of rain drops, instead of the bullets that filled the sky on Day Two, killing his loving wife. It was so unfair, he thought, grinding his teeth.

With hands together for prayer, he recited the Hail Mary out loud five times. Then, he asked Mary to look over his wonderful wife. He asked Mary to guide her to Heaven. He believed that of anyone he had known over his twenty-eight years, both Darlene and his mother best met the call from Jesus through the Gospels. They lived their faith completely. There was no selfishness, always helping others whenever possible.

Dylan made the sign of the cross to finish his prayers, then paused to consider what he was about to tell his dear departed wife. He looked around to see if anyone was near him. He didn't mind speaking to her out loud but preferred not to be distracted by others in the cemetery.

"Darlene, I know you wouldn't be happy with some of the decisions I have made since you were taken from me," said Dylan, looking directly down at the ground where his wife was resting only a few feet below the grass surface. "But there is no other choice but to be prepared to defend against those evil-minded killers.

"I hate it! You know I hate it! I'm hoping by the time I am called by the Lord that the world will have changed. Believe it or not, I've sort of become a voice people are listening to right now, which is incredibly ironic, since they only started listening to me once they saw how fast I am with a gun. Yes, please don't laugh too hard at that ridiculous fact, but it's true.

"Darlene, I miss you! I miss you so much! I hate life without you. I know it takes time and there is the mourning period. But right now, I just don't see any happiness in my future without you in my life. I don't!

"I'll be here all the time. I can certainly think about you in my head, but when I'm here, I know I am with you and that makes me feel a little better.

"But please watch over me. Give me a nudge if I am making bad decisions. I could use your help. I love you!"

Dylan recited ten more Hail Marys and made the sign of the cross.

"Goodbye, Darlene," he said then walked toward his car. A text began buzzing on his iPhone. As he climbed into his 2008 red Jeep Cherokee, he picked up his phone to read it.

"Dylan, help! The terrorists have taken me and Willie hostage. They want you to come with no gun. We are being taken to the Midwest Trade Building. They will kill us if you don't come. Please let us know you received this. Thanks, Dylan. And I'm so sorry about this. Georgie."

Dylan looked over through the passenger window at the black headstone.

"I may be joining you sooner than I thought, Darlene."

Filled with energy and determination, Dylan sped out the front gates of Good Shepherd Cemetery, intent on saving his friends, even if that meant giving up his own life.

CHAPTER THIRTY-ONE

The muffled sounds of the city outside of the Midwest Trade Building were quieting down about 7 p.m. on this Wednesday evening. Two well-built, tough-looking African American security guards were stationed at the front desk, where they had just begun their eight-hour shift. Both were former military men who had fought in Iraq. They were busy talking about going to the White Sox game together the next day to see the Pale Hose take on the star-studded Yankees.

The Midwest Trade Building was one of the most secure buildings in Chicago. Only two weeks after the terrorist attack on the 22nd floor, scaffolding adorned the front of the building. Heavy-duty dump trucks, large cranes, and bulldozers were parked in front of the legendary structure, where workers would bring them back to life early the next morning.

Ziad Haznawi returned that evening to carry out a different type of terrorist attack. He was going to use the building to kill America's newest hero.

The two uniformed guards were having a grand time talking baseball and never expected the teenage boy entering the front door to be a threat. The young man approached them asking for directions. The minute the guards began pointing Arman in the right direction, Ziad came through the door, firing his 357 Magnum at the unsuspecting guards, cruelly ending the lives of the two very brave men. With no remorse, Haznawi then waved in his other new recruit, Ali, holding Georgie and Willie at gunpoint, just outside the front entrance.

"Let's go. The elevators are right over here," said the demented terrorist, leading them all onto the elevator, destined for the forty-fourth floor, the top of the famed Chicago building.

It was now 7:15 p.m., well past office hours. Only cleaning personnel were scattered throughout the building. Unfortunately, two middle-age Polish ladies were working on the top floor when the elevator door opened and out walked the most wanted man in America.

Haznawi didn't pause when shooting the two innocent women, justifying his sadistic act saying, "Americans! Two more dead Americans! The world is now a better place."

As fearful as Arman felt at that moment, he was also horrified and outraged. How could that man just shoot innocent people? It just served to remind the young Persian-American that his parents were both at the gunpoint of one of Ziad's soldiers in their home, where they would be killed if Arman did not go along with this terrorist attack.

This was the typical protocol for Al-Qaeda or ISIS terrorist groups. Force the young sons out to kill, and if they don't obey, kill their family, the non-combatants. This is explicitly forbidden by the Quran. Yet, the terrorist justifies these acts of violence by cherry-picking statements from the Islamic sacred book.

Although a convert to Catholicism, Arman was well aware that true Muslims know the Quran requires a full reading. Quran 3:8 preemptively calls out people who cherry pick as "perverse" declaring, "Those in whose hearts is perversity seek discord and wrong interpretation of [the Quran]."

He was also well aware that the permission to fight, given in Quran 22:40-41, was only given to "those against whom war is waged." The guidance was clearly for self-defense against aggressors, not peaceful non-aggressors, like Arman, his parents, Georgie, Willie, the two security guards, and the two Polish cleaning women. None of what Ziad was carrying out was justified in the Quran. None of it!

At that moment, on the 44th floor of the Midwest Trade Building, Arman knew he would never be able to convince this misguided, brainwashed murderer of the real truth in the Quran. He just had to try and find a way to survive.

Ziad was determined to use Arman, who was now known throughout the world as a fast and talented gunslinger, thanks to his friend Omar's

YouTube post. Ziad planned to promote Arman as a new recruit of his terrorist cell in Chicago and record him killing Dylan and his two friends Georgie and Willie. He planned to post the video on the Dark Web to draw new recruits and send it to the Associated Press, which would no doubt produce a story and place it on the media outlet's website, as well as Twitter, Instagram, and YouTube.

Down the hall, Ziad directed Georgie, Willie, Arman, and Ali to walk around the corner into a large conference room with windows overlooking LaSalle Street, where his two associates had been gunned down by Dylan. This was an evening that would be focused on revenge. And Ziad planned to make it as excruciatingly painful as possible for the Americans.

Georgie and Willie were ordered to sit down in one of the impressive high-backed black leather chairs at the beautiful mahogany conference table. The rolling chairs were then pushed back against the window. This seemed like a dangerous idea, but their expectations couldn't be anything less, given the insane state of mind of their captor.

"Now when he gets up here, Arman, I will do the talking," said the fierce-looking terrorist. "But as we discussed earlier, you will toss him his gun and shoot him just before he catches it. Understood?"

"Yes," said the terrified teenager, who could have never imagined being in such a terrible predicament.

Neither could Georgie, who earlier that day was sitting in his office when he heard what sounded like gunshots in the hallway. When he stepped outside his office to investigate the commotion, he saw a wild-eyed Arab man walking toward him. He slammed the door shut, ran over to his phone to call 911. But two shots to the Yale lock opened the door for Ziad Haznawi, the "Most Wanted" man in America.

"Put that phone down," ordered Ziad, pointing the gun directly at Georgie's head. The petrified banker put the receiver down slowly. "So you are the man who helped that American swine get away, the murderer of my two friends. Is that right?"

"I don't know what you're talking about," pleaded Georgie, hoping the terrorist would not kill him.

"You were on all the television news stations when they showed the video from the bank robbery that day!" yelled Ziad, whose hair-trigger temper had just been triggered. "They showed your friend and said that he's the same man who killed my two comrades. And you helped him get away! You helped him!"

"I...I..."

"That's okay, because you're going to help me kill him," Ziad informed Georgie, whom he thought would be his one bargaining chip.

However, Willie showed up at Georgie's office around noon to surprise his high school pal and take him to lunch. Unfortunately, the surprise was on Willie.

When he walked down the hallway to his friend's office he didn't see the three dead co-workers lying on the floor. As he approached the door, he could hear loud talking, yelling, and wondered if he would be disturbing some important meeting.

For a moment, he waited outside the door, which was ajar. The wood and handle were torn apart. All of sudden the talking stopped. Willie knocked twice, and the door was pulled open quickly. Ziad pointed his 357 Magnum at Willie's face.

"Who are you?" demanded Ziad, waving his gun toward Willie, indicating for him to enter the office.

"Willie!" exclaimed Georgie, disappointed to see his friend, who he knew was now in just as much trouble as him.

"Oh, a friend of yours, huh?" said Ziad. "Well, that's good! Increases my collateral. Another hostage."

Seven hours later, the two friends sat side-by-side in the large conference room overlooking LaSalle Street waiting for their friend Dylan to arrive so they could all be shot and killed together. The iPhone Ziad was holding, Georgie's cellphone, buzzed with a text. Ziad read it and smiled. Using only his left thumb he began typing a message.

"He's here," Ziad informed Ali and Arman, typing in the location for Dylan, as if Georgie were sending the message. "Up to the forty-fourth floor conference room at the end of the hall, he shall come. And we shall greet him."

At this same time, Park Hills Police officers Matt Durkin and Donnie Joy were driving by the Farzan's residence and noticed an old beat-up blue Impala in the driveway.

"You know, my brother-in-law knows the Farzans," said Officer Durkin, pulling his impressive black Ford SUV police vehicle into the driveway, parking next to the Impala. "Says they are great people."

"Great!" said Officer Joy, typing the car's license plate into his computer. "You know I don't recognize that car."

"Yeah, neither do I," said Durkin, climbing out of the vehicle and putting his trooper's hat on his head. "I'm just going to say hello, let him know we are here to help, if needed."

"That car is registered to Hamid Hussein," said the younger, dark-haired partner. "Maybe it's a good thing we stopped by."

"Yeah, I'll check it out," said the sandy-haired, middle-aged officer, Durkin, walking up to the front door and ringing the doorbell. No answer. But the veteran policeman heard something, a commotion of some sort. He rang the bell again. A muffled voice was heard. No answer. He waved his partner out of the car.

"Hey, something's not right here," said Durkin, taking his gun out of his holster. "You cover the back door. You have your walkie-talkie?"

"Yeah," said Joy, hustling down the sidewalk on the left side of the red-bricked ranch-style home, toward the backyard, while taking out his Glock gun.

Officer Durkin radioed into the police station for backup while his partner moved to his position in the backyard of the Farzan home. Then the veteran glanced into the front window to see if anyone appeared. No movement.

"I'm in position," said Officer Joy over the walkie-talkie.

Durkin knocked loudly on the door. "Park Hills Police! Open the door!"

He clearly heard loud voices and what sounded like thuds, perhaps someone running. He spoke into his walkie-talkie, "Be ready. I'm going in."

Durkin, a former linebacker on the St. John's Academy football team, didn't think he had time to go back to his vehicle for the battering ram to knock the door open. Instead, he lowered his shoulder and smashed into the brown oak door, breaking it open. He pulled his gun out of his holster and held it in front of him, just as he had been trained, but rarely had to implement since he worked in such a nice quiet suburb outside of Chicago. His heart raced as he entered the home. Now he definitely heard voices in the back.

"Do you see them, Donnie?" he said over the walkie-talkie.

"Not yet. Oh, wait, here they come. Hurry!"

Durkin sprinted to the back of the home, where he saw two young men dressed in black with Arabic headdress, holding guns against the heads of Mr. and Mrs. Farzan.

"Drop the guns!" yelled Officer Durkin, now his energy at fever-pitch, holding his weapon straight out, ready to fire. One of the attackers quickly turned toward Durkin and began firing his gun. The suburban cop wisely dove into the bedroom on his left. Lying on the floor, he held his gun up, prepared to shoot the terrorist the moment he filled the doorway

"C'mon, get out! Get out now," he heard one of them yelling, instructing the Farzans to go out the back door.

"Drop the guns!" he heard his partner Donnie yell out. Then, bang, bang, bang! Bang, bang, bang! Loud shots rang through the hallway of the home.

Durkin jumped up quickly and ran toward the back door, his heart racing, each breath so loud, the smell of gun powder filling his nostrils.

The door was wide open. As he reached the doorway, he saw one of the Arabs holding his gun straight out, pointed at Donnie, who dropped straight down to the ground, making himself a harder target to hit.

Durkin fired his gun, round after round, hitting the terrorist in the head, the arm, the back, sending him flying to the side. He fell lifeless onto the green lawn.

Durkin looked over at his partner. "Are you hit, Donnie?" he asked, running over to check the combatant to make certain he was dead.

"No, he missed. They both missed," Donnie explained, jumping back up to his feet, walking over to his partner to embrace. "Thanks, man. You saved my life."

"I'm just happy I was able to get here in time," said Durkin, turning toward Amir Farzan, who was holding his distraught wife, crying uncontrollably.

"Are you okay, ma'am?" asked Durkin placing his hand on the upset woman's shoulder. She just continued to cry as her husband looked up and nodded at the officer.

Officer Joy was still breathing heavily from the confrontation.

"They came out the back door, holding the Farzans in front of them, using them as shields," he explained to his partner. "I told them to drop their guns, but they raised them right at me. I had no choice. I'm just glad

Mr. Farzan pulled his wife to the side and gave me a clear shot at the one shooter. I'm also glad he was a lousy shot. They both must have fired at least three or four shots at me."

"But you're sure you're not hit?" asked Durkin, looking over his partner for blood or wounds.

"Not even grazed, I don't think," said Donnie, checking himself to make sure he hadn't been hit. Many soldiers and cops who get shot don't realize it right away, because their adrenaline is running so high.

"They are going to kill my boy!" said Amir, anguish and fear filling his face. "They took him, and told him they would kill us if he didn't listen to them."

"Where is he?" asked Durkin.

"I don't know, but those two said he was going to help their leader kill Americans," said Amir, holding Sofia, who moaned loudly. "We need to let him know we are okay."

"Yes, right away, too!" said Officer Joy.

"That will change the game they are playing," said Durkin who could hear sirens getting louder, realizing his backup was getting closer. "Let's go inside. We have another team coming as well."

A few minutes later, Officer Matt Durkin sat with Amir and Sofia Farzan, while his partner alerted the station of the situation. An ambulance was dispatched to haul away the two dead terrorists. Four more police officers entered the home as Amir texted his son:

"Arman, we are safe. The police came and we are safe. Get away from them, if you can. Where are you?"

Arman was standing in the back of the conference room, furthest away from Ziad, who felt it necessary to punch Georgie across his pale once-freckled face more than a few times, before Dylan arrived.

"Understand something, you swine, you infidel!" he said, his eyes dancing, visually revealing his crazed mind to all in the room. "When your friend walks in here, you just sit there. Understand? Don't get up. Don't say anything. Don't do anything. Understand?"

A red-faced and battered Georgie nodded, fully realizing he was going to die that night. He needed a plan of attack once Dylan arrived.

If he was going to die, he was going to go down fighting. He looked over at Willie and nodded. His longtime friend read his unspoken intention.

Arman's phone was on vibrate and he felt it buzz. Not wanting Ziad to see him, he turned away to look at the message and read it. A huge sense of relief filled his heart and soul. Thank God, he thought to himself. "Thank God!" he muttered softly.

"What?" asked Ziad, staring at his new famous recruit.

"Nothing, I just said thank God this is going so well," said Arman, while Ziad looked at him, his eyes narrowing with curiosity. There was a knock at the conference room door. Ziad walked over with his Magnum held high. He opened the door and there stood the nation's hero, the man who stopped the terrorist attack and bank robbery.

"Get in here, you murderer! You devil!" demanded Ziad, stepping back a bit, still fearful Dylan may have a gun on him.

"Put your hands against the wall and spread your legs," Ziad demanded, then thoroughly frisked him. He found no gun, no weapon. He stood straight up relieved that he now held complete control. He was confident his plans would succeed that evening.

"Ali! Film all of this, all of it!" Ziad instructed his new twenty-five-year-old terrorist comrade. "We are not going to cut your heads off today, although I'd very much like to. We are going to show the world that you aren't such a great hero. They are going to see that you aren't so fast with your gun. They will see that my young friend, Arman, is faster. Much faster! And he is going to prove it and kill you."

Dylan looked over at the young man whom he recognized couldn't have been more than eighteen years old. He could have been a student of his at Watson College Prep.

Ziad pulled a brown holster out of his black leather bag and tossed it to Arman, telling him to put it on.

"Now you, Mr. Hero, step back there, with your arms to your side, just like they described you when you murdered my two jihadist friends," he told Dylan, who moved backwards, toward the far end of the conference room. He looked over at Georgie and Willie who were trying to read their friend, so they knew when it was time to charge the terrorists.

At this same time, the elevator on the 44th floor opened and out stepped Officer Gregory Panozzo and two young ex-military SWAT team officers. They were all dressed in full protective gear with bullet-proof vests, helmets, and 9mm submachine guns.

Dylan knew he wasn't allowed to enter that room with a gun, but had already decided that even if the terrorists killed him, he wasn't going to let them get away. He contacted Officer Panozzo, who he had become his friend since the incident in Union Park, where the loyal cop was somehow able to protect the hero's identity.

Dylan texted him from the cemetery after receiving the initial text from Georgie. Over the phone they coordinated a plan of attack. Once Dylan received the location, he passed it along and asked that the police not enter until they heard him shout, "Now!"

He had hoped to divert the terrorist's attention long enough for the police to break in and shoot them, hopefully before the terrorists could shoot Dylan, Georgie, and Willie.

Unfortunately however, Dylan wasn't aware of the terrorists plan to use the young boy to execute them. Now the scenario had been changed and there was no way to alert Officer Panozzo.

Dylan watched Arman strap on the brown holster as Ziad reached into his black leather bag, taking out a shiny silver Smith & Wesson pistol, identical to the one Dylan used. Then, he took out a Glock gun, like the one Arman used in the parking lot, except this was no BB gun. This was a real gun!

He made sure they were both fully loaded. He reached out to hand the 9mm black pistol to Arman, when doubt entered his twisted mind, and he quickly pulled it back.

"Ali, you keep your gun on Arman here, and I will do the same," said Ziad, pointing his Magnum directly at the teenager. "Remember, Mr. YouTube celebrity, you do what I tell you. Or I will call my two comrades sitting with your parents right now and your family will be dead before I can end the call. Understood?"

Arman nodded.

Dylan, Georgie, and Willie now had the full picture. Dylan gnashed his teeth, now realizing his plan with Officer Panozzo wasn't going to work. He was certain that under such pressure they would come through that door shooting at anyone brown, anyone Arab, including the kid. He most certainly didn't want that to happen and quickly tried to think of another way out of the life-threatening predicament.

"Now here's what going to happen," said Ziad, handing the gun to Arman, while continuing to point his Magnum directly at him. "Are you getting all of this, Ali?"

The newly chosen terror cell member who was proud to be there, nodded.

"Place that Glock gun into your holster," Ziad instructed Arman. "And here is the gun for our murdering hero. See, it is loaded. You will stand ten feet apart, both of you with your arms to your sides, just like gunfighters have always faced off.

"Arman you will toss him that Smith & Wesson. But just before he catches it, you are to draw your gun quickly, just like in the video at your high school, and shoot him. Shoot him several times. Shoot him in the chest! Shoot him in the head! Kill him!

"Then turn, and with the two bullets you have left, kill his two friends there. Put those bullets right through their chest, blasting them right through the window, falling to a horrible and certain death on the street below. I don't want you to have to reload. You're supposed to be that good. Understand?"

"I understand," said Arman, whose back was to Ziad. "Toss the gun but shoot before he catches it."

"That's right, then kill these other two infidel Americans. You will then be a jihadist, just like me and Ali. And like us, you will one day become a martyr and go to heaven and receive seventy-two virgins."

As Ziad spoke, Arman used his eyes, opening them wide, moving them quickly to his right, trying to indicate to Dylan that he was going to try and shoot Ziad. Dylan wasn't quite sure what the young man was trying to tell him, but he guessed that he wanted Dylan's help. Ziad handed Arman the pearl-handled Smith & Wesson.

"Now I will count to three and you toss the gun. Understand?" Ziad said, Arman nodding. Georgie and Willie prepared themselves to charge at Ziad once that gun was tossed in the air.

"Ready? One, two, three...."

Arman paused a second. Georgie and Willie watched, ready to charge.

"Three!" demanded Ziad and watched Arman toss the gun in the air toward Dylan. The shiny silver pearl-handled Smith & Wesson six-shooter wasn't spinning at all but was sailing through the air parallel to the floor with the handle pointed toward Dylan, giving him the best chance to catch it and shoot quickly.

As Dylan watched the gun flying toward him, he knew this may be his last moments on earth. Part of him was excited to know he would soon see Darlene again, while another part of him, a larger part, wanted to win this battle and save his two friends and the young Arab boy in front of him.

Georgie and Willie froze. As the gun descended, Dylan reached up to catch it and could hear Ziad yell out, "Shoot him! Shoot him!"

As the gun descended toward him, Dylan felt a strong tingling sensation run up his spine, just as he had during the previous attacks. God was with him.

"Shoot him!" demanded Ziad.

Dylan caught the gun in his right hand, his shooting hand. In a split second his finger was on the trigger.

Arman quickly crouched down and turned, firing three shots at Ziad, who yelled out, "Noooo!"

The office door burst open, as Dylan fired three shots into Ali, while Officer Panozzo and the two SWAT team officers charged into the room. They immediately saw the two dead terrorists on the floor. They turned toward Arman with their submachine guns pointed at him, ready to shoot the boy holding his small black pistol.

"No!" yelled Dylan, who fired the six-shooter twice, knocking the long heavy guns out of the hands of both SWAT specialists, while Arman shot the Magnum out of Officer Panozzo's hand.

"Stop! Stop!" Dylan yelled at the police, running in front of Arman, raising his arms up to protect the boy. "He's with us. They took him hostage and threated to kill his parents if he didn't go along with them. He's with us."

A great sense of relief was felt in the conference room, knowing the crisis had ended and the only ones injured were the two terrorists, lying lifeless and bleeding on the gray carpet.

Dylan turned toward Arman, while the three police officers tried to grasp what had just happened. "Are you okay, young man?"

"Yes, thank you sir," he said. "Thank you so much. You saved my life. I was trying to let you know what I was going to do…"

"Yes, I sort of picked up on that but wasn't sure. What about your parents?"

Arman just smiled. "I got a text a few minutes ago from my father. He said the police came to their home and they are safe. Once I knew that, I knew I could shoot Ziad but would need your help for Ali."

"Son, are you sure your parents are okay?" asked Officer Panozzo.

"I think so, but…." Arman quickly punched in his father's number on his cellphone and all in the conference room watched and listened.

"Dad…? Are you okay?" A bright smile grew on his handsome brown face. "Thank God! Thank God!"

Smiles lit up the room, hearts filled with joy and gratitude for one another. Good had overcome evil under the most difficult of circumstances.

Dylan would have to postpone his reunion with Darlene, although he knew he would be visiting her the next day at the cemetery. He would be talking to her once again under the shadow of the tall silver Good Shepherd statue.

CHAPTER THIRTY-TWO

A cool breeze swept over Grant Park on this beautiful autumn day, brown leaves scattered everywhere. The powerful sound of Lake Michigan crashing against the wall was heard across the lakefront, sending the remnants of waves hurtling over the cement landing in front of the couples sitting on the steps watching one of nature's most beautiful sights in a city offering so many wonderful views.

The Chicago Police Commissioner, Jerry McAdams, stood with Mayor Ron Carlisle and FBI Director Jim Toomey on the stage of the Petrillo Band Shell, which was decorated with signs reading, "Chicago's Call to Courage!"

Following the success of the press conference at City Hall a few weeks earlier to address the Midwest Trade Building hostage shootout, the mayor decided to use the momentum to invigorate Chicagoans.

He stepped to the podium and looked out at the expansive park packed with thousands of proud citizens. All were hoping to get their first look at the man who had been in the news so many times over the past month, saving lives and stopping bad guys.

"The time has come for all of us to take a stand against these killers!" pronounced Mayor Carlisle, wearing gray slacks, open-collared white dress shirt with sleeves rolled up, and shined black wing tips. He was hoping to promote the importance of being proactive against those who seek to hurt innocent people.

"In order to stop them, we are calling on all of you to have the courage to pay attention. We are calling on you to have the courage to call the police whenever you see things that look unusual. We are calling on you to fight back! All Americans are going to have to find the courage to stand up to the violence.

"And as you all know, the effort to fight back started right here in Chicago just a short time ago with a man who had violence devastate his life. We are hoping his story will encourage all of you to think about what you can do to help.

"Please welcome America's new hero, our own Chicagoan, Dylan Reilly!"

Over the sound system played David Bowie's song, "Heroes."

Dylan Reilly entered from the wings, walking to the podium, shaking Mayor Carlisle's hand as the crowd went wild with excitement, seeing the world's fastest gun.

As the applause rose, Reilly waved to the crowd from the podium with the Police Commissioner and FBI Director smiling wide, feeling like they finally had someone who could give them an advantage, helping them deter or destroy those who sought to kill innocent people.

Dylan lifted his arms trying to quiet the crowd, looking down to see his longtime friends Georgie Hanlon, Willie Mitrovich, and Teddy Webb in the front. Standing next to them, were his newest friends, Arman, Amir, and Sofia Farzan, along with recently decorated police officers Greg Panozzo, Matt Durkin, and Donnie Joy.

A spine-tingling sensation ran up Dylan's back, so happy they were there. And right next to Georgie Hanlon stood Sergeant James Henry, the man who gave Dylan the skills to defeat the terrorists. Dylan waved to his friends and saluted Sergeant Henry.

As he stood there, in the same park where his wife had been killed, Dylan couldn't help but think of all the tragic events that led him to that stage. His anonymity was gone forever.

After surviving the hostage crisis at the Midwest Trade Building, he knew that the world would soon find out the identity of the man with the fastest gun. There was no question in his mind that he had to participate in the Chicago Police press conference to support Arman, Officer Panozzo, and his two SWAT specialists.

Officer Panozzo tried to talk him out of it, but Dylan knew his testimony would be crucial to the credibility of the story. He provided the details of the communications with the terrorist and his recollection of the events that took place in the conference room that evening. Both Georgie and Willie attended as well to provide their eyewitness accounts, including the murder of the two security guards when they entered the building.

The Farzans attended the press conference to provide their account of the happenings. Amir and Sofia Farzan stood with their son, Arman, and new friend, Dylan, all feeling a bit overwhelmed by the number of TV cameras and photographers snapping visual historical records.

Driving to the press conference that morning, the Farzans discussed selling their home and moving away. But where could they move? They didn't know, but they talked about moving away from the dangers that seemed to be showing up at their doorstep, literally. As they discussed it, however, they realized that their eighteen-year-old son had it right. There was nowhere in America they could go to avoid the hateful looks and attitudes that had been generated for all people of brown skin by terrorists like Ziad Haznawi.

The Farzans agreed that they were lucky to be accepted in their community and at St. Michael's Church where they had made so many good friends. And, their two eldest children, Aaron and Miriam, lived in the area and they most certainly weren't going to move too far from them.

Plus, Amir's brother Ahmad had gotten over his initial anger about his younger brother's religious conversion. They reconciled their relationship agreeing to put aside their differences in order to live as brothers who love each other and will always be there to support one another. Family was at the heart of the Farzans' lives, and their home would always be where their heart was beating loudest, no matter where the family lived.

"I guess this is a time to appreciate what we do have and not what we don't have," Amir said to his wife and three children, so happy to be together again, as he drove the family's blue Dodge Stratus. "And we do have quite a lot to be grateful for, that's for sure."

That is exactly how Arman felt about his high school, where he and his friends were once social pariahs. But everything changed after the YouTube video and his exhibition of courage and skill. All of a sudden, his fellow students didn't see a brown-faced Arab boy, who was immediately visually-linked to terrorists. No, they saw a hero. And everyone loves a hero, regardless of their skin color and heritage.

So when Arman returned to school after his incredible acts of courage at the Midwest Trade Building, he was more than a YouTube web celebrity. He had become an international superstar, known in every corner of the world, as a very brave American high school student.

His greatest supporter at the school, Coach Neal Michaels, and the principal, Ben Leonard, organized a special presentation for Arman in front of the entire student body in the school's large orange and white-walled gymnasium. His high school wanted to show him just how proud they were of his courageous actions. It was Arman's proudest moment, as well as his four pals—Omar, Jahan, Gabe, and Dabney—who he insisted stand by his side during the presentation.

Friendships were extremely important to Arman, loyal friendships. The same was true for Dylan, who viewed loyalty and trust as the two most important character traits he expected of his friends. He demanded an even higher standard of himself. That is why he was so grateful that the break in his friendship with Teddy Webb had been resolved.

Following the shooting at the rally in Union Park, Dylan sat by the side of his seriously injured friend, Teddy, in the ambulance carrying them to Northwestern Hospital. Dylan called Willie and Georgie, who came to the hospital where they sat with Teddy, while he recovered from the surgery.

Northwestern was the last place Dylan wanted to be that day, the hospital where he watched his loving wife die. Unfortunately for Teddy, what had seemed like an easy-to-treat shoulder wound, turned into a far a more complicated injury that required two surgeries, removing the bullet, and then a small portion of Teddy's left lung, which had been pierced.

He almost didn't survive, due to the blood loss and infection that developed. Teddy was a strong man though, and he did wake up to see his wife, two kids, and three great longtime friends, sitting in his hospital room.

He smiled at the sight of the people he cared the most about in life. Teddy vowed that day to change. And he did, resigning from Slagle & Sharp and starting his own small law practice, where he could choose the clients he would represent. He knew he would be giving up the high level of wealth he had enjoyed for so long, working for a large powerful law firm. But his soul would be clean and he would sleep better at night.

After surviving the night of terror, Georgie, Willie, and Dylan vowed they would get together once a month, along with Teddy and Arman. No excuses accepted. By the time they were done discussing the monthly get-togethers, Amir and Sofia Farzan were invited, along with officers Panozzo, Durkin, and Joy.

The four high school pals also promised each other that they would travel to Washington, D.C. once a year to visit the gravesite of their fallen friend, Joe Doyle, the real hero in their collective minds. All four men were well aware that they each came close to having their lives cut short, and somehow, that reality provided them each with a new perspective, a new motivation for living each day like it were their last.

After the packed press conference came to an end that Thursday morning, and all statements were made, all questions answered, Police Commissioner McAdams told Dylan that a record number of reporters had been in attendance. Local, national, and international media were there to cover the story that had become of great interest across the globe.

A photograph of Dylan, with a cutline proclaiming him the "World's Fastest Gun," was distributed worldwide by the Associated Press. That photo, and the stories accompanying it, described Dylan's heroic journey and was published on the front page of newspapers in most countries across the world. The media attention resulted in an invitation to speak at events across America.

And his first event would be in his hometown, the city he loved. On this beautiful Saturday in October, he stood behind the podium in Grant Park. The exuberant and grateful crowd finally quieted down enough for him to speak.

"Just four months ago, I was just like all of you," Dylan began. "Just like you! Then my beautiful and loving wife Darlene and I went to New York City in June, a trip we had been planning for years. We wanted to see the site of the tragedy at the World Trade Center. Like all of you, 9/11 was such a significant event in our lives. Everyone knows where they were that day, many at that moment, when those two jets crashed into the twin towers. I was at my high school, St. John's, with my three longtime friends, who are standing right in front of me today."

Georgie, Willie, and Teddy, turned and waved to the crowd, who burst in applause in appreciation for the enduring friendships.

"The day my wife Darlene and I went to visit the tragic and historic site, and the Museum dedicated to the memory of the 3,000 victims, was a day I had looked forward to for many years. Unfortunately, the day we visited was the day of that homegrown terrorist attack I'm sure you all know about from the news reports.

"We could have been killed that day. We were so glad to get back to Chicago, where we have always felt safe. After my wife and I returned, we went shopping at Water Tower on a beautiful July Sunday. We were sitting near the historic Water Tower eating ice cream when we saw a disturbance across the street.

"A few minutes later, RPGs were being shot into the John Hancock Center and then bullets at innocent people running for their lives. Another terrorist attack, but this one was Al-Qaeda. We ran and felt so lucky to have gotten away alive. Again, I'm sure you all heard the reports.

"But all of a sudden, the city we had both felt so safe living in our entire lives, didn't seem so safe. Another month passed, and the fear and anxiety from that day somewhat subsided, but we did become more selective about where we went, avoiding major public crowds and events.

"However, we really wanted to attend the Midwest MusicFest and see some great live music, great bands! We thought we were possibly overreacting to the Water Tower attack and needed to start living our lives again.

"So on the evening of Saturday, August 3, Darlene and I were sitting right over there, just across Balbo, sitting on our blanket watching the concert," Dylan said, pointing toward the field at the corner of Balbo and Lake Shore Drive.

"Then we heard screams, not one scream, but a crowd of people screaming all at once. It was coming from the stage a full block west of us. Then we heard the pops. Pop, pop, pop! That's when we knew.

"Again, you know the story, but what you don't know is my wife was shot that night. She had been mortally wounded and died at Northwestern Hospital. Murdered!" he said, dropping his head, his voice now quivering as he wiped the stream of tears pouring down his cheeks.

"You can do it, man," said Teddy, encouraging his former hockey teammate to stay strong. Sergeant Henry nodded. Dylan glanced down at his supportive friends and smiled with appreciation.

"I was most certainly overcome by anguish that night. But let me tell you, I was filled with an anger that couldn't be measured," he said, now feeling the familiar sensation rising up his spine, as he looked up to the blue skies for a brief moment. "My living without the protection of a gun to defend myself ended that night. If I had a gun that evening, would it have saved my wife? No. The shooter was on the twenty-second floor of a hotel with an assault weapon that had a bump stock on it. Look at how far away we all were from Michigan Avenue, but his bullets were reaching us. How do you prepare for that? How do you defend against it? You don't. You can't!

"But what about the shooter in New York or the Water Tower shooter? Could I have stopped that from escalating? Could I have saved lives? Yes, I know for certain that if I had my Smith & Wesson, I would have saved lives.

"But make no mistake about the realities of the world we now live in. All of us, every single one of us, has to make a choice, determining which risk we are willing to bear. Will it be the pearl-handled dangerous freedom I have chosen and all the risks that come with that weapon? Or do you take the risk of having no gun, hoping danger doesn't show up in your life? Or do you move to a country with stricter gun laws, but accept all the other risks that come with the move? Those are the options for all of us.

"Believe me when I tell you that my wife and I had never owned a gun because of the many risks that come with that ownership. I met a man recently, Haydon Reuben Huff, whose father made history in this park back in 1968. He is the son of 1960s activist leader, Andy Huff, and unfortunately Haydon made some bad decisions about the use of a gun that got him killed.

"Please understand there is a big responsibility that goes along with owning a gun. Get educated. Get training, just as I did from this great war hero in front of me, Sergeant James Henry."

The crowd roared and Sergeant Henry turned and waved, a big smile on his face, overwhelmed by the incredible wave of recognition he was receiving.

"But when you are playing the odds against someone showing up in your life with a gun, and then all of a sudden, you find yourself in the wrong place at the wrong time, like we were, three times! When you are confronted by the dangerous realities of this world, that's the moment you know you have to make a decision. I made the choice of carrying this old six-shooter to stop the bad guys, thanks to Sergeant Henry. And I'm glad I did.

"I guess I gained a new perspective about the brave law enforcement professionals, like those right up front here," he said pointing to his new police friends, who turned and waved to the crowd, receiving a loud applause. "They see the worst side of gun violence. It makes their jobs much harder. It makes their lives much more difficult. They put their lives on the line for us every day.

"I just hope I can be of some assistance to their efforts to keep Chicagoans safe. All I can promise you is that I will be carrying my Smith & Wesson and trying my best.

"I hope my story helps you make your decision. And I also hope all of you will be proactive, as Mayor Carlisle said earlier. Keep your eyes open. If you notice something that doesn't look right, call 9/11. Don't accept it. Be proactive. It can happen anywhere at any time, so we all have to be vigilant and fight back.

"Maybe then, those bullies with their assault rifles and bump stocks will think twice before going out in public and shooting innocent people. Because those innocent people will be shooting back! Thank you. And God bless you all for your support!"

A loud applause erupted, two-fingered whistles, shouts of support, and a chant began, "Dylan! Dylan! Dylan!"

Dylan turned to thank Mayor Carlisle, Commissioner McAdams, and FBI Director Toomey. Hugs and handshakes were exchanged as the song, "Heroes" began playing again. The crowd reveled in the atmosphere, accentuated by the wonderful song and voice of the great David Bowie.

In the crowd, a tall, tough-looking, unshaven man in a black cowboy hat and tan Legacy Drifter coat, and high leather boots, stood among a dancing group of very excited and happy college kids. One of them noticed the cowboy, stopped dancing, and approached him, "Are you a cowboy? I mean, are you a real cowboy?"

"Yep!" he said, spitting some of his tobacco onto the green trampled grass, which completely grossed out two of the dancing ladies who witnessed it.

"You know he uses a six-shooter just like the old cowboys used back in the day," said the boy, a little too friendly with the snarling older, leather-faced man. "Is that what you use?"

"Nope!" said the cowboy.

"Oh, I see," said the young man. "You know, that man is the fastest gun in the world. The fastest!"

The cowboy turned slowly to look at the college kid, his eyes squinting. "He's not so fast. And he'll find that out real soon."

The college kid felt shocked by the threat from the cowboy and quickly walked away with his friends, while David Bowie's powerful voice echoed loudly through the park, singing the wonderfully uplifting chorus from "Heroes."

THE END

ABOUT THE AUTHOR

John Ruane is an author, journalist, playwright, and actor. He has written for the *Chicago Sun-Times*, *Chicago Tribune*, and *Atlanta-Journal Constitution*. He is a critically-acclaimed author of four books, including *The Earl Campbell Story* (ECW Press, 1999) and *Parish the Thought* (Simon & Schuster, 2008). Ruane's stage work began at the famed Second City theater in Chicago. He then went on to write four critically-acclaimed satirical sketch comedy revues and a rock-musical play. During college, John was an English major, wrote a column for the school newspaper, and played center on two college hockey championship teams. Later, he volunteered his time to coaching fifty-two youth sports teams over a seventeen-year period. He and his wife, Charlotte, have four wonderful children.

Made in the USA
Columbia, SC
01 August 2021